Bolan closed the cell phone with a click

The man had wished him luck. The Executioner shook his head at the sentiment. Right now civilization needed more than that. Balls and brains could only take a soldier so far; after that it was the draw of the cards. So far, his luck was holding, but for how much longer? Just one slip on his part and the bombs would disappear, until atomic fire burned a city to the ground.

A nuclear fireball bearing the technological signature of America and possibly starting a war that might never end.

The soldier hoped that Lady Luck would stick with him. He had to find the Zodiac in twenty-four hours.

Don Pendleton's Mack Bolan®
Stolen Arrows

A GOLD EAGLE BOOK FROM
WORLDWIDE®

TORONTO • NEW YORK • LONDON
AMSTERDAM • PARIS • SYDNEY • HAMBURG
STOCKHOLM • ATHENS • TOKYO • MILAN
MADRID • WARSAW • BUDAPEST • AUCKLAND

First edition May 2004

ISBN 0-373-61496-9

Special thanks and acknowledgment to
Nick Pollotta for his contribution to this work.

STOLEN ARROWS

In doing what we ought, we deserve no praise, because it is our duty.

—St. Augustine, 354–430

It's a soldier's duty to stand guard against the forces of evil and to shout that none shall pass. In this I will not falter.

—Mack Bolan

As always, for Melissa.
And a special thanks to Lucia Read. She knows why.

PROLOGUE

Archbishop Park, London

Distant thunder rumbled softly in the cloudy London sky, warning of a coming storm. Soon now, very soon.

Trying to act casually, heavily armed CIA operatives strolled through the budding greenery of the south bank parkland. No two were dressed alike, but each had a telltale flesh-colored wire trailing from his earplug to the compact transponder clipped to his gunbelt. A few smoked, one was eating an ice-cream cone, but all were razor-sharp and braced for the oncoming action.

Stopping to tie a shoelace, a man checked the digital readout of the Geiger counter strapped to his wrist as if he were comparing its time against the distant chimes of Big Ben. Satisfied for the moment that the combat zone was clear, he coughed twice into his hidden throat mike to relay the information, then moved onward to take a sip of water from a nearby fountain.

Scattered across Archbishop's Park, several families had spread checkered blankets on the freshly cut lawns while excited children ran along the footpaths darting in and out of the trimmed hedges and among the strolling pedestrians. Rising like a glass cathedral above the lush trees was the new Archbishop's Hospital and past the footbridge was the old baroque-style library, the once-clean Scottish granite blocks now stained a dull uniform gray with the passage of the long centuries.

Sitting on the steps of the library, a large man was reading a book in Portuguese, the volume positioned to hold down his loose windbreaker and to hide the gun in his shoulder holster.

"Falcon, we have a contact," whispered a voice from the radio in his ear. "Sector five, a Zodiac is approaching the park. Repeat, a Zodiac is near. All agents, full combat protocol at all times. Stay sharp and wait for my command."

Grunting in confirmation, Cirello Zalhares continued reading his novel, waiting for target identification. The voice on the radio was David Osbourne, the CIA operative who had hired his team of mercenaries for this dirty job. But then, black ops were what his group did best and the CIA always paid top dollar.

Just then a teenage girl walked by, her yellow print dress rising high in the river breeze to expose a lot of tanned leg and a hint of lace panties. Nice. Raising his sight, Zalhares admired the fullness of her young body and finally her face, loose, golden blond hair framing elfin features. Noticing his attention, the girl paused for a moment and pursed her lips in a controlled smile at the stranger, but as he smiled back she paled slightly and hurried away, fearfully glancing backward to make sure he wasn't following.

Unconcerned by her reaction, Zalhares returned to his reading. Although only in his early thirties, it had been many years since Zalhares could have been called handsome, the network of scars on his face and neck from his line of work reducing his looks to merely striking. Although the black hair and dark skin proclaimed a Spanish ancestry, his sharp eyes were swirls of different subdued colors. Egyptian, the effect was called, although he knew of no such Arab relative in the family tree. Just a genetic fluke, an abstraction that caught the attention of many beautiful women, until they saw the savage mind behind the beautiful eyes and their ardor cooled just as quickly as it had flared to life.

A small boy walked over to the man and

stopped directly in front of him. Hoping the boy would go away, Zalhares did nothing for a minute, but then when it was obvious he had to respond. The big man slowly raised his eyes from the book and looked at the child without any emotion.

"That's a funny kind of writing, mister," the boy said curiously. "Is it Latin?"

"Portuguese," Zalhares answered, closing the book on a finger to hold his place. In spite of the summer warmth, he was wearing expensive gloves on both hands. The leather was so pale that it resembled human skin.

The boy tilted his head. "You Portugeese?" he mispronounced.

Controlling his impatience, Zalhares started to answer but then paused as a well-dressed businessman in a Gucci suit walked into view, holding a briefcase. The killer relaxed at the sight of the alligator-leather trim. That wasn't a Zodiac. Those were plain brown leather, as ordinary and plain as humanly possible, virtually invisible in a crowd.

"Mister?" the boy repeated.

"I'm from Brazil," Zalhares said, giving an empty laugh. Stay loose, do not attract attention from the crowd. Bore the child with details. "The Archbishop library has the largest collection of books in Portuguese in all of Britain. I come here often for a taste of home."

"Don't they speak Brazilian in Brazil?" the boy asked, and then added, "I know I would."

Now annoyed, Zalhares controlled his temper and started to open his mouth to speak.

"Red alert," a new voice said in his earpiece. "We have a Zodiac in the park. Repeat, we have a Zodiac coming home from sector two."

That wasn't Osbourne, but a member of his Zalhares's team, Artero Mariano, also known as Dog by his many enemies because of his tendency to bite people in the throat during fights. An expert in Kodokan judo and high explosives, he was one of the most feared assassins in the S2, the dreaded secret police of Brazil. That was, until Cirello Zalhares had recruited the man from the government and into the Scion, his mercenary unit.

As surreptitiously as possible, Zalhares gestured behind the book toward the child standing directly in front of him.

"Better get rid of the kid, my friend," Mariano said urgently. "The Libyans will be here at any second and we'll have to move."

Keeping his expression neutral, Zalhares leaned forward slightly so that his windbreaker fell open, exposing the silenced Imbel .22 pistol in the holster to his team hidden in the nearby trees.

"No, just chase him away," Mariano suggested.

"There are too many people around. Killing the brat would only start a riot if somebody found the body. The English are very sentimental about their children."

"Well, I must be going now," Zalhares said, rising to his full height and closing the book. The adult towered over the child like a giant from a fairy tale. When the physical intimidation didn't frighten the boy away, Zalhares impatiently tried another tactic.

"Would you do me a favor and return this inside?" he asked, pushing the volume into the boy's grasp. "Thank you."

"Not late, is it?" the boy asked suspiciously, looking over the thick book. "Billy once asked me to return a book, and it was late and I had to pay the fine."

"No, it is not late," Zalhares stated, starting to walk away. "But I am. My…daughter is having a birthday and I'm late for her party. Thank you again."

The boy scowled in disgust. "Yuck, girls," he said, turning to charge up the flight of stairs into the library. "Goodbye, mister!"

Once safely in the crowd, Zalhares walked until two more people slipped into position nearby, never coming close, but now each of them was able to cover the other with gunfire if the need arose. Dressed in slacks and a turtleneck, Minas Pedrosa was a bald giant who sported a drooping red mustache. His companion was a muscular woman who wore gray pleated slacks and a matching vest over a loose black shirt to try to mask her ample chest. In their line of work her curvaceous figure was often a source of consternation for the team, but Jorgina Mizne was one of the best knife fighters in the world, along with being a superb interrogator, which more than made up for the minor inconvenience of her beauty.

Upon reaching a footpath, Zalhares turned into the trees and paused in a pool of shadow. The fourth member of the team, craggy-faced with a short ponytail, stepped out of the greenery. Once an escaping prisoner had foolishly grabbed that hair to try to subdue Artero Mariano, but the razor blades hidden inside had neatly sliced off his fingers. The prisoner had howled at the pain, but when Mariano got hold of him, the screaming really began.

Making sure they were alone, the four exchanged pointed glances, then nodded in readiness and checked their weapons.

"We're in the clear, Eagle One." Zalhares subvocalized into his throat mike, thumbing the control in the pocket of his windbreaker to change to the CIA channel. The unit automatically scrambled the broadcast, then shifted to another frequency and code so that even if MI-5 or the local police were listening in, they would never be able to decipher the transmission soon enough to stop what was happening in the peaceful London park.

"Our goat has arrived, Falcon," Osbourne said brusquely, his voice tense with controlled excitement. "Caucasian male, denim pants and shirt, portly, mustache, steel-rim glasses."

"Confirm, Eagle," Zalhares said, starting along the footpath. "We will engage. Want anybody alive for questioning, sir?"

There was a buzz of static in the earphone for a moment, masking the reply. "Hello, Eagle? Repeat, please, 10-2."

"Falcon, I said not this time," Osbourne said tersely. "Our psych department says that it will scare the hell out of the others in their group to have a team simply vanish off the face of the earth. No bodies, no news coverage, just gone. It makes the next batch of killers move a little slower, and thus easier to stop. Terminate with extreme prejudice."

The word is "kill," Zalhares thought snidely to himself. How can the CIA order something done if they're too cowardly to even speak the word? Americans were rich, but foolishly sentimental. A combination he found to be highly conducive for business.

"Confirmed," he said out loud. "Falcon out."

The rest of the Scion dispersed into the greenery as Zalhares turned toward the street. Reaching the corner, he saw a double-decker bus pull to a halt at the curb with a hiss of air brakes, the over-size vehicle gently rocking for a few seconds as the shocks rode out the inertia.

A short, fat man with metal glasses and tightly carrying a plain leather briefcase stepped quickly from the bus. As he started toward the park, several men rose from parked cars and headed after the plump courier. They were dressed in ridiculously loud sports coats with noticeable lumps under their arms from holstered weapons. Zalhares tried not to frown at the sight of the rank amateurs. These Libyan fools were a threat to America?

Hurrying down a footpath, the fat man darted into a break in the bushes and disappeared from sight. Only seconds behind, his pursuers quickly followed.

"Now," Zalhares said, entering the bushes from another direction.

"Confirm," Mariano replied.

Moving with silent grace, Zalhares slipped through the manicured hedges and entered a small clearing in the heart of the park. There he saw the four Libyans converge on the fat man, each of them carrying a stun gun or pepper spray. As they tried to cut off his escape, the courier simply dived to the ground, hugging the briefcase.

Zalhares and his people charged the circle of Libyans from behind. At the sound of their footsteps, the men turned from the cringing courier and the members of the Scion moved like lightning, each choosing a target and ramming a knife upward into the bottom of the jaw to pin the mouth shut.

As the startled Libyans began to choke on the blood filling their throats, they dropped the stun guns and spray cans and tried to pull real weapons, but it was too late.

Zalhares grabbed an arm of the biggest man and broke it with a twisting gesture, making him drop the 9 mm Glock pistol. Mariano did the same. Pedrosa crushed another man's neck in his bare grip, the bones audibly cracking. Mizne stabbed her target with another knife, leaving the blade buried deep in his chest to stem any possible gush of blood from the ruptured heart.

Only yards away from cheerful families having a picnic on the village green, the Libyan terrorists died, drowning in their own blood, not so much as a whisper escaping their lips. Rising from the ground, the fat courier nodded at the members of Scion in frank appreciation, then calmly walked away and out of sight. The moment he was gone, the mercs shifted the bodies behind some bushes instead of lugging them to the open sewer grating deeper in the parkland as they had the other corpses. Then they pulled their weapons and carefully checked the sleek sound suppressors attached to their Brazilian-made Imbel .22 pistols.

The mercs clicked off the safeties and racked the slides to chamber a round for immediate use.

"Eagle, this is Falcon," Zalhares said, touching his throat mike. "All clear."

"Confirm, Falcon. Another good job," Osbourne said. "And so ends the British cell of the Libyan National Front. Hell of a day, people. Forty-five terrorists killed and no breakage. Not an agent lost."

"Well, sir, a live Zodiac is a hell of a bait," another CIA agent added on the encrypted channel, a trace of a Southern accent in his voice. "Too good for those sons of bitches to pass up."

"Damn straight it is," Osbourne chuckled. "Good job, Falcon. You handle the bodies, and we'll cover the Zodiac to the truck. We'll meet you back at the Savoy Hotel for a debriefing."

Holstering his piece, Cirello Zalhares looked at his people and they nodded.

"Confirm, Eagle," he replied, giving a rare smile. "See you real soon."

But as the mercs began to leave, the bushes rustled near the stacked corpses and a London constable pushed his way into the clearing.

"What's going on here?" he demanded firmly.

Without pause, the Scion pulled their guns and fired, the silenced weapons whispering death. Grunting at each impact, the patrolman folded over and tumbled to the grass, bleeding from a dozen small wounds.

"Sorry, I was once a police officer myself," Mariano said, advancing close to press his weapon directly to the temple of the dying man. "But business is business."

Struggling to breathe, the unarmed constable clawed for the radio microphone hanging over his shoulder. Mariano fired the pistol. Jerking backward, the patrolman trembled for a moment, then lay still.

"Quickly! Get him into the bushes," Mizne directed, removing the partially used clip from the Imbel .22 and quickly inserting a fresh one. "We must not deviate from the plan!"

"Wait," Zalhares said slowly, glancing at the park beyond the thick hedges. "Maybe we can use this dead man to our advantage."

As THE PLUMP COURIER reached the footbridge near the bank of the Thames, six other men moved smoothly from the surrounding crowd to form a protective ring. Standing shoulder to shoulder, the CIA agents kept everybody away from the man and his battered old briefcase.

From on the footbridge, Osbourne keenly watched the milling civilians for any suspicious movements. But nobody seemed to be following the group or paying them any undue attention. Good. Everything seemed to be under control. Although Osbourne grudgingly admitted a faint unease at his inability to locate the constable who patrolled the riverbank. But since neither Scotland Yard nor the local bulls were privy to the covert actions here today, the fellow could just be having lunch, or was otherwise occupied.

Reaching into a pocket, Osbourne switched channels on his radio. "Nest, this is Eagle, all clear, we're on the way with the egg."

"We're ready, Eagle," a woman replied. "Hawks are live and ready for anything."

"Good. Stay alert, see you in five."

"Roger that, Eagle. Nest, out."

Passing a fish-and-chips vendor, one of the CIA agents scowled as an elderly woman liberally doused her chips with vinegar and salt.

"What the hell is a 'toad in the hole'?" he muttered. "Sounds like something you get from a Hong Kong hooker for fifty bucks."

"God, I want a hamburger so bad my dick hurts," another man answered curtly.

One of the other agents snorted a laugh. Everybody was starting to relax. This was the last Zodiac, they were in the clear now and it was smooth sailing. The project was completed and a total success.

"So after this, we'll hit the McDonald's in Piccadilly Square," the first agent said, scratching his chest to keep a hand near his gun. "Burgers and fries sounds good to me."

"Amen, brother."

"Please, I have not eaten American food in thirty years," the courier said, shifting his grip on the briefcase. "I would kill for a hot dog right about now."

"Then lunch is on the Agency. You guys did a hell of a job and deserve a bucket of medals. The least we can do is buy lunch."

"Yes, it is almost over," the courier said, sighing deeply. "Only a few more minutes and I shall be free."

At the base of the footbridge Osbourne joined the others and all conversation stopped. Staying in tight formation, the group swung around the library, to find an unmarked armored truck in the parking lot, the engine idling softly.

The two uniformed guards in the front nodded at Osbourne. One raised a mike from the dashboard to speak a single word, then tucked it away again. A few seconds later, heavy bolts could be heard disengaging before the thick rear door of the truck swung ponderously aside. Inside the vehicle there was a squat lead safe bolted to the floor and surrounded by six more CIA agents wearing flak jackets and armed with M-16 carbines. More weapons hung on the metal walls, along with medical kits, metal netting and ABC breathing masks. No chances were being taken this day.

As Osbourne and his team approached, the six guards assumed a firing stance.

"Blue skies," Osbourne said. "You can stand down."

At the all-clear signal, the guards moved away from the safe as the courier climbed into the truck. Kneeling on the floor, the plump man nervously wiped a sweaty palm on a leg to dry it first before pressing it to a security pad on top of the box. The indicator lights blinked twice, then the door loudly unlocked to swing aside, revealing several identical briefcases. Placing the item into a numbered slot, the courier closed the safe with a satisfied expression.

"Done," he whispered. "It's finally over."

A crackle of static sounded over everybody's earphones, followed by muffled gunfire.

"Red alert!" Zalhares shouted. "We have a situation in the drop zone. A police officer is down… shit, Dog is hit! We're under attack by an Iraqi backup team. We need immediate assistance Eagle! Now, goddammit, right now!"

Drawing his piece, Osbourne now realized why the constable had been missing. Poor bastard. "We're on the way, Falcon," Osbourne said, jumping out of the armored truck. "Let's move with a purpose, people!"

Pulling their weapons, the CIA agents poured onto the parking lot, then impatiently waited for the guards to close and lock the armored door. As the agents raced around the library, the strolling

civilians started to scream at the sight of armed
men running through the park.

Seconds later the Scion came charging around
the other side of the library, their weapons drawn
and Zalhares adjusting the preburner on a U.S.
Army M-1 flamethrower. Halfway to the armored
truck, he crouched against the recoil and pressed
the lever on the insulated wand to send out a
stream of napalm. The burning lance hit the rear
grille of the thick door and sprayed through to fill
the vehicle. Covered in flames, the guards and the
courier shrieked wildly and dashed around, slamming into the walls and one another in a blind
panic to escape. A few moments later the ammunition in the rifles began to cook off from the
mounting heat, the hardball ammo ricocheting off
the walls in a hellish clamor, cutting short the ag-
onized wails.

Seated in the front cab, the driver and uniformed guard couldn't see what was happening on
the other side of the steel wall in the rear of the
truck, but they could clearly hear the hideous
screaming. Grabbing a Remington shotgun from
a ceiling mount the uniformed guard racked the
slide to chamber a shell as the driver pulled a .357
Magnum pistol and threw open the sliding panel
covering the conversation grille. Broiling waves of
flame poured instantly into his face, searing his
skin and setting his hair on fire. Recoiling in a

wordless scream, the driver accidentally discharged his pistol, blowing a hole in the seat. He threw away the weapon to wave his hands at the flames engulfing his head.

"Jesus Christ!" the other guard cried, jerking backward against the door and raising the shotgun for protection.

Moving without conscious thought, the burning driver clawed at the handle of the cab door and shoved it open to throw himself outside to try to escape the flames. Tumbling to the cool pavement, the driver beat at the fire with his blistered hands and only vaguely noticed some people coming his way. There was a metallic cough, a flash of pressure, and his pain ended forever.

BURSTING THROUGH the hedges, Osbourne and his people found the dead Libyans and the constable. But there was no sign of the Scion or anybody else.

"Son of a bitch, we've been tricked!" Osbourne cursed angrily, grabbing his throat mike. "Nest, this is Eagle. Evac, now! Scion may be compromised! Repeat, Zalhares may have turned! Acknowledge!" There was only the soft hiss of background static as a reply.

"Nest, do you copy!" Osbourne demanded, pushing through the foliage and starting back toward the distant library. He could see a plume of dark smoke rising from behind the building and doubled his speed.

Police and fire department sirens were growing louder as the CIA operatives circled the library. Tendrils of smoke sailed through the air, which carried an aroma oddly reminiscent of roasted pork. The older agents scowled as they identified the stench of burned human flesh mixed with the telltale reek of napalm.

The hot wand and pressurized tanks of a flamethrower lay discarded on the pavement. Sprawled nearby were two bodies; the uniformed guard, obviously shot in the head, and what appeared to be the driver, although the face was burned beyond recognition. There was no sign of the armored truck.

"The bastards got them," an agent whispered. "Zalhares and his crew stole the entire shipment of Zodiacs!"

"Kissel, take two men and sweep the neighborhood for that truck or any more bodies," Osbourne growled, slowly holstering his gun. "I'll handle Scotland Yard. Wallace, grab a cab and get your ass to the American Embassy and call the White House."

"We'll need top authorization before we can brief the Brits on what's loose in their city," the agent replied, buttoning his jacket closed. "If then."

"Yeah, I know," Osbourne said woodenly as squads of police cars raced into the parking lot. "How can we tell anybody that the world just lost a battle in the war on terrorism?"

CHAPTER ONE

Aberystywyth, Wales

An old, dilapidated truck bearing two members of Scion trundled along the cliff road, the vast gray expanse of the Atlantic Ocean spreading in front of them to the distant horizon. No ships were in sight and no commercial jet planes flew overhead. Zalhares hadn't even seen another car for the past hour, but he still kept a sharp watch on the sky for any sign of a Harrier jump jet. That's what the British would send, the merc realized, something that could strike from the sky, then land to check the debris. He knew that the CIA would prefer a shoot-on-sight order, but with the Zodiacs in the possession of the Scion that would be far too dangerous. No, the orders would be to contain the merc unit and to call for reinforcements. But Zalhares had already taken steps to counter the event should it occur. Everything was under control, or rather, it would be in just a little while.

Hours passed as the two people in the battered vehicle bounced along the rough roadway, accompanied by the rattling of chains from the rear of the truck. A squat wooden box roughly the size of an office safe was securely chained in place on top of a thick bed mattress, the price tag still attached.

"Is this the best you could steal?" Jorgina Mizne muttered from the passenger seat, adjusting the baby blanket covering the 9 mm Uru submachine gun cradled in her arms.

"It will suffice," Zalhares said, braking in the middle of the road to check the hand-drawn map. Ah, the turn was over there. Aberystywyth Avenue. Good.

"Welsh, ha! And I thought English was spelled oddly." Mizne snorted in amusement.

"The English think of the Welsh the same way we do Bolivians," Zalhares said, tucking away the map. "Idiot cousins who should not be allowed to play with sharp things."

She flashed a predator smile. "Then they will not work well together to find us? Excellent."

"It is why I chose here," he said, shifting gears and starting forward.

Maneuvering past a pair of wooden markers

that bracketed the gravel road, Zalhares shifted gears again to the accompaniment of loud grinding noises as the truck started along the steep incline that wound down the face of the cliff. He had heard that the locals often referred to the road as Dead Man's Curve, but compared to the impossible mountain roads of western Brazil, it was a wide highway.

Reaching the rocky ground, a side road extended to the sleepy hamlet of Aberystywyth, which was so reminiscent of his home village of Botcaku it made Zalhares momentarily homesick. The bitter memories of wearing dirty rags for clothes and going to bed hungry for countless years killed the gentle recollections of playing with his brothers and sisters. His mind returned to the task at hand. Making money.

Soon the gravel became dirt, which abruptly turned into smooth pavement again as the truck rolled along the prehistoric-looking granite dock. Wooden jetties reached out to sea, the thick planks shiny from the constant spray of the waves crashing on the pillions underneath. A motor launch was moored at the farthest slip, guarded by several large men in raincoats. Two were smoking pipes, one was eating an apple, all were carrying Uzi submachine guns slung beneath yellow slickers.

More guards occupied the launch. A lone figure stood on the foredeck armed with an American surface-to-air Stinger missile, while another watched the skies through compact Russian military binoculars. American weapons, Russian equipment, Australian-registered cargo ship, the smugglers were the UN of crime operating in these waters, a covert cartel that dealt in the oldest currency in history—human misery.

Parking the truck a safe distance away, Zalhares got out as Mizne removed the blanket and leveled the Uru out the open window. The men on the dock reacted, then relaxed slightly as Zalhares stepped between them and the unusual weapon.

"Who the hell are you?" one of the smokers demanded, resting a hand on the checkered grip of the Uzi. The bolt was already pulled, the weapon primed and ready to fire.

"I hear this town used to mine tin for a living," Zalhares said loudly to be heard over the endlessly crashing waves.

The man with the apple tossed it away and stepped forward, wiping his hands on his pants. "Now we sell trinkets to the tourists," he said carefully. "But it's a living."

Code phrases exchanged properly, Zalhares touched a gloved finger to his ear to let Mizne know to stand down.

The leader of the sailors pulled out a military radio and hit the transmit button. "They're here," he announced, then turned it off.

Not a phone, but a radio. Zalhares approved. With so many high-orbit satellites scanning the transmissions of cell phones, it was safer to use a short-range radio for local communications. The signal was too weak to be intercepted by the military satellites and their damn code-breaking computers.

"The cargo is in the truck," Zalhares said, nodding in that direction. "You'll need a forklift."

"Jones, Smitty," the man shouted over a shoulder. "Get humping, boys."

The two men walked off, the third staying near the launch, puffing steadily on a briarwood pipe that looked older than the granite dock.

"So where is the *Tullamarine* anchored?" Zalhares asked, glancing at the rough sea. There was nothing visible to the horizon.

"Just past the ten-kilometer mark," the man replied gruffly. "That puts her in international waters and will be hard for the Brits to get on board without a bloody good reason."

"Then do not give them one," Zalhares said, locking eyes with the sailor for a moment.

The other man tried to match the gaze and had to turn away. His crew were professional smugglers, hardcases and killers from a dozen countries, but this dark foreigner had the look of a buttonman, a stone-cold assassin, and the boson knew that he was out of his league here.

Standing on the dock, the two men watched as the crew of the *Tullamarine* removed canvas sheeting from a forklift parked at the base of the cliff, far away from the corrosive salt spray of the surf. With the Uru in hand, Mizne stood guard as they dragged out the heavy wooden crate and hauled it over to the waiting launch. Everybody stayed alert until it was firmly lashed into place again with ropes and more chains.

Checking the lashings himself, the boson grunted in satisfaction, then climbed back onto the wet jetty and pulled out the radio. "Clear," he said before turning it off and tucking the transmitter into a pocket.

On the launch, the sailors started to release the mooring lines. The craft's big gasoline motor purred to life.

"Anything else?" the boson asked, pulling out another apple and polishing it on the front of his shirt before taking a bite.

"Yes," Zalhares said unexpectedly, pulling his flesh-colored gloves on tighter. "If there's any trouble, destroy the cargo. Just firing a few rounds into the wood should do the trick. The crate is packed with thermite charges so it will burn even if you toss it overboard."

"Fair enough," the boson replied, taking a juicy bite. "Not going to get a refund though."

The armed sailors laughed at that as they stored the lines in preparation to leave. Only the guard with the Stinger didn't join in, his hard eyes never leaving the clear blue sky.

"Don't worry about it," Zalhares replied, turning to walk back to the waiting truck. "We have already gotten our full money's worth from you."

Still chewing, the boson frowned at that and glanced nervously at the packing crate in the launch. Just what the hell kind of contraband were they smuggling out of England this time?

Washington, D.C.

HAL BROGNOLA SAT hunched over his desk, looking at a picture of his family, then at the clock, and back to the telephone, silently willing Mack Bolan to call. As he stared at the photograph of his wife and two children, he felt a momentary pang of remorse over spending too much time on the job and not enough with his loved ones. But such were the demands of his career. He had no choice, really. So here he was again, behind his desk at the Justice Department on the weekend. The big Fed sighed loudly. No rest for the wicked.

The phone rang. Darting out a hand to grab the receiver, Brognola forced himself to wait until the trace circuits finished their work. It only took a few seconds before the small plasma indent screen showed the phone call was coming from a delicatessen in Brooklyn, then switched to a motel in

Staten Island, a synagogue in Long Island, gas station in Harlem, Queens, Empire State Building, 42nd Street subway station, and so on, the location steadily changing every two seconds. Good, that meant it was Bolan and the Farm had tracked him down. Any phone call could be traced in time, but Aaron "The Bear" and Kurtzman the electronic wizards at Stony Man Farm had cooked up a device about the size of a pack of cigarettes that gave a hundred false identifications along with the legitimate location. It was classified as President Eyes Only and very few people in the entire world even knew of its existence, much less possessed the scrambler. Mack Bolan had the very first model released.

"Brognola," he answered, lifting the receiver.

"It's me," Bolan said.

"Thank God, Striker," Brognola exhaled, leaning back in his chair. "Do you know what Project Zodiac is?" he asked without preamble.

There was a brief pause. "I have heard rumors," Bolan replied. "Some sort of doomsday plan from the cold war."

"Damn close. President Kennedy wanted something to put the fear of God into the Soviets, and the CIA cooked up Project Zodiac. Twelve deep-cover agents scattered across Europe, with wives, jobs, children. They lived undercover for years before receiving their Zodiac."

"Twelve agents, each with a code name after a sign of the Zodiac," Bolan said. "Capricorn, Virgo, and such. Cute. Sounds like the kind of nonsense the CIA thinks is clever."

"Yeah, you hit the nail on the head. Only these sleeper agents weren't saboteurs sent to blow up certain targets, they were equipped with a compact nuclear device that fit into a standard-size briefcase."

"Can it be that small and achieve threshold?"

"Different configuration," Brognola stated, "and they work just fine. I've seen the films from the White Sands bomb range. Each of these has a full one-quarter kiloton yield, just about enough to vaporize six city blocks and destroy six more with the concussion and heat flash. Very nasty stuff, and as dirty as hell."

"So if America fell to an enemy sneak attack, these sleeper agents walk their Zodiac to some military target and blow it up," Bolan said, clearly thinking out loud. "How did they handle the blast? With a timer or by radio detonator?"

"A Zodiac detonates by hand," Brognola said without emotion. "It's a suicide device. After you set the internal trigger and close the lid, the agent only has to grab the handle tight and the next time he releases it, the bomb detonates."

"The handle is the trigger. So shooting the agent would only set off the Zodiac when he let go. Just like shooting a man holding a primed grenade," Bolan said, the disgust strong in his voice. "America strikes back from the grave. So what went wrong? Somebody find a list of the agents? Or did one of them turn and sell a Zodiac to some terrorist group?"

In reply, the big Fed inhaled, then let it out slowly.

"Or is it worse than that, Hal?" Bolan demanded.

"It's worse," the man admitted. "Last month the President canceled Project Zodiac. But when the CIA recalled the Zodiacs, they deliberately let the information slip out."

There came a soft rustle of cloth as if the man on the other end of the line was shaking his head. "They used the nukes as bait, a damn stalking horse," Bolan stated, not needing to hear any more. "Okay, what went wrong?"

"At first, nothing. The CIA was blowing away terrorist groups from across the globe, and then…the perimeter guards stole the truck of bombs right from under their noses."

That only took Bolan a second to translate. "So the cheap bastards were using mercs again," he growled.

"You got it. Save a buck and lose the war. Those guys spend too much time playing politics and trying to look good to Congress than they do getting the job done."

"Preaching to the choir here, Hal."

Softly in the background, Brognola could hear people chatting and machinery moving. Was it a recording, or was Striker actually calling from an airport or bus terminal?

"So the mercs now have twelve atomic bombs."

"No, only four," Brognola corrected. "The CIA may screw up big sometimes, but they're not complete fools. Nobody but the mission chief knew that identical armored trucks were going to carry away every third collection. The mercs probably thought they were stealing all twelve, but they only got four."

"Only four," Bolan said in a graveyard voice.

"Yeah, I know. And that's about the only goddamn good thing about this whole mess."

"So why call me? Can't find them?"

The man's mind moved like lightning. "That's about the size of it. The rendezvous point was in London somewhere and the Brits are having a fit over this going down in their backyard without their okay. MI-5 has every agent on the hunt, with the city sealed tighter than a virgin on prom night. The SAS and the CIA are tearing the countryside apart trying to find the mercs, but so far nothing. Meanwhile, the PM is screaming bloody murder at the White House."

"Can't blame him," Bolan said calmly. "If another country had tried that here, we'd tear them a new one."

"At least one, maybe two."

"Got an ID on the mercs?"

"Yeah." Brognola sighed, leaning forward in his chair and lifting a Top Secret file from the clutter on his desk. "I'm holding their Agency dossier in my hand. The Scion. Know them?"

There was a short pause. "Never heard of them before. Give me the basics and have the full dossier sent to a drop site at Grand Central Train Station."

"No problem," he said, opening the file. "Okay, their leader is a guy named Cirello Zalhares—"

Interrupting, Bolan grunted at that. "Wait, big Brazilian guy, used to work for the S2," he said. "Works with Dog Mariano, Minas Pedrosa, and a woman, Jorgina something. A real looker, loves knives."

"Jorgina Mizne, that's them."

"So Zalhares now calls his group of mercenaries the Scion? Yeah, that sounds like right. He always did enjoy grandstanding."

"Christ, Striker," Brognola said with a dry chuckle. "Have you got every freelance killer in the entire world locked in that mental file of yours?"

"Only the live ones," Bolan said humorously. And yeah, he knew them. An elite group of mercs who were all former S2 agents cashiered out of the service for various crimes against their fellow police officers: murder, rape, blackmail, torture and worse. During the communications blackout, Phoenix Force had had a brief encounter with the S2 when they tried to flee Brazil. They were serious hardcases, tougher than any of the street soldiers from the Mafia or the defunct KGB.

"Is this intel hard?" Bolan demanded.

"Confirmed and double-checked," Brognola replied. "Now we have the Middle East sealed tight, and the leader of every known terrorist group under surveillance, along with the arms dealers and top smugglers."

"Now you want the unknown groups covered," Bolan said slowly. "Then I'm in the right town. If anything big like this is coming into America, I have contacts in New York who will know."

"Just one more thing, Striker. You should know that these are kamikaze models. Shoot one, and even if its not already armed, the bomb detonates automatically. The Zodiacs have to be recovered intact and undamaged."

"Then the sooner I move, the better the chances they won't be damaged," Bolan said unruffled. "Talk to you later, Hal."

"Hold the line, Striker," Brognola said as the encrypted fax machine whined into life on his desk. "I have a report coming in from the Oval Office…. Well, I'll be a son of bitch. We found them! The Brits got an anonymous tip from a reliable source that an Australian cargo ship, *Tullamarine*, is ferrying the Zodiacs out of England. The captain has refused to turn around for an inspection and now they're pretending the radio and cell phone are all dead. RAF fighters are on the way to do a recon."

For a moment Bolan said nothing.

"Looks like this was a lot of excitement over nothing, old friend. We have them cornered."

"Hal, recall those planes," Bolan stated firmly. "I'm betting that anonymous tip came from Zalhares."

"But why would he do that?"

"Trust me, Hal. It's some sort of trick. Recall those planes."

Just then, the fax whined once more, extruding another encrypted report. "Too late," Brognola said out loud, reading fast. "The RAF has already engaged the Scion."

CHAPTER TWO

Norwegian Sea

Dropping out of the clouds at 990 mph, the five RAF jetfighters streaked toward the Atlantic Ocean until they were skimming along the water barely above the waves. At these speeds, a single twitch of a hand on the joystick or an unexpected thermal, and the multimillion dollar fighters would go straight into the drink. However, the risk was worth it. At this height, the jets would be practically invisible to any ship's radar until it was far too late and they were in camera range.

"Wing Commander Lovejoy, this is Vivatar," a nasally voice said into the earphones of the pilots. The RAF controller was using the code name for the local UK air base. "Permission to fire has been granted by the PM. Repeat, you may arm all weapon systems."

The Prime minister? Bloody hell. "Roger, Vivatar, confirm," Captain Adrian "Lovejoy" Scott said into his helmet microphone. "Will recon first for friendlies, then proceed to disable engines. Over."

"Roger and confirmed, Lovejoy. Good hunting, chaps!"

"Disable their engines, my arse," Shadowboxer said on the pilot-to-pilot channel. "We should blow the bastards out of the water. Miniature nukes, just how crazy are those damn Yanks?" From the rear seat of the two-man Tornado G1-B, his navigator wholeheartedly agreed.

"Cut the chatter, Shadow," Lovejoy ordered as the radar beeped and a tiny image appeared on the horizon. Preset, the video screen on the dashboard did a zoom to show a cargo ship bearing Australian markings. "Okay, there it is. I'm going in for an ident, Merlin and Red Cat stay on my wings. Shadowboxer, Crippen, maintain position."

Dropping out of Mach, the front three delta-shaped Jaguars slowed their speed as the two sleek Tornados folded back their wings to peel away at full throttle, soon reaching Mach 2.5, and began to widely arch around the target zone.

With the cool air whispering past the bubble canopies of the Jaguars, the choppy Norwegian Sea below was sable in color, the dull gray cargo ship almost lost in the sheer vastness of the ocean. Which was probably the whole idea, Lovejoy thought.

Still slowing their approach, the three Jaguars flew past the *Tullamarine* with their video cameras on automatic. The wide cargo ship was probably moving at its top speed, but compared to the British jetfighters it might as well have been nailed in place.

On the dashboard of his jet fighter, Commander Lovejoy studied the relayed pictures from the belly cameras. The infrared scanners had focused on every human-size thermal and showed only sharp images of armed men on the decks. No women, or children, and nobody who appeared to be held as a hostage. Nothing but a room-by-room search would ever truly show if the vessel was completely clear of innocent people, but this was the best the RAF pilots could do at the moment. With any luck, the crew would surrender and the question of civilians would never arise.

"It's the *Tullamarine*, all right," Red Cat said, slowing even more. "I can read the bow."

Just then there was a fast series of flashes from all over the cargo ship and a flurry of Stinger missiles rose quickly on smoky contrails.

"Incoming," Lovejoy reported calmly, dropping chaff and flares in his wake. The other Jaguars duplicated the tactic and the Stingers detonated harm-

lessly in the open air, the expanding halo of shrapnel never even coming close to the speeding jets.

"Target is hostile. Repeat, target is hostile,"
Lovejoy announced grimly, banking into a turn.
"Shadow, take out their radar."

"My pleasure, Lovejoy!"

An ALARM missile streaked inward from out
of the distance, locking on the signal of the ship's
radar and striking the rotating dish dead center.
The explosion blew it apart and damaged a good
section of the bridge, windows shattering for yards
in every direction

"Good shooting, Shadow."

"Roger, Commander!"

The crew was running madly around, firing
more Stingers and what the RAF computers soon
identified to the pilots as LAW and SRAW rockets.
The smugglers seemed to be throwing anything
they had into the sky and hoping for a lucky hit.

"Shadow and Crippen, keep those Stingers busy
while we hit the engine," Lovejoy directed, dropping into an attack profile and checking the readouts
on his console. Fuel good, weapons hot, no damage.

In tight formation, the five jets streaked toward
the cargo ship and cut loose with their cannons,
the 27 mm rounds of the two Tornados raking the
vessel from bow to stern, the fusillade sending a
score of men diving for cover as the fat rounds

deeply dented the deck and chewed several lifeboats to pieces.

Meanwhile the Jaguars concentrated on the flat stern of the wide ship, their larger 30 mm rounds stitching lines of holes across the steel achieving full penetration. Soon, smoke was pouring from the portholes and the turbulent wake of the vessel went still, the great props rotating to a slow stop.

"She's dead in the water, boys," Lovejoy said, then banked sharply as yet another flight of Stingers rose from the disabled ship. "But we don't yet have their full cooperation."

"Let's give them two deadheads in the north," Crippen suggested, spreading his wings to match speed with the slower Jaguars. "That'll put the fear of God into them."

"Sounds good. Splash two hot pickles," Lovejoy stated. "But this is their last chance. Afterward, we start them hard. Dover, take the bow, Red Cat, take the stern. Shadow and I will fly the midship to draw fire. And keep it tight! We want them scared, not dead."

"Shitless, not spitless," Red Cat said. "Will comply."

Flying in a staggered line, the fighters raced past the cargo ship, Crippen and Red Cat cutting loose a pair of Sidewinder missiles. With the guidance systems of the missiles turned off, the deadly heat-seekers simply flew straight past the cargo ship, knifing down into the ocean where they violently exploded. Twin plumes rose to throw a spray of hot salt water across the ship, knocking several of the crew overboard.

"Damn good shooting, boys!" Lovejoy stated, but then, incredibly, saw the stuttering fireflies of small-arms weapons being fired from around the open cargo hatch.

Oh surrender already, blokes.

"What is the ETA for the Harriers, Commander?" Merlin asked, slipping sideways in preparation for another attack run.

"Harriers from the HMS *Edward III* should be here in five minutes," Lovejoy replied. "RAN helicopters in fifteen, and a Yank Los-Angeles-class submarine will arrive in about half an hour."

"Thirty minutes? Too slow, chicken marango!" Red Cat quoted with a laugh. "It'll be all over by…. Wait, what the hell are they doing? They're dumping something overboard."

Once again, fireflies danced along the starboard railing of the ship, but this time the crew pointed their weapons low, as if shooting at the water.

"Did they toss something overboard?" Lovejoy asked, dropping lower for a closer inspection when a blinding white light rose from the cold Norwegian Sea to fill the universe.

The expanding fireball caught Merlin and Shadowboxer, vaporizing the jet fighters instantly.

Just far enough away from the blast to survive, it took Crippen and Red Cat a full second to realize what had happened. The pilots shoved their joysticks to the stop as they desperately punched for the sky. Their ships were shielded from the EMP blast of a nuke, so if they could just get outside the thermal flash and...

The physical shock wave of air compressed to the density of stone slammed into the RAF fighters, ripping off their wings, the fuselages crumpling around the men and trapping them inside the smashed jets. The damage activated the ejector seats, crushing the pilots into bloody jelly as the charges hurtled the seats directly into the wadded canopies. A split second later, the ruptured fuel tanks detonated, igniting every missile.

In a strident series of explosions, flaming debris rained from the clear azure sky to vanish below the radioactive waves, where soon there was nothing remaining but the empty, boiling ocean.

42nd Street Subway Station, New York

IT WAS QUIET and dark at Mack Bolan's end of the old subway platform where graffiti covered the walls. The stairs were closed off with a folding iron grating padlocked into place and the door to the access tunnel was equally protected. Aside from the bank of old pay phones, half of them missing all together, there was nothing and no reason for anybody to go to that section of the subterranean platform so far away from the bright lights and busy crowds. Which made it just about perfect for Bolan's needs.

"Hold on, Striker," Brognola said over the receiver. "Another fax is coming. Be right back."

"I'll wait," Bolan said, leaning against the dirty tiled wall. In the Executioner's opinion, there was no way the Scion would have been caught in that stupid a move.

Bolan's combat sense flared, and he felt that he was the center of someone's attention long before hearing the approach of boots on the dirty concrete.

"Hey, you!"

Turning slowly, Mack studied the group of six teenagers coming his way. They were shabbily dressed in torn clothing, but the damage seemed to be more deliberate than natural wear and tear. That assessment was compounded by the fact that they were wearing hundred-dollar sneakers and ten-dollar pants. Two were smoking, one was chewing gum with his mouth open and a third was an acne-scarred kid moving to the beat of the music thumping coming from his stereo headphones, a fancy CD player hanging from a wide leather garrison belt. However, despite their youth, each was smiling at the easy mark standing in front of them, a lone man in a secluded section of the subway without a cop in sight.

Stopping a short distance away, the tallest of the group flicked his wrist and a switchblade snapped into existence at the end of a fist.

"Give us your fucking wallet," he said, sneering. "That fancy watch, too!"

Still holding the phone receiver, Bolan turned sideways and lashed out with a shoe, the tip stabbing the boy hard in the stomach. The air left his lungs in an explosive grunt and the teen dropped his blade to stagger away, clutching his stomach and looking as if he was about to vomit.

As the rest of the gang stared hard at their intended victim, the Executioner gave them a look from the pits of Hell. The would-be predators shifted uneasily under his stern gaze, and most began to back away, splaying their hands in a sign of surrender.

"What are you waiting for?" the leader snarled, forcing himself to stand upright. "Kill that motherfucker!"

"Striker, you still there?" Brognola said over the receiver.

Bolan grunted in reply, watching the scene play out. How much authority the leader of the street gang held over his people would decide if blood would be spilled. Did they follow him out of simple fear, or respect?

"Hey, mister, we didn't mean nothing," a bald kid said, backing away. "Be cool. No corpse, no crime, right?"

"Wrong," Bolan said, the one word hanging in the air between them like a rumble of thunder.

"You punk-ass bitches leaving?" the leader snarled. "Then I'll ace him myself!"

Lurching forward, the teen threw an overhand haymaker at Bolan that would have broken bones if it hit. Dropping the receiver, Bolan went under the swing, then stood again with coiled-steel speed, driving two stiff fingers directly in the teenager's armpit.

Yowling in pain, the gang lord staggered backward, tears running down his face, the arm dangling impotently at his side like meat in a butcher's window. Bolan swept back his sports jacket to expose the Beretta 93-R riding in a shoulder holster.

"Go home," he said in a voice from beyond the grave. "Now."

The rest of the gang simply turned and ran, one of them scrambling so fast he slipped on some trash and almost went over the edge of the platform onto the abandoned tracks below. Only the leader sneered hatefully in reply and staggered away, cradling his damaged arm.

"Striker?" Brognola's voice called through the receiver in concern.

"Right here, Hal," Bolan said, drawing the

Beretta. Reaching up with the weapon, he used the sound suppressor to smash the exposed fluorescent lights overhead. As darkness crashed around the man, Bolan stepped farther into the shadows and leveled the weapon in preparation.

"Okay, I just got a report from the President. Goddamn it, how did you know?" Brognola said irritably. "The NSA just relayed a message to the Oval Office that the thermal flash of the blast registered only one Zodiac. Not four, just one. Zalhares and his people nuked an entire cargo ship, plus a full wing of RAF jets just to fool us into thinking they were dead."

There was a movement behind the iron grating covering the sealed-off stairs; the gray muzzle of a gun stuck out a few inches at about waist level. Bolan did nothing, waiting for the kid to make the choice. In a rush of speed, the teenager stepped into plain view holding a Glock .45 pistol. Bolan fired once, the muzzle-flash of the Beretta brightening the shadows as the 9 mm Parabellum round smashed into the Glock. The damaged pistol went flying onto the train tracks with a loud clatter. Cradling his broken hand, the gang lord staggered away, sobbing and cursing at the same time.

"If there hadn't been a Keyhole satellite sweeping the area, it might have worked, too," Brognola continued.

"Not for me," Bolan said, holstering the

Beretta. "The Scion is famous for its traps, and for playing dead. That's Zalhares's favorite trick. Whenever possible, he strikes from behind."

"That's not mentioned in his personnel file, but I'll take your word."

For a brief moment Bolan gave a rare smile. "Smart man. What I need now is a good description of a Zodiac, with as much detail as possible."

"Better than that. The design was taken from the most popular briefcase sold by an upscale luggage manufacturer. I can tell you the exact number of the model the Pentagon used."

"Good. Start talking," Bolan said, brushing some flecks of broken glass off his sleeve. Listening closely, the Executioner filed away the information as the big Fed told him the make and model of the matching briefcase, then how to arm and disarm a Zodiac. The process was slow and complex, but then these weren't battlefield weapons where speed of operation was considered an imperative.

"Got it," he said at last. "Thanks, Hal."

"Stay hard, Striker. These people mean business."

"I'm depending on it," Bolan answered. "A merc's lust for money is what always brings them down."

Disconnecting, Bolan then lifted the receiver and dialed randomly to scramble the memory on the machine.

Leaving the subway via the main entrance, the Executioner melted into the crowds and walked directly to a major department store downtown. He used cash to make a few purchases, then exited the building, pausing in a nearby alley to open the packages and throw away the wrappings. He then roughened the shiny leather of the new briefcase by rubbing it against a brick wall. When satisfied, Bolan returned to his car and plugged a small soldering iron into the dashboard outlet to quickly assemble an array of electronic components into a maze of wires and circuit boards that wouldn't fool anybody trained in nuclear ordnance, but might do the job on the Scion.

According to the CIA dossier, most of Zalhares's people came from farms and had little or no education, aside from military training. They may not know a mock-up from a working nuke. More importantly, the weight should be about the same because of the addition of two blocks of C-4 plastique and a fully functioning radio detonator. Bolan might never have any use for the decoy, but it was always wise to plan for what an enemy could do, not for what they might do.

Grabbing a cup of coffee and a sandwich at a corner deli, the soldier mapped out a battle plan while eating lunch. He was interrupted when a group of businessmen walked by carrying briefcases and, from out of nowhere, a raggedly dressed man darted from the curb to grab one of the cases, wrestle it away from the owner and take off at a run holding the prize. Furious, the owner shouted after the thief.

The incident had just been a simple robbery; nobody was even hurt. But if done to the Scion, a city would be obliterated from the map.

No longer hungry, Bolan left a decent tip for the old waiter and headed across town. New York City was the nerve center of international crime, and he could find out almost anything if he asked the right people, using the right kind of persuasion. The numbers were already falling on this, and it was time for him to start the hunt for Zalhares.

CHAPTER THREE

Central Park, New York City

A gray-haired man was sitting on a park bench tossing bread crumbs to the cooing pigeons. His clothes were clean and well pressed, the crease in the pants sharp, almost as if he were wearing a uniform of some kind. It was a peaceful, secluded section of park, near enough to see the lake, but well off the bike trails. There was nobody around but the old man and the pigeons.

A short, wiry man walked into view along the lake. He was neatly attired in a dark suit that was extremely out of date.

Strolling along, the newcomer detoured widely around the flock of pigeons to finally sit at the other end of the park bench. For a few minutes neither man spoke.

"Okay, Pat, nobody seems to have followed me. So what the hell is going on?" Brian Kessel, the director of the New York branch of the FBI, demanded in a soft, conversational tone. "Why the secret meeting away from our offices?"

"Too many ears," Police Chief Patrick Donaldson said, tossing another handful of crumbs to the fluttering pigeons. Then he rolled the bag shut and tucked it into a pocket of his coat. "Heard the news lately?"

Spoken that way, the news could only mean something in their line of work, and there was only one topic of conversation these days—the unsolved string of murders.

"Bet your ass I have," Kessel said, not looking at the other man. "But it's not us, if that's what you're hinting about. I can assure you of that."

"Thirty-six hours," Donaldson said, leaning back in the bench. The birds were gobbling up the crumbs and strutting around looking for more. Such a little act of kindness, feeding the hungry birds, it brought a sense of balance into the violent life of the top Manhattan cop. "It has been less than thirty-six hours and nineteen of the top weapons dealers in the world have been whacked in my town. I'm not a happy man, Brian. This smells like a goddamn secret government kill team."

"No way," Kessel replied curtly. "Impossible.

If the CIA or some black ops group tried that, I'd have their balls for breakfast."

"I thought that'd be your response."

"Look. It could be the Yakuza, the Russian Mob, the Chinese Tongs, Rastafarians, Colombians," he growled softly. "It's been a fucking feeding frenzy the past few years."

Watching the pigeons peck for more bread crumbs, the police chief shrugged. No matter how much he gave, they always wanted more. Sort of like his job. There were goals, but they were always replaced with more goals. In police work, the reward for a job well done was always a tougher job.

"Let the creeps blow each other away, that's fine by me," Donaldson stated in frank honesty. "I don't give a shit. Twenty little mobs are a hell of a lot easier to control than one huge invisible empire. Just ask the OCD."

"The Organized Crime Division can kiss my ass. Vigilante justice undermines the very fabric of society," Kessel stated with an angry growl.

"So it really isn't the Bureau?" Donaldson asked.

"No."

"Damn."

For a while the two lawmen sat on the concrete bench, listening to music from somewhere nearby and the shrill voices of children at play. Opening the bag again, Donaldson tossed the birds another handful, then offered it to Kessel. After a pause, the FBI director took some and sprinkled it across the pavement. The birds flocked around the cops, utterly ecstatic.

"So, who do you think is next on the list?" Kessel asked.

"What the hell," the cop replied wearily. "I don't know of anybody left."

Tyree Building, Staten Island

THROWING BACK his head, Alexander Tyree inhaled sharply and then relaxed. Crawling out from under the conference table, the naked blond woman padded over to the mirrored bar set into the wall and poured herself a short Scotch whiskey. Draining the tumbler, she gargled first, then swallowed the rest of the drink.

"You're the best, baby," Tyree said, closing his zipper. "See you tomorrow. Same time, eh?"

"No problem, sir," she said woodenly, rinsing out the glass before placing it in the sink. Stepping into black high heels, the hooker slipped on a full-length mink coat and walked out of the penthouse office, closing the door tightly behind her.

Rubbing his face for a moment, Tyree reached into a pocket and withdrew a small vial of white powder. Thumbing off the cap, the man poured the cocaine onto the polished mahogany table. Taking

out a pocketknife, he was about to neatly cut the
pile into lines when he heard a wet smack on the
window. What the hell? Damn birds had to have
flown into the glass again.

Glancing over a shoulder, Tyree blinked in confusion at the sight of a small gray lump of clay-
like material stuck to the bulletproof glass. There
was a nylon rope attached, as if it had been lowered from the roof. Then he spotted the flashing
red light of the remote detonator set into the wad
of C-4 plastique.

Throwing himself out of the chair, Tyree hit the
carpet a split second before the high-explosive
wad cut loose and the window stridently imploded
across the office, flipping over the conference
table and sending the line of wheeled chairs spinning crazily in every direction.

The concussion brutally shoved Tyree hard
against the marble wall. He was fighting to regain
his breath when a dark figure lowered into view
from above and swung in through the smoking
ruin of the window.

LANDING ON HIS crepe-soled shoes, Mack Bolan
slapped the release buckle of the safety harness
around his waist and anchored the line to the splintered ruin of the thirty-foot-long conference table.
Dressed for full urban combat, the Executioner
was in a black combat suit. A web belt of ordnance

and ammo circled his waist, a Beretta 93-R rode in a shoulder holster and a big-bore .357 Magnum Desert Eagle claimed the opposite hip.

A muffled pounding came from the other side of the door to the office, but Bolan ignored it. This was Tyree's private retreat, his secret bolthole, and the only place in New York where the international arms dealer could relax completely safe. The entire building was a fortress, and this particular floor his personal bunker, the floor, walls and ceiling each composed of two full yards of steel-reinforced concrete. According to the engineering blueprints, the foot-thick titanium door would stop a 60 mm shell, and the magnetic locks could be turned off only from this side. Bolan estimated that Tyree's bodyguards wouldn't be able to get through in under an hour. More than sufficient. It had taken Bolan an entire day to track down the hidden location of the retreat, and less than an hour to crack its five-million-dollar security system.

Hauling the crime boss off the ripped carpeting, Bolan slammed him against the Italian-marble wall and pressed the cold pit of the Beretta's sound suppressor into the man's stomach.

"What the hell," Tyree mumbled, clearly still disorganized from the explosion.

Keeping the Beretta in place, Bolan slapped the man across the face. "Get it together, Tyree. This is judgment day."

Rubbing his stinging cheek, the man sneered at that. "So this is a raid," he said. "Well, go ahead, cop, read me my rights. Arrest me. My lawyers will have me on the street in an hour!"

Shifting the aim of the weapon, Bolan fired and blood erupted from the man's shoulder as the 9 mm slug grazed the skin and ricocheted off the cracked marble.

"Stop! You can't do that!" Tyree shouted, grabbing the shallow flesh wound. "Cops can't shoot prisoners!"

"I'm not a cop," Bolan said bluntly, shifting the Beretta to center on the man's heaving chest.

The implication was clear and Tyree went pale. "It's a hit? B-but I got connections! I pay protection!"

"Not against me."

Starting to understand the gravity of the situation, Tyree nervously licked dry lips. "Look, I'm just a businessman. We can cut a deal here," Tyree said, keeping a palm pressed to his bleeding shirt. "There's money in the wall safe behind the mirror in the bar. A hundred grand in cash. It's yours. Take it and go."

"Wrong answer," Bolan stated coldly.

"Look, I know the Dragon missiles were shit, but the buyers were al-Qaeda," he said, the words gushing out in a torrent, "and this is New York, for Christ's sake! Whack me if ya want, but screw those Afghan dirtbags and the hairy-ass camels they rode in on."

For one of the very few times in his turbulent life, Mack Bolan found himself caught absolutely by surprise. Then he looked hard into the man's sweaty face and saw it was the truth. Incredible.

"You sold fake missiles to terrorists," Bolan repeated slowly.

Filled with the bravado that comes in the face of inevitable death, Tyree gave a snort. "Yeah, fuck him, and fuck you, too!" he retorted, rubbing his aching shoulder. "Go ahead, shoot me! Get it the fuck over with!"

"Not today," the Executioner said. "Maybe we can cut a deal."

Hope flared in his eyes and Tyree glanced at the bar.

"Not for cash," Bolan countered, keeping the weapon level but shifting it off center. "But I'll trade information in exchange for your life."

"Done," Tyree agreed quickly. "What do ya want to know?"

Smart fellow. No wonder he seized control of the East Coast weapons traffic from the Jewish mob. "Some Brazilian muscle is smuggling weapons into the country," Bolan said, deliberately being as vague as possible. He'd give more details if necessary, but only what was necessary.

"Big stuff, small package. Who would they approach to broker a sale? I want a name."

Gingerly massaging his upper arm, Tyree listened to the thumping on the armored door for a while, but said nothing, deep in thought.

Was he cooking a lie or digging for a name? Bolan wondered. He sincerely hoped the man was going to play it straight, because there was nobody else to ask. This was the end of the line, which was why he had opted for a stunt like swinging in through the window instead of ambushing the man in the elevator.

"Brazilian," Tyree said slowly. "So it's the Commies, the rebels, or the S2? Right?"

Bolan nodded.

"The Communists and the rebels ain't got shit to sell. They're buyers, but so broke they can't afford anything important, so that means it's the S2," Tyree said at last. "Okay, there's a guy, lives out in Belmore, Long Island. Deals a lot with those assholes. Name is Michael Prince. Fat guy, silk suits, uses a cigarette holder."

Yeah, Bolan knew the name, but not much more. Michael Prince, the self-proclaimed Prince of the City. So he was handling weapons now. The rope suddenly had some extra length.

"Call anybody, and I'll come back," Bolan said, tucking the Beretta into its holster. "Only next time, we don't talk."

"Hey no problem." The man smiled weakly. "Time for me to retire anyway."

Attaching the safety belt as a prelude to rapelling down the side of the building, Mack Bolan paused at the window to glance over a shoulder.

"Dummy missiles?" he said, giving a brief hard smile.

"What the hell." Tyree sighed, looking past the Executioner at the distant Manhattan skyline with a noticeable gap in the line of towering skyscrapers. "It's a new world."

Richmond, Virginia

EVENING WAS starting to fall across the lush Virginia countryside as the dark gray sedan rolled off the highway and into the suburbs of Richmond. The streets were astonishingly clean and lined with old trees, the front lawn of each house wide and immaculately maintained, with dogwood flowers sweetly scenting the air. Every car was in a garage or parked on the driveway; nobody was using the street.

"Jeez, it's like something out of a Disney movie," Cliff Maynard complained from behind the wheel. "I keep waiting for the music to swell and credits to roll."

"Got to be a tough commute to D.C. every day,"

Eliza Linderholm replied, checking the power-pack in her Taser. Tucking the electric stun gun away, the CIA agent pulled out a Glock 21 pistol and carefully threaded on a sound suppressor. Mr. Osbourne wanted the woman alive, undamaged if possible, but that wasn't carved in stone.

"Maybe Dupont likes the peace of the countryside," Cliff continued, reaching under his jacket and snapping off the strap of his shoulder holster. "It'd drive me crazy."

"Amen to that, brother." Linderholm smiled. "I'm a big-city girl and plan to stay that way."

Back in Langley, the Agency was at its most busy when the place was quiet. Casual conversations and laughter meant that nothing important was happening in the world, an uncommon event. To any CIA agent, peace and quiet always meant trouble.

"This must be it," Maynard said, checking the map on the dashboard display. He turned off his navigational computer and it folded back out of sight.

"You sure this is the right address?" Linderholm asked, sliding a medical pack into her skirt pocket. The boss had sent her along in case Helen Dupont was found in the shower or the agents had to strip search for weapons. After the debacle in London, the Agency was toeing the line on every government regulation. At least, for the present conflict.

"Got it out of her personnel file," Maynard said, parking the sedan on the street a few houses away. Down the block, a old man watering his lawn studied the strange car in frank disapproval, then turned his back on them to concentrate on the weeding and fertilizing.

Pulling out a monocular scope, Linderholm swept the vicinity for anybody standing guard. The house was a modest two-story. Fake wooden shutters sat alongside the windows for purely artistic effect, which was ruined by the addition of a plastic gnome in the flower garden. Returning the scope to her pocket, the black woman shrugged at the sight. At least it was better than those racist Civil War lawn jockeys.

"Looks clean," she reported.

"Good enough," Maynard said. "Then let's go catch a traitor."

A low-level G4 clerk in the records department of the Agency, Helen Dupont was rather plain-looking, but known for getting overly friendly on the weekends. Fair enough. Nobody cared about sexual peccadilloes, as long as they were discreet. Consenting adults, and all that. However, a routine security check revealed that Dupont seemed to only be going to bed with people in the technical repair department. And the technicians had been among the very first people told about the plan to recover the Zodiacs so that they would be ready to safely disassemble the bombs.

However, in the opinion of Special Team Leader David Osbourne, that sounded suspiciously like sexual backpay. A crude spy would offer sex in exchange for secret information. Sometimes that worked, mostly it didn't. On the other hand, a good spy would have sex with the target several times, hundreds of times over many years if possible, to build a good rapport and then have emotional leverage on the victim. Now the requested intel seemed more like a favor, with the implied threat of ending the affair if denied. The Agency did that themselves, and the ploy worked more often than not. To discover it was being done to them was extremely disturbing.

New rules for sexual conduct were already being drafted, but that wasn't the pressing problem at the moment. Plain, sweet, sexually repressed until the weekend, Helen Dupont had left the office complaining of a migraine headache exactly when the Scion had stolen the truckload of Zodiac bombs.

It could just be a coincidence, those did happen. But the team was taking Dupont to the section chief for questioning. Just routine. Unless she cracked, and then the traitor would be hauled down to the Tank, the soundproofed room in the basement where enemies of the nation could be strenuously interrogated without undue interruptions.

Getting out of the car, the agents started for the house, but froze at the sight of the slightly ajar front door.

Returning to the car, Linderholm pulled out a radio and called for more agents as Maynard moved along the driveway and to the side of the door. Openly pulling his piece, the man waited, holding his breath to try to hear any noises from inside. But the house was silent. A few moments later Linderholm was at the other side of the door, weapon drawn. The agents nodded three times in unison counting down before she kicked open the door as Maynard rushed inside.

The living room was immaculate, not a speck of dust in sight or a book out of place on the shelves. Linderholm eased beside him and jerked her Glock at the hallway when they both caught a familiar smell. Oh, hell.

Rushing into the kitchen, they found nothing out of order. They moved fast down the corridor and into the bedroom. Dupont was tied spread-eagled on the bed, a soup bowl on the nightstand containing her fingernails, teeth and ears. The woman was almost naked, her clothing slashed off her to expose the bare skin, then left there to partially drape the mutilated corpse. Both of her breasts were covered with the circular burn marks of a cigar, the left leg covered with round bruises where the bones had been broken by some sort of blunt instrument, a hammer, or perhaps a baseball bat. As per regulations, Maynard checked her pulse, but there really was no need. The woman was dead, and had been for hours.

"It's Dupont," Linderholm said. "But this doesn't make any sense. There is no way Zalhares could have gotten here yet to do this."

"And why torture her?" Maynard demanded, making to holster his pistol, then moving to the closet to check. It was empty. "If she was working for them, and it now certainly seems that way, they might kill her to plug the leak. But why torture their own contact?"

Even as he said the words, the truth hit them both.

"Zalhares was a double agent," Linderholm said, pulling out her radio again.

"Playing us and some other group against each other so that he could steal the bombs? Damn, sounds solid."

"Hello, base? This a priority two report," Linderholm said quickly. "Inform Internal Affairs and the chief that our contact has been neutralized, and we now have gate-crashers at the party. We'll be back in an hour to report."

Closing and locking every door, the CIA agents returned to their car and raced for the highway.

Helen Dupont had only been a pawn and Cirello
Zalhares was a double agent. Yeah, made sense.
Unfortunately, it didn't require any great leap of
logic to guess who his employers were. Or rather,
who they had been, since it seemed he had also cut
them out of the deal. The Agency was finally
going to go directly against the Brazilian S2. And
there was no doubt that the breakage in innocent
human life would be very high before this mess
was finally settled.

CHAPTER FOUR

Atlantic Ocean

A steady thumping pervaded the small metal room and the air smelled strongly of machine grease. A rack of beds covered the far wall, a folding table stood in the corner, and in the middle of the room was a lead-lined safe draped with a fine wire mesh netting attached to an array of car batteries.

Kneeling by the apparatus, Zalhares carefully checked a voltage meter to make sure the Faraday Cage was working properly. Driving the armored truck into a private garage, there had been plenty of time to burn open the armor and then breech the safe. However, he suspected the CIA of having planted a tracer or even a repeater circuit in the Zodiacs, and thus had taken the precaution of having a Faraday Cage ready. With a steady current moving through the fine mesh, no radio signal could possibly penetrate.

Satisfied for the moment, Zalhares took a seat on the lower bunk and leaned back against the steel wall. The regular beat was oddly soothing, like the rhythm of a living heart.

Sitting at the table, Jorgina Mizne was sharpening a knife, her strokes unconsciously matching the pulse in the walls. Minas Pedrosa was drinking from a bottle of beer, while Dog Mariano groaned softly, holding a bucket between his shaky knees.

"Feeling any better, my friend?" Zalhares asked, crossing his arms behind his neck for a cushion. The thumping eased into a gentle background vibration.

Breathing for a moment, Mariano finally shook his head. "No," he muttered. "How…soon…."

"Until we disembark? Quite some time."

"Why couldn't we take a plane?" the man muttered, closing his eyes. "I like planes."

"Every airport was covered ten minutes after we left the park. No, my friend, this was the only way."

"I hate the sea," Mariano groaned.

"And yet you love the beach," Mizne said, inspecting the edge on the blade. "One of God's little jokes, eh?"

Unexpectedly, there was a knock on the hatch that served as a door for the small water-tight compartment.

"Fine," Mariano corrected weakly, placing the bucket aside. "I hate submarines. Better?"

"Of course." She smiled, sliding the blade into a sheath behind her back.

The knock came again, more insistent this time. Still drinking his warm beer, Pedrosa walked to the hatch and pulled it open on squealing hinges. The air tasted greasy, yet the metal was rusty. And this was considered a reliable transport?

In the corridor stood an unshaven slim man in rumpled coveralls, the tarnished insignia of a Taiwanese naval lieutenant pinned to his limp collar. Nodding to the passengers, the officer stepped through and tossed a casual salute to Zalhares. It wasn't returned.

"Sir, there is a problem," the lieutenant said, smiling widely.

Pushing away from the wall, Zalhares sat upright but said nothing, waiting for the man to continue.

"The captain has learned of your identity." He glanced at the safe. "If not that of your cargo, and believes that our deal needs to be—how shall I say it?—adjusted properly." The man grinned again, pretending to be embarrassed. "You are very wanted men by a great many people. Rich, powerful people."

"A deal is a deal," Zalhares said flatly. "We paid enough to buy this craft, and he wants more?"

With a sigh, the lieutenant shrugged, displaying both palms upward. "What can I say? My captain disagrees."

For a few minutes the members of the Scion exchanged glances.

"Fine. You leave us no choice then," Zalhares said. "Dog, pay the man."

Pulling out a wallet, Mariano removed a wad of cash and offered it to the lieutenant. His eyes bright with greed, the man eagerly reached for the cash. Mariano Dog extended his arm past the hand, a stiletto snapping out from his sleeve to ram into the officer's stomach. As the lieutenant's mouth flew open wide to scream, Zalhares stuffed in a bunched glove, careful to not be bitten.

Still sipping the beer, Pedrosa stepped to the hatchway, a silenced Imbel .22 pistol in his other hand. Meanwhile, Mizne grabbed the bleeding sailor by the shoulders to hold him steady as Mariano slowly sawed the razor-sharp blade back and forth straight up the middle of the torso. Thrashing against the grip of the muscular woman, the officer was helpless, his eyes rolling back into their sockets from the incredible pain. Blood poured from the yawning wound as his intestines began to slither out, most of them plopping into the waiting bucket.

With professional detachment, Zalhares watched as the life faded from the man's eyes and the body went limp, twitching a few times before finally succumbing to death. They all died so easily; it wasn't even interesting anymore.

"Still feeling seasick, old friend?" Zalhares asked, retrieving the saliva-streaked glove.

"Not any more," Mariano said excitedly, easing the gory blade out of the corpse and wiping it clean on the coveralls.

"Good," Zalhares said, sliding the glove back on his hand to cover a curved scar of teeth marks. "Get the guns. We're taking over the ship. Minas, you stay with the safe."

"And if the crew resists?" Mizne asked, opening a metal locker and removing an Uru caseless rifle from the collection inside.

"Kill them," Zalhares ordered, accepting one of the weapons. "But save the captain for me. Understood?"

"Make it quick," Mariano suggested, catching an Uru in one hand. "He's a fellow Brazilian."

Flicking off the safety, former Sergeant Cirello Zalhares looked at the mercenary with eyes as dead and empty of life as a child's grave.

"Then he should have known better than to cross me," the S2 operative rumbled deep in his throat.

"Leave the damn hatch open when you go," Pedrosa finally spoke, sitting in the corner and resting an Uru on his lap. "It stinks in here."

Staying low and fast, the Scion moved out of

the storage compartment and soon the sound of gunfire filled the submarine, but not for very long. Then the screaming started and it lasted all through the long night.

Belmore, Long Island

THE TRAFFIC in Belmore was heavy, with stop lights at every intersection, taxi cabs, delivery trucks and station wagons fighting for every inch of space. Every street was lined with crowded stores and full parking lots, with cars hunting for any available spot. Long Island seemed to carry the impression that everybody was in a big hurry to get somewhere else, and you were personally in their way.

Mack Bolan turned down a side street, the traffic immediately thinning to a more conventional level. Bolan increased his speed. The Jaguar hummed around the man as if every piece of the luxury car was directly involved in generating speed. Bolan had chosen the X-series because the vehicle blended well into the wealthy suburbs of Long Island and because the four-wheel drive gave it amazing traction at high speeds. A good soldier always planned a retreat route in case the enemy had unexpected reserves of strength. Michael J. Prince was a twenty-first-century monster, and those always had a cadre of devils around to hold back the just. The question was how many devils did he have. Honestly, Bolan didn't know. This was a crap shoot, the worst kind of a fight to go into, but there was no other way.

Unfortunately, while all of the downtown arms dealers had been mere facilitators and brokers, merchants in the selling of destruction, Prince was a dealer. A hands-on kind of guy who actually moved the physical weaponry, storing a lot of his stock in a warehouse strategically set between an elementary school and a shopping mall. Any kind of an armed assault by the feds or the police, would almost definitely result in civilian casualties. Unless the area was sealed off first, which would give Prince all the time he needed to escape and burn his records. No, this had to be a blitzkrieg, a lightning strike directly into the heart of the enemy.

Parking the Jaguar directly in front of Pierson Importers, Bolan fed the meter some quarters to show that he was planning to be here for a while, then, whistling tunelessly, strolled to the front door of the warehouse and rang the bell.

Bolan knew that he had been under video surveillance ever since he'd turned the corner onto this street. So he wasn't surprised when the door was instantly opened by a large man in work clothes, two more gorillas standing close behind.

"Private property," the first man growled, already starting to close the door.

Moving with lightning speed, Bolan drew and fired, the Beretta coughing tribursts of death to the three men. The bodies were still tumbling to the concrete floor when he slipped inside and bolted the door tightly behind.

Pulling out a second Beretta, Bolan moved down the corridor firing at anyone carrying a gun. There could be civilians here—accountants, secretaries—so he had to stay razor sharp. A man stood holding a cardboard box; Bolan shot him in the leg. But as he fell the box went flying, revealing a .38 Walther PPK in a fancy shoulder rig. The Beretta whispered once more and the man no longer felt the pain in his leg.

A big guy swinging an ax charged out of a bathroom, and Bolan ducked fast, feeling the breeze of the blade swish above his head. Still crouching he stroked both Berettas and sent the man tumbling backward to the floor. A shotgun roared and the desk near Bolan exploded into splinters. He dived out of the way, firing both guns, tracking for the target. Across the room, a woman in a crimson-stained business suit collapsed, her shotgun discharging wildly into the ceiling.

Reloading quickly, Bolan swept into the corridor again, catching two more men running his way. They died without even seeing him. Moving deeper into the warehouse, Bolan broached a cross corridor, finding only a spilled cup of coffee steaming on the floor. Listening hard for sounds of movement, Bolan proceeded to the nearest office and found a set of steel doors marked with No Smoking signs in several languages. This was it.

Glancing through the plastic window, he could see that nobody moved among the stacks of crates and endless boxes filling the cavernous room. A billion dollars' worth of armament sat neatly packed in cushioned crates, waiting to be shipped out. A single loose bullet could start a chain reaction of explosions that would level the elementary school next door. Only a chain-link fence separated the buildings and would do as much as a wall of tissue paper to stop the hellstorm of shrapnel. Even as the dire assessment was made, Bolan accepted the onus. He'd take some lead himself before letting the warehouse explode.

Just then, a scuffling noise from the corridor caught his attention and Bolan turned to fire both Berettas at the left wall. Plaster puffed as the 9 mm Parabellum rounds punched through the drywall and then a bloody man staggered into view dropping an Ithaca shotgun.

"Shit, he got Tony!" another man shouted, swinging around the corner and firing an Uzi machine pistol.

The 9 mm rounds stitched Bolan across the chest and he grunted in pain as his NATO body armor stopped the slugs from penetrating. Then Bolan returned the favor, his own 9 mm rounds smacking the other man backward, but yielding no blood, as the enemy gunner also wore a Kevlar vest. The Uzi fired again as Bolan tracked for the head. The machine pistol dropped from lifeless hands as a third eye appeared in the gunrunner's forehead.

Dropping the spare Beretta, Bolan pulled the Desert Eagle and headed for the stairs. As he neared, the Executioner fired the Beretta into the dark shadows under the steps and a man grunted in pain, staggering into view and still holding an M-16 assault rifle. Without hesitation, Bolan fired once more. The Magnum rounds smashed the rifle out of the little man's grasp and he crumpled to the floor.

"Please," he sobbed, raising his hands for pity, "I only w-work here. I don't sell the stuff. I'm not one of them!"

Right, just a clerk who carried an M-16 in an easy hold exactly like a pro.

"Where's Prince?" Bolan demanded.

"B-back room, second floor," he stammered, jerking his head. "Just take the stairs."

"You lead the way."

The gunner looked at the stairs in fear. "No, please, my leg…I can't walk."

"Get up," Bolan ordered, "or die where you are. It makes no difference to me."

"Okay, okay," the gunner said, standing easily.

"Up the stairs," Bolan ordered.

"Please. I only—"

"Move!"

"Jesus, okay already, they're a trap! Rigged to blow!"

Bolan stepped closer. "Yes, I know."

He did? Shit. "There's another set of stairs," the man said, looking around nervously. "The one the staff uses, ya know."

"You're still leading the way," Bolan said, both weapons held in rock-steady hands. "Get moving."

CHAPTER FIVE

Pierson Importers

Running footsteps echoed along the corridor on the second floor of the warehouse and an office door was thrown open as an armed man rushed inside.

"Boss, we got trouble," Oswaldo Fontecchio said, quickly closing and locking the door. "There's some lunatic running around shooting everybody. He's got Tony, Leo, Ira and—"

"Tell me something I don't know," Michael Prince growled in a strained tone.

Whirling, Fontecchio reacted at the sight of a big guy in a dark suit holding a huge silver Desert Eagle to the side of his boss's head. Prince's shirt was torn open, exposing the shoulder holster he always keep hidden, the little Remington .22 au-

tomatic pistol missing. Slumped over in a chair at
the computer was Little Bill from the loading
dock. The guy had a lump on his head, but was still
breathing.

Fontecchio scowled at the sight. So, Bill had
shown this guy the back stairs. Fucking coward.
He would be praying for death after Prince was
finished with him. Lousy bastard!

"Drop the piece," the stranger demanded.

Shifting his gaze, Fontecchio weighed his options and finally did as he was ordered.

"So what's the deal?" he demanded. "You an
unhappy customer come for a refund? Tough."

"Who is he?" Bolan demanded, shoving the
gun harder against Prince.

The fat arms dealer grunted. "My second in
command," he muttered, incensed at the treat-
ment. "Handles all of my security matters."

"Not very good at your job, Os," Bolan said.

"Fuck you, cop!" he snarled, then stopped.
"You know my name, then why…" Shit, it was a
test to see if he would tell the truth!

"And now I know that your boss will cooperate," Bolan said. "How about you?"

"I don't know anything!" Fontecchio snarled.
"So there's nothing I can tell you, even if I fucking wanted to, punk!"

"Then who needs you?" Mack asked, raising
his other gun.

As the Beretta fired, Michael Prince recoiled as his bodyguard's shoulder gushed blood from the front and back, the man clutching the wound with both hands trying to staunch the flow of his life. Swearing loudly, Fontecchio staggered around slowly bleeding to death.

"You just going to let him bleed like that?" Prince demanded, removing the cigarette holder.

"And how much is mercy worth today?" Bolan asked.

The guy was cutting a deal? "So what do ya want?"

"Information."

"Done. Help him, please."

Weapon trained on Prince, Bolan carefully removed two field bandages and tended to the now unconscious Fontecchio as best he could.

Walking around the desk, Bolan stood with his back to the file cabinet and looked hard at the fat man in the expensive chair.

"That will have to be good enough. So, the S2," he said. "Start talking."

"Who are they?" Prince asked, trying to sound confused.

But his eyes betrayed the truth and Bolan fired the Beretta, flame stabbing across the desk, and the cigarette holder exploding into a million pieces.

"Okay, okay, I do business with them," Prince cried, holding his bleeding hand. "What do you want? I can give you names. All you want. I'll rat them all out."

"More."

Taking on a crafty expression, the arms dealer inhaled sharply and let the breath out even slower, buying time to think.

"It's that goddamn submarine," Prince said at last. "Right? Sure, no problem. Always knew the damn thing would be trouble. Now I didn't make the sale, but I know who did. Just come back tomorrow and I can—"

The Executioner stroked the trigger and the Desert Eagle roared, the desk in front of the fat man shifting as it kicked out a spray of splinters. Crying out, Prince grabbed his face to find slivers of wood sticking out of his cheeks.

"You crazy son of a bitch!" he started, grabbing a pocket handkerchief and holding it to the wounds.

Without comment, Bolan fired again and the headrest of the chair was blown off. Then the Beretta coughed and the collar of the silk suit was tugged hard, making the man jump.

"Okay, okay!" Prince cried, raising both hands in surrender. "Enough already, I get the message. I've got to make some phones calls."

"I'll wait," Bolan said. "And this is your only chance at life. Don't waste it."

Sweating profusely, Prince hauled the telephone closer and started making calls.

Bolivia

RISING ABOVE the teeming city of La Paz was a low hill of manicured grass, land mines and razor wire, the granite-block wall patrolled by armed guards and dogs. Safe behind a protective cover of thick trees, far from the stink of the open sewers in the village below, a mansion sprawled luxuriously through landscaped hedges and perfect green lawns decorated with imported Italian statues.

The president of Bolivia, a former general, was lying on a table on the eastern terrace, two women massaging scented oils into his muscular frame. He had seized the country in a military junta and planned never to relinquish control. He refused to become a victim of those he subjugated on a daily basis.

The French-style double doors swung open and a butler approached the man, waiting to be recognized before daring to speak.

"Yes, what is it, Jose?" the president said, his face buried in his arms.

Not having been told to stop, the women continued to rub the older man's body, never slowing nor increasing their speed. Both actions were punished severely. Soft music played from somewhere in the mansion, along with the occasional crack of a bullwhip followed by a muffled scream of pain.

"Sir, we have a message from the Scion," Jose whispered, glancing briefly at the nearly naked women. One was wearing only the bottom half of a bikini, while the other was dressed in the matching top. He found the combined effect to be quite stimulating.

"We have no work for them," the president murmured peacefully. "Tell them to call back in a few months when the big push starts into the mountains."

"If I may, sir," Jose said. "This is about some other matter."

"They're not looking for work? Then why are they calling?"

"Apparently, sir, Mr. Zalhares has an item to sell." Jose scowled. "Although I do not understand why we should want to buy some broken arrows. Yet he seemed quite serious in the matter."

The president jerked his head up at that and the girls retreated quickly to get out of his way. "Repeat that," he growled, swinging his legs around to sit upright on the table.

"The Scion has some broken arrows for sale."

That was the code term used by the Americans for a lost or stolen nuclear device. The Scion had a nuke for sale?

"How much did he say?" the president demanded urgently. "What was the price? Do they have more than one? Speak to me, man!"

Trying not to glance at the man's exposed genitalia, Jose stared him directly in the face. "Sir, Zalhares said he would call again soon with the details about an auction."

"Bah, that would send the cost through the sky. Unacceptable, fool!" the president snarled, slapping the steward to the stone-work floor. "Call him back! I must have it at any cost! By God, I could destroy the rebels in one air strike! Burn their entire valley to the ground!"

Cringing on the floor, Jose paused before standing again. "But he did not leave a return phone number, sir."

"Find him," the president roared, shaking a fist. "Or I'll feed your head to the dogs!"

Scrambling out of range, Jose got hastily to his feet and headed back inside past the imaginary safety of the delicate French doors.

Snorting in frustration, the president rubbed the scar on his prominent jaw for a while, lost in thought.

"Enough," he said at last, rising from the table and wrapping a towel around his waist. "Both of you come to my room, where we can finish this in private."

Wordlessly, the women simply followed after the brutal government leader.

Pierson Importing, Long Island

"FINE, THANKS, Bob, owe you. Yeah, sure, later. Bye." Prince hung up the phone and swiveled to face his capture.

During the phone calls, the big man had sat like a statue on a folding chair, the Desert Eagle never wavering.

"Okay, a friend of a friend…" he paused. "You know how it goes."

Bolan scowled impatiently.

"Right. Anyway, RDCS—that's the Rotterdam Dockyard Company Submarines—had a couple of Zwaardvis-class subs, diesel electric, that they were trying to unload for years. Good ships, based on the old Barbel model of the U.S." He stopped, seeing the anger in the man's blue eyes. "Yeah, well, I made the sale to Taiwan for them, and then resold one of the subs for Taiwan to Brazil."

"At a modest profit, I'm sure," Bolan said.

At that, Prince snorted a laugh. "Modest, hell, I soaked them good. But that's just good business, huh? Get them before they get you. The law of supply and demand."

More like the law of the jungle. So the Scion had a submarine. Hell of a getaway car, he had to admit. Unfortunately there were a hundred customers for a hot-ticket item like a miniature nuke. A regular nuclear warhead cost about forty million, but these could easily bring double that price, maybe triple. For half a billion dollars Cirello Zalhares had better stay sharp from his own people. As a professional soldier, Bolan held mercs in low esteem, even if he did admire their abilities. Some of the best soldiers he had ever encountered had been mercenaries, and some of the most evil bastards, too.

"Blueprints, weapons," Bolan said.

"No weapons. The Dutch won't sell them that way, and Taiwan doesn't have the dockyard to retrofit."

"But Brazil does."

"Sure."

Yeah, it was armed, most likely with very modern MK37 or NK37 torpedoes. So much for calling in the Navy. Made sense, if you were going to steal half a billion dollars in weapons, who cared about spending a couple of million more to get the job done right?

"Crew size?" Bolan demanded.

"Originally the Zwaardvis held seventy, but it was modified for cargo hauling, deep-sea probes, shit like that. The Dutch won't sell fighting subs the way we do. Say, thirty people tops. But it's just a guess. There's no way to know for sure."

A crew of twenty-five then, with the Scion along. Bolan went to the fax machine and studied the sheets detailing the size and length of the submersible craft. Tear-drop design, very fast and quite advanced for its day. Diesel-electric motors, short range nowadays with the environmental-safe catalyst converts on the exhaust. The original ten thousand nautical miles cut to seven. Still a hell of a range for a getaway car. Brazil had to have been planning this for years. But then, so had Zalhares, which raised an interesting question.

"Where is it registered?"

Prince tried not to show his disappointment. So he figured that out already, eh? Damn. "Miami," he said, sounding surprised. "It's got a good deep-water harbor. I do lots of shipping business down there."

Yeah, drug dealers and slavers. But for the Scion it would be easy sailing to Brazil if the plan failed and they had to maintain their cover as loyal S2 agents.

"Company?" Bolan said it as a question.

"Black River Shipping and Exploration. Black River, like in the Amazon. Cute, huh?"

"Adorable. Address."

Checking some notes, Prince started to read off a piece of paper, but Bolan reached over to take the paper and fold it away into a pocket of his black suit.

"Is that the lot?" he demanded.

"That's everything," Prince said. "Now I kept my part of the bargain, how about you?"

The stranger in black didn't move in response and the arms dealer waited, listening to the sound of his own breathing. There was really little else that he could do with the cannon pointed at his head.

"I keep my word, even to scum like you," Bolan said, sliding the Desert Eagle into a holster under his coat. "You live for now."

Looking up in desperate hope, Prince couldn't believe it when the guy dropped the clip out of the sleek little Beretta and started rummaging in a pocket for a spare one. He was unarmed!

Seizing the chance, Prince grabbed the snub-nosed .38 out of its holster under the desk, but the stranger simply leveled the Beretta and stroked the trigger once more. The round in the chamber discharged with a soft chug and punched out his left eye, the searing ice pick of pain driving Prince backward into an inky blackness that lasted forever.

"Bad move," Bolan said, slipping in the fresh clip, then racking the slide to chamber another round. "Especially for a weapons dealer."

Taking out a handkerchief, Bolan lifted the receiver and started dialing.

"Hello?" a tired voice answered. "This is the Belmore Police Station, Desk Sergeant Buckley speaking. How may I help you?"

"This is the Pierson warehouse on Sixth," Bolan said. "We've got some bodies here."

"What was that, buddy?"

"People are dead. I shot them."

"Aw, for Christ's sake." The sergeant sighed. "Look, asshole, prank phone calls are a felony offense!"

"Come see for yourself," Bolan told him, then placed the receiver on the table and fired the Desert Eagle into the air. That should make the cops come running.

Leaving the phone off the hook to make the trace easier, Bolan went downstairs to remove the videotapes from the surveillance cameras, and gather a few choice items from the warehouse for his own use, before calmly driving away at just below the speed limit.

He was still in sight of the warehouse when a black-and-white patrol car rolled to the curb and two police officers climbed out to start for the front door. They stopped as they spotted the first group of bodies.

Following the rush-hour traffic, Bolan stayed with the flow and left the matter behind. Miami. That could easily be a dead end, but it was also the best shot he had at finding the Scion. With a sub, Zalhares and his people could go almost anywhere in the world, so he just had to go with his instincts on this and keep digging until somebody tried to make him stop.

Turning on the headlights, Bolan moved into the gathering darkness alone with his dark thoughts.

still alive after all this time. The sailor had begged for his life and helped the Scion take control of the ship, in exchange for a solemn promise that he wouldn't be harmed. Amused by the coward, Zalhares agreed and the engineer hadn't been harmed, aside from being sealed alive with the rotting corpses of the men he had betrayed. Minas Pedrosa wanted to pump in some air to keep the fellow alive longer to prolong the suffering until eventual starvation drove him to cannibalism. But Zalhares had strongly vetoed that. Not out of sympathy, but common sense. If they broke the seals to pump in air, the stink would also get out, and it had to be pretty ripe in there after three days.

On the horizon, a large speedboat streaked by, dragging a group of water-skiers behind, their cries of terror or pleasure lost in the sheer distance of the ocean. There had been a bad squall the previous day that had almost driven the submarine into the coast, but the weather was clear again now, and the gulls were out in force scavenging the shoreline for the fish killed during the storm.

As several birds wheeled overhead, Zalhares remembered how as a child he used to toss them seltzer tablets to watch them explode from the build-up of fizzing gas in their bellies. His father had beat him for that, of course. Not for killing the birds, but for wasting money buying the seltzer tablets. That was how he learned to beat the smaller children into stealing the tablets for him from the local store. It was a valuable lesson in learning that strength yielded pleasure. Now that little boy was one of the most powerful men in the world. How proud his father would be today.

With a great deal of noise from below, Dog Mariano started to lumber up the ladder, his broad shoulder barely able to pass through the access tube of the conning tower. His size was an asset in the field, but a liability inside the cramped submarine. The Norwegians had to be small people compared to the Brazilians. Then again, the boat would be gigantic for the diminutive Taiwanese. Everything was relative. Only death made men equal.

"Any word on the radio about the *Tullamarine*?" Zalhares asked, keeping his face to the wind. The gulls were so close, such easy throwing distance. "It would be a pity if the smugglers landed safely and eventually found themselves the owner of a free nuclear bomb."

"Nothing so far," Mariano replied, lowering his head against the constant spray. "And there would be major coverage if a seaport had been destroyed by an atomic blast."

"Unless the Americans moved faster than we thought possible and destroyed the ship at sea," Zalhares muttered. "That was the risk in the transaction. One for three is good odds in any wager."

Mariano shrugged. "I suppose."

"Are the torpedoes rigged to blow?"

"Of course. It required little of my expertise. Ten minutes after we flip the arming switch, the torpedoes in the launch tubes will detonate, setting off the tanks of diesel fuel and the rest of the torpedoes in the armory. There will not be enough of this tub remaining to stuff into a thimble."

"Good. You have done well, my friend."

"Jorgina helped," he said in simple honesty.

Keeping a hand on the railing of the platform, Zalhares turned to smile. "Then you should both be congratulated. But come now, you should be happy. We shall be landing soon, and put you back on firm ground. That sounds good, eh?"

"It is not a concern," Mariano replied, his ponytail whipping around in the salt wind. "I have finally gotten used to traveling this way, and would not mind we if rode this all the way to the rendezvous point."

"That would not be wise," Zalhares stated in a stern tone. "Wherever we go, the U.S. Navy tracks our every move, as they would any foreign submarine just off their coast. But if we do anything suspicious, we could be surrounded by the Coast Guard and ordered to surrender. Then we have to kill them and arm a Zodiac in preparation for a U.S. Navy submarine to challenge us and we have a standoff and they would respond with some foolish but brave gesture."

Shaking his head, the leader of the Scion frowned. "No, my friend, we need another form of transportation. Something a little less noticeable than a billion-ton submarine.

"No, we must stay low-key," Zalhares added. "Until after we have made our deliveries and are long gone from America."

"But they will remember that we were here." Mariano smiled coldly.

"Oh, yes, my friend, they will remember," Zalhares said, watching the gulls. "And so will their grandchildren for a thousand years."

Miami, Florida

IT WAS EARLY in the morning when Bolan arrived at Miami airport. The small Cessna Skylane rolled along the reserved landing strip at the far end of the busy airfield, far away from the terminals or other planes.

"Welcome to Miami, CR-57-D," the flight controller said through the ceiling speaker in the sunlit cockpit. "Hope you have a pleasant stay."

"Roger, Tower," Bolan replied, easing back on the throttles. "I'll do my best, CR-57-D, out."

Coasting the seaplane off the field, Bolan moved onto a paved area surrounded by blinking warning lights. It was the VIP field for visiting dignitaries. A phone call to Brognola had secured the necessary clearance. His arsenal in the locked trunks in the rear of the seaplane would have caused a stir, and just in case of any red tape, Bolan still had the FBI commission booklet from New York, but he envisioned no hassles from the local police. They were used to DEA, CIA and ATF agents using the airport for covert assignments and knew when to back off and let the agencies have some privacy.

Shutting down the engines, he locked the brakes and stepped outside to stretch and wait for his ride to arrive. On the plane ride down, Bolan had made use of the autopilot and used his new U.S. Army laptop with its cellar modem to scan the Internet for business registrations in the greater Miami area to locate the address of the Black River Shipping and Exploration. Surprisingly the Scion had their company located, not in the plush and luxurious downtown skyscrapers along the Gold Coast, but out in the dirty ghetto of Liberty City. A ghetto that boasted more street-gang violence than south Los Angeles and Detroit combined. It was a savage human jungle where the brutal killers from Brazil would fit in perfectly. The Scion may have even recruited some of the local gangs to work as additional security. The odds could be stacked against him, but it wouldn't be the first time.

A horn sounded in the distance and Bolan could

now see a couple of vehicles coming his way. He waited as a windowless blue van and a brilliant-orange-colored Jeep pulled to a stop a few yards from the seaplane. Both drivers were wearing Miami Airport Security uniforms and wearing sunglasses against the harsh glare reflecting off the white concrete access roads. Those seemed perfectly normal, but also made great disguises.

With sea breeze tugging on his jacket, Bolan keep a hand near the Beretta in his pocket until the driver got out of the van to toss him a casual salute. The driver then got in the Jeep and the two men drove away.

Warily going to the van, Bolan ran an EM scan to make sure there were no listening devices installed, checked for bombs, then killed the lowjack with a simple short circuit. Throwing open the rear double doors, Bolan loaded the equipment trunks into the van, removing a fat Multiround Projectile weapon from the array of death dealers and placed it under the passenger seat for easy access.

Changing his jacket to something more casual, Bolan carefully pulled off his mustache and goatee, wiped his face with a moist towelette to remove the last of the spirit gum and slid on sunglasses. Better.

Starting the engine, he checked the fuel and oil gauges, turned on the air conditioner and drove away. Circling the airport, he reached the concrete access road and merged effortlessly into the streaming downtown traffic.

Settling in for the drive, Bolan found himself thinking about all of the other times he had visited the city. Lots of memories in Miami, most of them bad. He could still remember the sweet smile of brave Margarita… The Man in Black shook his head to disperse the memories. She was long gone and he had personally dealt with the monster who had stolen her life.

Less than an hour later, a grim Bolan parked in a strip mall filled with liquor stores and massage parlors, most of the signs printed in both Spanish and English.

From here could see the building that served as the home office for Black River Shipping and Exploration, a small, one-story, white stucco building of unknown origin. The sign was faded almost to obscurity and, like most of the buildings in the area, it had steel grates over the windows and doors to keep out the gangs. But the place also had illegal wiring to the grates to deliver a potentially lethal shock. The front door was metal, not wood, and concertina wire coiled along the roof three layers deep. It wasn't an office, it was a fortress. And it said a lot that in a shabby ghetto of filth and destruction, Black River Shipping and Exploration was the only structure free of graffiti.

Using a sniper scope from a rifle, Bolan dialed for computer enhancement and checked the building for thermal, but the infrared showed nothing moving inside. The building seemed to be empty. Checking his weapons, Bolan added a few burglary tools to his pockets and climbed from the van.

As he started across the hot street, Bolan noticed a group of teens watching from the shade of a pool hall awning. The gritty teenagers wore head bandannas of the exact same color and stood close together, like a platoon of combat soldiers catching a rest between missions. Bolan had seen troops in that exact same pose in battlefields across the globe. This had to be the local gang that owned this street.

Stopping respectfully in the middle of the street, Bolan removed his coat to show the double rig of his shoulder holsters underneath. The teens tensed at the display of hardware and a few dropped into a gunfighting crouch, hands hidden in their own windbreakers. Bolan understood their unease. He wasn't acting like a cop, Mob hit man, or drug dealer, and that was confusing. These were the mean streets of the vacation wonderland where armed cops only traveled in packs, not the peaceful subways of New York with its purse snatchers. These were hardcore criminals who killed almost every day. The only thing they respected was brute force, and nothing else.

Slinging the coat casually over a shoulder, Bolan threw what he hoped was a neutral gang sign showing that he was here on personal business and not about to interfere with the gang in any way.

A small black girl walked out of the gang and threw back the same sign to Bolan. He nodded in thanks and continued across the shimmering pavement.

Going around the building, Bolan used the Beretta to shoot off the power cable to the building, then slipped a key-wire gun into the lock. A few seconds later the mechanism yielded to the locksmith tool and he eased inside. Standing motionless, Bolan strained to listen with his entire body, trying to sense any sign of life. But the office felt utterly still. The air tasted stale with dust and the heat was stifling because of the closed windows. Nobody had been in there for weeks, maybe even months.

Pulling a slim aerosol can from a pocket, he sprayed fog into the air, but there was no sign of infrared or laser beams. His EM scanner showed no proximity sensors in the vicinity. Could he have been wrong about the place?

Doing a quick recon, Bolan found only a front room with a cheap Formica counter, a large office and a storage closet full of supplies—a suspiciously large amount of flammable cleaning solutions, paint thinner, and even a large can of kerosene. A couple of bullets through the thin plywood door and no fire department on Earth would be able to stop the blaze from consuming the building down to the ground. Just a coincidence, or was the place rigged to blow to destroy the records?

The bathroom was clean, with nothing hidden in the tank or the flotation bulb. The file cabinets were mostly empty, only a few letters dealing with buying the house, installing the grates, phone service, installing the sign outside, business license and such. Nothing unusual or even suspect.

The computer was turned off, but a quick check revealed it was operational and not even protected by a password. Accessing some files, Bolan skimmed the spreadsheets for anything useful. According to the accounts, the company had been spending a lot more than it was making carrying machine parts to a series of oil rigs in the Outer Hebrides for a Scottish petroleum company. Every dime went for upgrading the submarine. That put the Zwaardvis sub in the right area to rendezvous with the Scion and carrying them back to Miami, then on to…where? There had to be more here.

There were shortcuts for other files, but those were on the zip drive and that disk was gone. Probably the real records for the covert operation.

Inspecting the fax machine, Bolan found a stack

of papers, with a few spilling onto the floor. Mostly they were spam, advertising sent through fax machines for get-rich schemes, and pornography. Flipping through the shiny pages, Bolan discovered that a few were business related, requests for a list of their carrying charges, a reminder to renew their local business license, and some receipts for fuel. Fuel bought only two days ago in Newfoundland.

That was the closest point on the North American continent to England. The Scion was already here! They had refueled in Newfoundland, and twenty-seven hours later at Georgetown at the intercoastal waters. While the military of the world searched Europe for them, the mercs had been leisurely cruising the Eastern Seaboard. Bolan had to have passed them somewhere along the trip down here. The P3 sonar of the Atlantic defense grid would have spotted them immediately, but the sub would have stayed close to shore, pretending to be recording fish migrations, salvaging wrecks or something similar. If discovered, the Scion could threaten to detonate a Zodiac, the blast sending a tidal wave of radioactive water inland to kill hundreds, maybe thousands if they were near a major city like Atlantic City or Charleston. No Coast Guard or Navy ship would touch them under those circumstances. Yeah, Zalhares was smart. Too smart. The denser the population, the safer he was. The Scion was good at this game of cat and mouse, so Bolan would just have to be better, and faster.

Turning to leave, he spotted a fax stuck inside the machine. He paused for a moment, then removed the top to take a look. It could be anything, even a plane or hotel reservation. With any luck, Zalhares might not even know that the fueling docks were sending receipts to the home office in Miami. The sheet tore getting it loose, and Bolan wasn't surprised to see that it was just another receipt for…no, not fuel this time, but docking charges for Biscayne Bay Harbor. That was right here in Miami, and the date was today, less than an hour old. They were in town!

As Bolan tucked the receipt into a pocket there came a thundering explosion from the front of the building, and searing light washed down the hallway heralding a rapidly expanding wave of flame. Ducking behind the heavy wooden desk, the Executioner opened his mouth and covered both ears to try to save his hearing as the blast shook the office. A split second later the water sprinklers in the ceiling came on, but the deluge had no effect on the writhing flames filling the hallway. Bolan sniffed hard, but there was no smell of napalm or white phosphorous, so that had to have been a thermite grenade. Damn, those were unstoppable. The blasted stuff actually burned hotter underwater.

More grenades bounded from the front of the structure, and Bolan rode out the double blast, feeling the heat seep through the desk. Suddenly, the closet erupted, the door blowing off the hinges and adding more fuel to the mounting inferno. The temperature was rapidly becoming unbearable, the air painful to breath.

He had to move fast. Pulling out his only grenade, Bolan pulled the pin and flipped the spoon to then wait a precious three seconds before tossing the bomb across the burning hallway and into the bathroom. The antipersonal grenade detonated while still in the air, the halo of shrapnel blowing out the window grating as water gushed from the ruptured pipes.

Grabbing the plywood door from where it lay on the smashed fax machine, Bolan tossed it into the hallway on top of the searing chemical flames. Instantly, the thin wood began to char. The soldier raced over the makeshift bridge into the watery bathroom, then crawled out the window to land on the cool ground, gasping for breath.

Something hit the ground near him and he instinctively rolled away and came up with the Desert Eagle in his hand.

A rifle barrel jutted from the open window of a black Cadillac on the street and an AK-47 gave a stuttering roar, the 7.62 mm rounds striking the shingles of the office building and the ground.

Momentarily trapped in a box of fire, Bolan had no choice but to charge the machine gun, shifting from side to side to try to avoid the incoming lead. Firing the Desert Eagle, he hit the Cadillac and the AK-47 fell silent long enough for him to reach the street.

The Kalashnikov gunner cut loose again, the hardball ammo throwing sparks as it hit the pavement, tracking for a kill. Pulling the Beretta, Bolan threw himself to the left and hit the pavement rolling and firing both handguns. Coming up behind a parked car, he dropped the spent clips, hastily reloaded and adopted a weaver's stance to blow high-velocity death at the Cadillac with the Desert Eagle. The sideview mirror shattered, the door dented and a slug glanced off the window.

The whole car was armored! Bolan cast a look at the van sitting in the strip mall with its mass of weaponry, but it might as well have been on the moon for all the good it could do him right then.

Black smoke billowed, making it difficult to see, so Bolan took a gamble and tossed the loaded Beretta to his right onto the street. He remained silent, but the driver's side door of the Cadillac was thrown open and a big man climbed into view thumbing a 40 mm grenade into the fat launcher attached under the main barrel of the Kalashnikov.

The Desert Eagle roared and the man dropped the AK-47, tumbling backward into a tree. He grunted from the impacts and jerked his hand forward, a derringer appearing from his sleeve and discharging loudly. Dropping to the ground, the soldier heard the slugs hum by, knowing he had escaped death by mere inches.

After the second shot Bolan stood and emptied the Desert Eagle at the other man as he scrambled into the car and ground metal, throwing the vehicle into gear. As the Cadillac raced away, Bolan chased after the vehicle, shooting on the run, hitting the rear bumper and catching the left tire. But there was no effect whatsoever, and the luxury car sped away and out of sight.

Standing in the roiling clouds of smoke from the Black River office, Bolan knew that pursuit was out of the question with the van, and dismissed that option. He had gotten the license plate, but if it wasn't fake, or stolen, Bolan would be extremely surprised. The Executioner didn't know who this new party was, but he was very good. On the flight down, Hal Brognola had told him about the Dupont woman being tortured. If that was the same person who just attacked him, then he was probably here to merely burn down the building and remove any connections between himself and the Scion. Bolan had simply gotten in the way. Right place, wrong time. So the question was, was this man working for the S2 of Brazil or somebody else entirely?

Dropping the spent clips, Bolan reloaded his handguns and gathered the dropped AK-47 to head for the van. On the way he noticed the street gang still lounging against the side of the poolhall, smoking and drinking beers. They had done nothing to help or hinder the fight between the two strangers as it had been none of their business. Nobody even seemed to be paying any attention to the office building enshrouded by clouds of dark smoke, writhing flames licking high into the sky. Once again, not their concern.

Opening the door, Bolan tossed the Kalashnikov onto the seat and started to climb inside when there was a shout. A hand going for the Desert Eagle, Bolan turned expectantly.

"Not bad, old man," the teenage girl said, flashing a smile.

Nodding in reply, Bolan climbed into the van and started the engine. At this very moment, the Scion could be at the city dock and, if he hurried, it might be possible to end this whole thing this day. The identity of his assailant could wait until Bolan took out the Scion and got control of the Zodiacs. That was, if Zalhares was still on board that sub.

CHAPTER SEVEN

Miami Dockyard

Parking at the dock was impossible, and time was pressing, so Bolan placed a government business card in the window and parked in a fire zone near a hydrant. Slipping on a pair of dime-store glasses, he carefully attached a small mustache to his upper lip, then checked his reflection in the mirror against the picture on a new FBI commission booklet. Not a perfect match, and that made it appear to be real. Acceptable.

Tucking the FBI booklet into a shirt pocket so that the photograph was displayed, he took the briefcase and locked the van. Once he was a few yards away the intruder systems automatically activated with a subdued hum.

Briskly cutting through the crowds, a couple of

stevedores gave Bolan a hard look, then shrugged
and went on with their animated conversation.
The smell of salt was strong in the air, the Biscayne Bay facilities bustling with shouting people,
trucks, vans and crowds of rushing people.
Wooden crates and steel cargo containers were
stacked to the sky in the yard of the docks. Workers in hard hats drove by on forklifts.

The dockyard was huge, extending for dozens
of blocks along the coast, so the soldier did the
sensible thing and went to the harbor master office. Controlled chaos, that was the only possible
description, Bolan thought. If the sub was still in
a slip somewhere, the master would know its exact
location. No sense searching for a needle in a
haystack when you could ask the farmer.

Large signs pointed the way and he soon located the office in a three-story building with a
roof covered with microwave receivers and radio
antennaes. Bolan headed that way just as a hard
breeze smacked him in the face and the entire
world seemed to shake as a thundering explosion
rocked the yard. Shielding his face with a raised
hand, Bolan looked between the fingers to see a
roiling fireball rise over the buildings from the
southside of the bay, a corona of debris flying
wide and high, black specks in the air that resembled people and vehicles.

The sailors and workers on the dock shouted

and cursed in alarm at the incredible sight, every-body but Bolan flinching as more explosions oc-curred with triphammer force. Secondary detonations were to be expected in a blast that powerful, but the Executioner felt his blood run cold as he slowly raised his wrist to check the Geiger counter. If that was a Zodiac, then he was dead al-ready. Time seemed to stand still as he waited a few seconds to get a reading. The CIA device was only registering standard background radiation. Clean. It wasn't a nuke.

Another blast shook the docks and debris began to fall from the sky, impacting everywhere. A blurred motion overhead caught Bolan's attention and he sprinted forward to grab a man and forcibly drag him out of a forklift. A split second later some sort of fuel pump the size of a mailbox slammed into the forklift, mashing it flat.

"Incoming!" Bolan shouted through a cupped hand.

As if waiting for the command, a dozen or so men and women lurched into action, dragging friends underneath concrete lintels and behind brick walls. More flaming objects plummeted from the sky to smash into the pavement like ar-tillery rounds. A man screamed as a length of steel rod speared him through the chest; he wriggled horribly, alive but trapped like a bug on a pin. A propane forklift was hit with an unrecognizable mass, and it erupted into a blast that knocked a dozen running people to the ground, most of them never to rise again.

"Seek cover!" Bolan shouted at the top of his lungs as a swarm of falling litter rained upon a Quonset hut, punching straight through the corrugated steel roof with the sound of high-caliber bullets. Surprised yells erupted from inside and a man ran out covered with flames and waving his arms. A woman threw a bucket of sand on the victim as another man rushed out with a fire extinguisher to cover him with a cloud of CO_2 fumes.

Weeping and cursing, people ran mindlessly as fire sirens began to build into a strident howl. Then more explosions sounded, and Bolan's guts tightened as a mushroom cloud began to form above the distant conflagration. Almost any ground fire would create that effect if it was hot enough, but the sight was still unnerving, a hellish reminder of what exactly could have happened here.

There was no doubt in his mind that this explosion had been caused by the Scion. Their sub was here and something major had exploded. There had to be a connection, and the very last place to find out anything would be the blast zone itself. Zalhares would have been long gone before igniting a blast of this magnitude.

The wail of ambulances could be heard, along with fire trucks and police cars, the noises overlapping with the screams and explosions into a background roar that sent the warrior back into combat just for a moment.

Watching for falling debris, Bolan moved quickly through the crowd to reach the exposed brick staircase that led to the third-story office of the harbor master. He ducked for a moment as a cloud of dense smoke blew over the area, then moved onward. Time was against him, and this was his best chance to get the information needed.

People were streaming down the stairs, carrying fire extinguishers and medical kits, calling on cell phones or shouting orders. Bolan tried to stay out of their way to not slow the rescue operation. This was a battle zone, exactly the same as the jungle of Vietnam or the desert of Iran. Chaos and blood and noise, but with a core of professionals moving through the madness working hard.

A wooden railing encircled the third floor, the outer walls composed of huge Plexiglas windows to give a panoramic view of the harbor and the hundreds of ships moored at the complex docking facilities. Most of the windows were intact. Only the ones facing due south were out of their frames, lying across desks, smashed computers and fallen file cabinets like a lake of ice blown into the rooms by the concussion of the first explosion. Although built to withstand the worst Florida hurricane, a blast like this had simply not been in the design specifications.

Bolan found a pretty young woman moaning softly at the reception desk while a janitor expertly bandaged her head wound with strips of cloth. Lying on the dirty carpet nearby was a still form covered with a suit jacket, the material soaked through with blood.

Proceeding deeper into the offices, Bolan grabbed a disheveled man by the arm but the fellow only stared back, hugging a ream of copier paper. After a moment, Bolan released the man and watched as he shuffled away, clutching the ream as if it were the most important thing in the world. Bolan recognized the symptoms as shell shock, his mind gone for the time being from the harsh reality of so many violent deaths. He had seen it before in combat and knew the man would be fine again, after an extended period of peace and quiet.

Most of the other rooms were deserted, but at the end of the corridor there was a large office with a wide view of the harbor. A woman in utility-green clothing was shouting on a telephone. Fire tugs were cutting across the waves heading for the rampaging maelstrom to the south, the black cloud spreading over the yard like a death shroud. Smoke, it was just smoke, nothing more. At the dock, a dozen sailing ships moored at the jetties were listing badly, gaping holes in the decks from the falling wreckage. On the main deck of a cruise liner, the crew was battling an out-of-control blaze with hoses, the arching spray creating a rainbow across the vessel. Down in the ocean, the waves were full of people swimming in no discernible direction and, as Bolan watched, more passengers jumped into the ocean to start swimming for the shore.

The combined noise from outside was deafening, and Bolan couldn't make out what the woman on the phone was saying until he was directly beside her.

"What in hell do you mean, you didn't hear it?" she shouted, a hand covering her other ear. "I would have thought the concussion would have blown the governor off his chair in Tallahassee! Lost every window we have facing south and… yes, we have casualties, you freaking moron! Dozens are dead, maybe more, the place is a disaster zone."

She paused and looked up in fear as a rain of debris sprinkled onto the roof. She visibly relaxed when nothing happened. "What was that?" the woman barked into the receiver. "No, send us everything you can spare, medical helicopters, National Guard, the works. And move fast or I'll be using your balls for chum!"

Slamming down the receiver, the woman muttered curses as she opened a drawer in the desk and pulled out a S&W .38 revolver. With sure fingers, she ripped open a cardboard box of Remington ammunition and started loading the cylinder.

Protection against looters, Bolan noted in approval. Smart move. The dock would have security personnel, but who knew if they were alive, much less functioning at the moment.

"Are you the harbor master?" he asked, resting the briefcase on the floor. Bolan was forced to repeat himself as another blast from the southern destruction drowned out his words. "Harbor master?"

"Yeah, I'm in charge here," she said, closing the cylinder and tucking the revolver into a pocket. "Assistant harbor master, Rebecca Weeks. Hell of a time for the boss to go on vacation, eh?"

She stopped and looked directly at the big man. A cop? "So who the hell are you, and what are you doing in my office?"

"Special Agent Matthew Cooper," Bolan said, tapping the FBI commission booklet. "I need some information."

She arched an eyebrow. "Now? You've got to be kidding!"

"It's important."

"No, the fire is important," Weeks retorted, then frowned. "Oh crap, is this the work of terrorists? Is that what we got here?"

"I don't know yet," Bolan replied honestly, then lowered his glasses to look over the black frame. "What blew up?"

"Hell, what hasn't?" Weeks growled, glancing out the missing southern window. "Looks like the big explosion was the main fuel storage tanks, but I can't say for sure yet."

"Diesel?"

"No, those are over there," she said, jerking a thumb in another direction. "That is—was the gas tanks. We keep them separate for safety reasons. Thank God for that."

But Bolan frowned at that news. Could he be wrong? The Zwaardris-class sub was a diesel, so there was no reason for it to take on gasoline as fuel. Maybe this was only a diversion so the Scion could leave unnoticed.

"Look, I'm busy," Weeks said, pulling on a cloth cap. "So grab a firejacket and lend some help, or come back some other time."

"I'll wait," he said, pulling up a chair.

"Wait? This could take days to sort out. Weeks!"

Bolan merely smiled in reply.

Casting a look at a closed safe in the corner where she kept the petty cash, Weeks frowned, then took a handheld radio from a recharging rack on the wall and strode outside shouting orders.

Bolan waited until the office was clear then set

to work on the file cabinets. The folders were up to date and in alphabetical order, so it took him only a few minutes to find what he was looking for. There were three submarines in port: a DVR doing some salvage for the U.S. Navy, an oceanographic vessel for a marine biology firm in Los Angeles, and a cargo carrier, the RDN Zwaardvis. The captain had paid the docking charges in cash, no supplies, or even lines charges for using the local electricity.

That's when he saw it. The only other charge was for sixteen thousand gallons of gasoline. There was even a memo from the fuel station operator that he thought it odd for a sub to run on gasoline, but since only an idiot would fill a diesel with gasoline the engines had to have been modified for some reason. Angrily, Bolan looked out the window at the chaos below. They rigged the sub to blow. Even filled the fuel tanks with gasoline to make the blast bigger.

But their one mistake had been paying in cash, and they had probably done that to avoid using a credit card and leaving a trail for the CIA computers to trace. However, that only forced each harbor to fax a receipt to the home office for the company records. Just standard business courtesy.

On a hunch, Bolan pulled out the signed faxes from Black River and compared the signatures. Yeah, he'd thought so, they were different. The man who signed as the captain in Newfoundland wasn't the same person who signed in Miami today, which meant the original Taiwanese captain was dead, along with most, if not all of the crew, too. Most likely the captain had discovered that he was hauling a hot cargo, decided to pressure for a larger fee and the Scion had taken over the sub. Brazil had a submarine fleet, two dozen or so vessels, so it was possible that at least one member of the Scion knew how to operate the submersible. Could have also kept a couple members of the crew alive. At least for a while.

Replacing the files, Bolan knew that Zalhares wouldn't cause a disturbance like this if he was planning on traveling through Miami. Homeland Security, FBI, state and city police were on terrorist watch by now, sealing the airports and train stations, with the Coast Guard and U.S. Navy moving in to cover the ports and dockyards. Which meant the Scion was already gone. The logical choice would be to use the most convenient venue, so they would be at sea again on a speedboat or a yacht, something fast that they could land easily. Simply set the sub to blow, choose their craft, kill the crew and sail away as the dockyard went up in flames, the blast removing every trace of the killings and theft.

A familiar throbbing from overhead caught his attention, and Bolan looked out to see National Guard helicopters starting to land on the dock to carry away the worst of the wounded. The Miami emergency measures team moved fast. Their lights and sirens clearing a path, an army of city ambulances and fire trucks was beginning to arrive, people running and shouting in the thick black smoke.

Turning away from the turmoil, Bolan scrutinized the peaceful city of Miami, its world-famous hotels standing along the coastline like the remains of some prehistoric wall built to hold back the sea. The golden sands of the beaches were coated with people enjoying their vacations, retired couples, young families, ten thousand college kids, each of them a shield for the Scion to hide behind. Any move on the part of the military placed their innocent lives in terrible jeopardy. And the nukes had been here.

A million civilian lives in danger, and Bolan had been at the wrong location, one deadly step behind the Scion. Dammit, he had to move faster and catch the mercs when they were not ready for trouble. But how? Where?

"Excuse, please," a gruff voice said from the doorway.

Assuming a friendly smile, Bolan turned to see a large, burly man standing at the open door. Although only seen through the billowing smoke, Bolan instantly recognized him as the gunman from Liberty City.

"I am looking for the harbor master…" the man began, then his eyes went wide in recognition. "You!"

Dropping the files, Bolan went for his piece as the stranger did the same thing. Both men were fast, but the soldier drew first and shot the other man in the stomach. He staggered but didn't fall. Pulling the trigger as fast as possible, Bolan kept firing into his stomach until the breathless man fell to his knees and dropped a large automatic pistol.

"Freeze, or die," Bolan growled, advancing upon the giant. "Your call."

His face a mask of hatred, the stranger stayed where he was, leaning against the wall with one hand holding his no-doubt aching guts.

Keeping the Beretta aimed at the man, Bolan kicked the dropped pistol away, then closed and locked the door.

"Empty your pockets," he directed.

The man spit on the floor. "Go ahead and shoot," he rumbled. "I have nothing to—"

Moving forward, Bolan slapped the sound suppressor against the man's temple, and he crumpled like old newspaper. Rifling through his adversary's pockets, Bolan found an Imbel pistol in a double shoulder holster and a Remington .44 derringer tucked up his sleeve in a trick slide. A CIA invention abandoned decades ago, Bolan knew of

only one nation that still used the gimmick—
Brazil. Not surprisingly, the man's watch was a
Geiger counter, there was a miniature blade hidden inside his wallet, along with a lock-pick key
perfect for police handcuffs, and several hundred
dollars in large bills. He also had a money belt carrying thousands more, and several passports from
an assortment of countries, each made out to a different name—Jose Ramariez from Mexico, Al-
dolfo Lars from Spain, and so on.

As the stranger groaned softly, Bolan unbuttoned the man's shirt to expose a bulletproof vest,
the quilted Teflon garment dotted with flattened
9 mm slugs. Using a knife, Bolan cut away the
garment and found one more passport taped to
the badly bruised flesh underneath.

Keeping a careful watch on the stirring prisoner, the Executioner stepped back to examine
the hidden passport. It had been issued by the
Brazilian federal police, Department S2, to a
Miguel Santarino. The picture matched and the
country stamps showed he traveled extensively in
South America, but had recently been to England
and Newfoundland. Interesting.

Removing one of the man's shoes, Bolan pulled
up a chair and took a seat to wait for Santarino to
awaken. But after a few minutes, the soldier impatiently got a paper cup of water from the cooler
and tossed it into the Brazilian's face. The S2

agent abruptly came awake, sputtering and reaching for his gun.

With the Beretta in hand, Bolan watched as the man jerked his other arm forward to activate the trick derringer, only to grunt when nothing happened. Leaning against the wall, Santarino very slowly raised a hand to touch his temple and massage the darkening bruise there.

"Amazing. Why am I still alive?" he mumbled, lowering his hand to examine the fingertips for any signs of blood.

"Because we're after the same people," Bolan stated.

Santarino ignored the deliberate distraction and concentrated on Bolan. "Good. Then we are allies," he said, starting to stand then pausing as he finally noticed the missing shoe.

"Damn difficult to rush somebody when you're off balance like that, isn't it?" Bolan asked, the barrel of the silenced Beretta staying rock-steady.

Sighing in grudging acceptance, Santarino crossed both legs with the practiced ease of a yogi. But his right hand moved too quickly over a pant cuff and Bolan extended the Beretta to point-blank range. Without any change of expression, Santarino dropped a throwing spike onto the floor, its tip glistening with some greenish chemical.

Santarino noticed the briefcase near Bolan and

recoiled for a split second before assuming his practiced calm.

Studying the S2 agent carefully, Bolan felt as if he were defusing a land mine. One wrong move and it would remove his head. The man had figured out the briefcase was a fake in two seconds flat. This was a dangerous man.

"I am listening," Santarino said, using a sleeve to wipe the excess water from his pockmarked face.

"Your team has gone rogue," Bolan stated as a fact, then paused. When there was no reply, he went on. "The captain and crew of the sub are dead and Zalhares has taken the cargo for himself."

"Who?"

Drawing the Desert Eagle, Bolan thumbed back the hammer. "Don't waste my time, Miguel."

Only the man's eyes betrayed a reaction to his real name.

"And what makes you think the Scion work for us?" Santarino said slowly. "Where is your proof?"

"I don't need any," Bolan answered coldly.

The Brazilian considered that for a few moments.

"Then you are not FBI?" he said as a question. "In spite of the badge in your pocket."

Not falling for that ancient trick, Bolan didn't

glance at the commission booklet in his shirt. "No, I'm not."

Now the big S2 agent grinned. "Ah. I was unaware that the United States also had a secret police force."

Bolan smiled coldly in return, and the man frowned, unsure if his remark had scored a bull's-eye or not. This American was revealing nothing.

"We do not approve of the cargo," Santarino said slowly. "The Scion was to infiltrate the CIA and relay political information to us, nothing more. This theft was entirely the plan of Cirello Zalhares. My nation has its own program to develop such weapons and does not wish to make America an enemy. If we accept delivery of the…items, the United States will cancel its trade agreements with Brazil. My country would lose billions for stealing weapons worth only a few million."

Make that, half a billion dollars on the black market for all four nukes, Bolan corrected privately, but it was still a point to be considered.

"Try again," Bolan growled. "The Zodiacs are priceless because the atomic signature of nuclear weapons is easily identifiable by satellites in space. These are more than just stolen nukes, they're American nukes. If Brazil used them to obliterate a rebel stronghold, no revolutionary force would ever dare to attack you again, but we would get all the blame."

"That theory has some small amount of merit," Santarino conceded, barely moving his lips. "But then the financial wrath of America would be crippling. America is rich, while Brazil is most definitely not."

The S2 agent shook his head. "No. If the weapons came to us, we would be forced to give them back purely for the sake of our political survival."

Bolan could see that the man was telling the truth. So the Scion was on the run from the most powerful nation in the world, and the most ruthless. Brazil made China look like Canada when it came to murdering its own citizens. Which also meant Zalhares was cut off from his official sources and would need to make new contacts for weapons, revenue, and contacts to sell the nukes.

Bolan also knew for a fact that the S2 agent would kill him the moment he could. But until then, they were uneasy allies. With the decision made, Bolan lowered the Beretta and kicked over the man's shoe.

"We're done here," he said brusquely.

Nodding in agreement, Santarino tugged on his shoe and started to reach for the pile of his weapons. Bolan stopped him with a curt gesture from the Beretta.

"Leave them," he ordered. "I'm sure you have more."

Rising slowly, Santarino started to rub his stomach but stopped the motion, unwilling to show weakness. Turning his back on Bolan, he walked stiffly to the door and worked the latch, then paused, the firelight from outside coloring his pitted features like an autumn moon.

"I must be the one to kill Cirello," the S2 agent said without looking backward. "You may have the others, but Cirello is mine."

"No. What they carry is mine," Bolan said sternly, holstering the Desert Eagle, fully aware his reflection could be seen in the frosted-glass partition. "Don't get in the way of me getting it back, and afterward I'll gift wrap Zalhares for you and the S2 boys to play with in the backroom all you want. Understood?"

Grunting in a noncommittal manner, Santarino swung the door aside and strode into the empty hallway, leaving it open in his wake.

Watching until the giant man disappeared down the external stairs, Bolan holstered the Beretta and gathered the rest of the weapons, tucking them into the accordion pouch inside the briefcase. Then crossing the office, he laid the money belt on the desk of the harbor master. The paltry few thousand wouldn't go very far in the rebuilding, but every little bit helped.

Bolan studied the milling crowd below. Santarino's size made him stick out, and the soldier

watched through a window as the big S2 agent disappeared into the rolling smoke. He wasn't sure
if he had made an ally or a new enemy. But either
way the heat had just been turned up on the Scion.

CHAPTER EIGHT

Stony Man Farm, Virginia

Carmen Delahunt was grimly patrolling the Internet for any sign of the Scion. Brushing away a loose strand of her fiery red hair, the woman adjusted her virtual-reality visor, surfing for any abnormalities. With the theft of the Zodiacs, she had fed one hundred keywords into search programs being run by the massive bank of Cray SV2 supercomputers located under the Farm's Annex Computer Room. Anybody sending e-mail, an IM, graphics, visual, or vocal transmissions on the Web that used a combination of any two of the keywords would trigger an automatic trace.

So far, the Internet was clear, with only a few odd t-bursts that she was trying to track down but without much success. Ultra small and superfast, the microtransmissions were gone in a nanosecond and even her extensive software couldn't nail them without help.

The armored door to the room opened and a tall, distinguished-looking man entered the room chewing on the stem of a pipe. Smoking was forbidden in the Computer Room, but Huntington "Hunt" Wethers still enjoyed the feel and smell of the pipe even when he couldn't light his favorite briarwood.

He walked briskly to his workstation and turned on the monitor to review the work in progress. After assuming control of a NORAD military satellite Wethers unleashed some specially designed software to gather information for Brognola. As he watched the files open and close, he made copies of the more interesting data.

"Fresh coffee, anybody?" Aaron "The Bear" Kurtzman offered, using one hand to push his wheelchair along, the other holding a mug large enough to be used as a weapon.

"Did you make the coffee?" Akira Tokaido asked, both eyes closed as his hands moved across the keyboard like a concert pianist's.

"Of course!"

"Then no thanks." Carmen Delahunt chuckled, lifting her visor to glance sideways with a bemused expression. "I have plans to live long enough to see my children graduate college, and that concoction you call coffee wouldn't help me make it there alive."

"Nonsense!" Kurtzman scoffed, proffering a mug. "This is real coffee! Kills every germ known to science and puts hair on your chest!"

Arching an eyebrow, Delahunt demurely ran a finger along the neckline of her blouse, exposing a hint of cleavage.

"Oh, just try some," Kurtzman chided in mock seriousness. "You'll never have to buy another sweater!"

"Now there's a splendid visual. Pass," she said with a snort, sliding her visor back into place. Delahunt sat upright in her chair and started tapping on her keyboard. "Curious. There it is again."

"Trouble?" Wethers asked.

"Could be. I just had another t-burst," Carmen said pensively. "That's the third within an hour."

A t-burst was the newest scourge of the Internet, a computerized version of a blip transmission over a radio; a massive amount of information condensed into a small tone that lasted for only a second, sometimes even less. There were a lot of heavily encrypted transmissions going over the Internet, and every one of them had a fake ID and source code. Something big was going down in the cyber world, and that was always trouble.

"Do you get a recording?" Kurtzman asked,

slaving his console to hers to start receiving duplicate reports.

"Of course," she replied, biting her lower lip. "But it's heavily protected; quadruple layers. Weird stuff. Aaron, I need a Cray assigned to handle just this data, or else it will take me a week to bust the code."

"If ever," Tokaido added, glancing at a submonitor. The screen was scrolling madly with alphanumeric figures. "I'm not familiar with this configuration of encryption."

"Could it be about the Zodiacs?" Kurtzman asked, scowling at the monitor.

"Damned if I know," Delahunt replied, then added, "Not yet, at least."

Good enough. Flipping some switches, the chief hacker brought online the only spare Cray. A few seconds later a section on Delahunt's console came to life.

"Number three is yours. Get cracking."

"Would you care for some assistance?" Wethers asked, shifting his pipe to the other side of his mouth.

"All I can get," the redheaded woman replied honestly, lowering her visor and becoming fully immersed into the swirling artificial reality of the World Wide Web.

The Gulf of Mexico

THE CESSNA SKYLANE BUZZED across the blue sky. Sitting behind the steering yoke, Mack Bolan adjusted his sunglasses and checked the altimeter to make sure he was maintaining the assigned height of five thousand feet above the Gulf of Mexico.

The sky was clear, and a gentle southerly wind blew steadily at five knots. Excellent flying weather.

Glancing at the military radar, Bolan saw that the Doppler screen was clear, as was the computer-enhanced civilian KNH-880 multihazard warning system. He was alone in the sky, except for some commercial jet liners twenty thousand feet above.

The problem was down in the ocean. The fires were still raging at the Biscayne dockyard, and so far more than one hundred assorted crafts were unaccounted for. Ignoring the smaller speedboats, the oddball hovercrafts and such, Bolan chose to concentrate on the seagoing yachts. They had long range and lots of room belowdecks where nobody could see what was happening.

Zalhares wouldn't have taken a full yacht, those two hundred footers always carried an armed crew in case of pirate attacks. That would have been too much trouble to try to steal quietly in the middle of a busy harbor. No, they would have gone for something smaller, but not too small. Say, a fifty-foot yacht, certainly no larger than a seventy-five. These days, every yacht had a lowjack built into its hull, a hidden radio set to broadcast its location in case it was stolen. However, the lowjack couldn't be turned on until the yacht was reported stolen to its security company. And with most of the owners dead, or in the hospital, that wasn't possible.

Bolan had asked Brognola to turn over every lowjack off the coast of Miami area and to have the computers at the Farm start removing the legitimate signals. In less than an hour the choices had been reduced to a mere handful: three that seemed just out for a pleasure ride going nowhere, two headed in the general direction of the Cayman Islands, one heading due east into the Atlantic Ocean, and one heading full-speed toward Jamaica.

Unfortunately there was no way of telling which it might be aside from monitoring the progress of the yachts, or having the spy satellites in orbit do a visual recon with their telescopes, which was taking far longer than hoped for. Most of the satellites had already been on assignments, monitoring troop movements in Cuba or drug shipments in Colombia and had to be realigned. That took time, and then, a visual recon would only tell them who was on the deck not down in the hold.

"Calling Hawk One," Brognola said over the speaker on the dashboard. "Hawk One, come in please, this is Uncle Harry."

"I read you loud and clear, Harry," Bolan said into the hand mike. "How's the fishing?"

"Not so good. Go to setting two. Over."

"Setting two. Confirm."

Bolan slid back a panel on the radio and flicked a switch to activate the encoder, then set the dial to setting three. Even using codes, it was foolish to give the setting. This hour, they went up one every time they used the radio. In the next hour, it would be down two. There were a lot of electronic ears in this part of the world and most of them weren't friendly. It paid to be careful.

"Okay, Hal, do you read me?" Bolan asked, adjusting the squeal slightly.

There was a brief crackle of static before the speaker started working loud and clear. "Like you were in the next room," Brognola replied. "Okay, the news isn't good. The sats checked the yacht heading for Jamaica. And unless our runners have hired a dozen teenaged girls as cover, it's exactly what it seems to be, a party boat full of drunk college students heading for fun in the sun."

Five to go then. "I'm heading for the Caymans," Bolan said. "Can you get a pass on the other four?"

"The declination of the Watchdogs is already

being changed by the NSA to check that wild card heading into the Atlantic," Brognola said, then there came a chuckle. "Although they're pissing blood over not being told why. But that's good for them to be knocked down a peg or two every now and then. It keeps them humble. I'll let you know once we have a visual."

"Roger that, Hal. Good luck. I'll report every hour until I hear from you. Over and out."

Returning the mike to its clip, Bolan flew on in silence, listening to the steady rumble of the engine and the whining hum of the propellers. With no exact destination, he was currently headed for the Caymans to refuel. The Cayman Islands were a good rendezvous point for any criminal activity in the Gulf of Mexico. The small country had no military at all, only the Royal Cayman Island Police with a few assault rifles, some rescue boats, and that was about it. But then, an armed military wasn't really needed as people rarely attacked their own bank.

A former British territory, now a free state, the Cayman Islands had no marketable crops, no natural supply of clean water, no minerals to mine, no manufacturing, no heavy industry and yet its population had the highest standard of living in the entire world. That was because the Caymans were the money laundering capital of the world. The vacation paradise was in truth a secret hellhole of vice and murder. There were a lot of honest cops who thought blowing the islands off the map would cripple every criminal operation in the world for the next decade, and Bolan heartily agreed.

Years ago, he'd been there on a rescue mission that had turned out to be a lot more difficult than expected. But it gave him an intimate knowledge of the islands. The capital city, Georgetown, had the best airport, absolutely state-of-the-art in comfort and efficiency, but also tight security, so Bolan optioned on refueling at a private airport on the Lesser Cayman Island. Things were more lax off the main island, and a fistful of cash averted the attention of the local police without any questions asked.

As Bolan settled down for the long flight, the radar screen rippled and went blank. Reaching for the reset button, he frowned as the KMH went down and the crackle of the radio turned into a soft, steady hiss. Quickly pulling out his cell phone, Bolan got the same results. There was a jamming field working in the area, covering the full EM spectrum. That took a lot of power and equipment.

After checking the Desert Eagle strapped under his windbreaker, Bolan pulled out some Navy field glasses and swept the ocean for any yachts below, but the water was clear. From out of nowhere came a rumble that built to overwhelm the steady buzz of his monoplane, then something eclipsed the sun and Bolan automatically veered off into a steep dive.

Banking hard, he glanced out the rear window to see that a C-130 Hercules transport had nearly crashed into him. If the pilot had wanted Bolan dead, he merely needed to cut a tight pass and the turbulence of the gigantic propeller-driven monster would send the Skylane into a tailspin that would end in a watery crash.

Suddenly there came the faint crackle of gunfire as bullets dented the cowling over the engine. Moving fast, Bolan threw the joystick to the left and angled into a screaming dive. Okay, the Hercules was hostile. Thumbing up the locking mechanism, he slid open the small access window set alongside the side window. The cold wind rushed inside despite the warmth of the sun. Titling the Cessna slightly, he caught sight of the Hercules and banked into a sharp turn. This was going to require precise timing on his part.

His briefcase lay on the passenger seat. Reaching over, the soldier flipped open the case and got a grenade. Keeping one hand tight on the yoke, he armed the bomb and dropped it out the side window. Eight seconds later an explosion blossomed just behind and slightly below the Hercules, the wind sheer taking the grenade off target.

More gunfire crackled from the Hercules as Bolan circled for another pass, but this time the gunner missed completely.

Only two more grenades remained in the briefcase, so he chose a canister charge and waited a moment after pulling the pin before dropping the bomb out the window. Six seconds later, a white phosphorous fireball detonated directly above the Hercules, missing its target by a heartbeat.

In response, the Hercules slowly turned sideways in a bank, showings its left side to Bolan. As he watched, the access door slid back to reveal two men with safety lines around their waists and a M-60 machine gun attached somehow to the floor. One of the men dropped behind the M-60 and it began sputtering flame, the spent brass shells sailing in a golden arch. The incoming barrage missed the tiny Cessna completely as Bolan flipped his belly to the Hercules and cut away in a hard turn.

Bolan scowled as the rear cargo hatch began to lower. Knowing what to expect, he was already climbing above the Hercules when a group of men was revealed attached to a spiderweb of safety lines. Ten, twelve soldiers, maybe more, it was hard to tell with their clothing whipping madly from the force of the wind. In unison, the group raised assault rifles and cut loose.

Pushing the Cessna engine to its limits, Bolan managed to catch the wind and get above the Hercules where the gunmen couldn't get a clear shot, although small-arms fire still continued from the open windows of the cockpit.

Swinging the monoplane back and forth, he quickly reviewed his options as the Hercules started to pull away in front. Okay, say, twenty men with automatic weapons, which was more than enough to tear the Cessna apart once they got the range, and only one grenade left in the brief-case—a smoke canister he had planned to use to pretend the Cessna was on fire to crash into the yacht. Plummeting into the sea was fast becoming a real possibility. There were the two C4 blocks still wired to the remote detonator in the briefcase, which would blow the Hercules in two if he could get it through the open hatchway. Small chance of that happening. On top of which, with the jamming field in place, the plastique couldn't be triggered by a radio signal; it would take far too long to disengage the wiring and reset the blocks for an impact detonation.

Wheeling through the unfriendly skies, Bolan reviewed his combat options with lighting speed. Both the Beretta and the Desert Eagle lacked sufficient power to do any real damage to the titanic airplane. But, in the space behind the rear passenger seats, was one of the equipment lockers, mostly containing small arms and extra ammunition. The other two trunks were stored in the aft baggage compartment. Considering they could only be reached from the outside of the plane, they might as well be on the moon for all the good they could do for the soldier right now. Small arms was all he had, but maybe the Saber OICW could do the job.

Suddenly the muted rumble of the Hercules grew in rapid volume, along with the sound of machine guns. Looking around, Bolan saw the huge plane in a steep climb on coming right at the Cessna. They were trying for a ram again. Slamming the yoke all the way forward, he did the unexpected and nosed into a full-power dive straight at the Hercules. For a moment the two airplanes headed directly toward each other, and Bolan got a fleeting glimpse of the pilot and co-pilot in the high cockpit of the C-130 transport. The co-pilot was unknown, but the pilot was Miguel Santarino. Apparently their truce was off before it ever really even started.

Waiting until the very last moment, Bolan cut the dive into a bank and dropped his port flap to skim sideways beneath the Hercules and avoid the gunmen in the rear. But the wash of the four turbo-props shook the monoplane, rattling every loose item inside and cracking the glass on a side window. Then he was past the winged behemoth and heading almost straight for the silvery waters of the Gulf.

Leveling the flaps, Bolan feathered his props, then fed the engine more power and started to pull back on the yoke to fight the descent. Pushed to its limits, the sturdy engine almost stalled from the conflicting g-forces, and the waves of the ocean came sharply into focus before he could feel the plane start to rise again to fly level above the Gulf.

However, trapped against the ocean would be suicide, so Bolan started climbing for distance, pushing the Cessna for the maximum ceiling of ten thousand feet. Safe for a moment, he flexed his hands on the yoke and took a breath. That suicide maneuver bought a few minutes, but not much more, and Santarino wouldn't fall for the trick again. Next time, the S2 agent would have his people ready to drop grenades as the Cessna cut under the wings and that would settle the matter permanently.

Accepting the hard truth, Bolan knew that he was in a bad spot. The Hercules was much faster in a straight flight than the Cessna, its four huge engines easily overpowering his one-lung 230. Plus, the mighty Herc could also climb higher, had greater range and a lot more firepower. There was no way the Cessna could escape, but there were a few points in his favor. The Hercules had only the one big hatch in the rear that its crew could safely use to shoot from and the open doorway with the M-60 machine gun. With both of those wide open, the plane was taking in a lot of drag that was slowing it. And since this seemed to be a civilian model, there was no access door on the right side, so the Hercules had a blind side. That was good news. Even better was that the Cessna cockpit was small enough for Bolan to fire out both side windows, doubling his attack vectors. Also, the little monoplane was a lot more maneuverable than the lumbering transport. Bolan didn't have much of an edge, but it was something.

Reviewing the plane for any damage, Bolan checked the engine temperature, gas and oil. The Cessna had a few holes in it, but was otherwise fine. Good. Setting the autopilot for full speed in a gentle climb, he unbuckled the seat belt and turned to open the equipment trunk. Kneeling on the sloped floor, he keyed the lock and flipped open the trunk to start releasing the straps holding a LAW to the inside of the lid. The armor-piercing rocket would blow a hole in the Hercules large enough to drive a Hummer through, but the back blast from the tube would blow the Cessna apart. It couldn't be used from inside the plane. Lying the LAW next to a parachute, Bolan went back to the trunk and chose his best weapon for this fight: a brand new, state-of-the-art weapon called a Saber.

Looking like something from a sci-fi move, the Saber had two barrels and one trigger, a thumb switch on the frame controlling which of the weapons to be used. The main barrel fired 5.56 mm hardball ammo, with a standard 30-round clip. The second, fatter, barrel was located directly above the machine gun and launched 20 mm grenades, fed by a 6-round clip. The scope had all sorts of impressive night-vision and computer-enhanced utilities, but those were useless unless the duel went into a cloud bank. Unfortunately, the tropical sky was clear to the horizon, not even a stray stratus formation in sight, much less any fat cumulous clouds or a good thick bank. Bolan was caught in the open and there was nothing he could do about that.

Checking the double clips in the Saber, Bolan tucked some extra into his pockets and returned to the pilot's seat just in time to see the Hercules rise on his side like some prehistoric leviathan from the depths of the sea. Never before had the soldier truly appreciated just how large the plane was. Thankfully, he couldn't see any Bofor 40 mm cannon barrels sticking out of the nose gunports. If Santarino was armed with those, Bolan would have no choice but to jump and risk setting his parachute on fire when he launched the LAW. And although the giant plane carried Brazilian markings, it was a civilian model, unarmed except for the twenty or so gunmen inside.

As the Hercules swung its left side toward the

Cessna, Bolan rammed the Saber out the right side window and sent a long burst of HEAT rounds. The tracers stitched a bright line across the sky, curving into the wind and away from the enemy plane.

Angling the weapon higher, Bolan managed to hit the left wing, but the incandescent ammo didn't achieve penetration, merely splattered on the metal surface. Now the gunmen had a clear view and cut loose with the M-60 machine gun again.

Thumbing the selector switch, the Executioner pumped out a grenade that directly hit one of the gunmen standing in the open hatchway, but there was no explosion. One man staggered and fell backward into the plane, the other kept shooting.

Biting back a curse, Bolan now remembered that the first round had been a stun bag to try to capture Zalhares alive. That blasted scenario load may have cost him the battle.

More gunfire came from the Hercules, then a dark object sailed past his propellers. Bolan couldn't tell for sure, but he was willing to bet that it had been a 40 mm round from an M-203. Slipping sideways over the Hercules to escape the gunmen, Bolan dropped the spent 5.56 mm clip, reloaded, then sloped sharply to the right, reaching the blind side of the Hercules and pumping all five of the Saber's remaining 20 mm rounds at the big plane. The first two hit only air, but then the one of the engine cowlings exploded to fall away, revealing the naked machinery.

Switching to hardball ammo, Bolan peppered the engine until it caught on fire, thick orange flames whipping back in the wind. The Hercules noticeably slowed as the propeller went dead, then foam gushed over the burning machinery, drowning the flames.

Slapping in another 20 mm clip, Bolan tried for the other engine, but only blew holes in the main fuselage just behind the bank of windows that framed the main cockpit. With his bare arm sticking outside the plane, Santarino was firing an SMG at the Cessna. Bolan responded by concentrating the 5.56 mm rounds on the blast holes in the hull. Unlike the glass in the Cessna, the Hercules's windows would be nearly bulletproof to withstand the massively higher wind pressures. As the clip became exhausted, Bolan lowered the flaps and tried to outdistance any possible response from the tail gunmen while he reloaded again. The cargo ramp was set below the tail section and back there the Hercules had another small blind spot. But staying in the protective shadow of the moving tail was difficult, and every time the Cessna came into view, the Brazilians opened up again. Suddenly a fiery dart streaked by to arch high above and explode into brilliant colors. Mo-

mentarily blinded, Bolan reacted instinctively and
sent the Cessna into a circling dive. The enemy
was shooting flares to get the wind! He had hurt
them, but now the Brazilians were coming in for
the kill.

As his vision cleared, Bolan slapped in a fresh
clip of 20 mm rounds and worked the arming bolt.
With one engine dead, plus the drag, the Cessna
and the Hercules were roughly capable of the
same speed now, so escape was an option. But if
he did, Santarino would be on his tail every step
of the way. Bolan had offered a truce, but Santarino had chosen death instead. So be it. Time for
him to pay the price of that decision.

More flares came soaring skyward from the
co-pilot, as Santarino maintained a steady hammering from his SMG. Pumping six more 20 mm
rounds at the Hercules, Bolan scored a couple of
hits in the top of the tail section, damaging the rud-
der, and then bluish smoke started to pour from the
rear hatch. The color of the smoke told it was an
oil fire. Maybe he had set fire to one of their vehicles parked inside or caught an auxiliary pressure line. Either way, an oil fire was hard to
control, and the gunmen in the aft section would
be nearly blind and choking on the fumes.

Slapping in the last 20 mm clip, Bolan swung
back and forth above the lumbering plane, while
the men in the cockpit raked the sky with small-

arms fire. A chance round pinged loudly off one of the Cessna floats, and another flare streaked by to burst so close that Bolan clearly heard the hissing aftershock.

Dropping to the right side behind the Hercules, the soldier thumbed the selector switch and peppered the craft with 5.56 mm rounds, the tracers curving in the wind to impact all over the slowing plane. Tiny dots of fire now clung to the hull and the smoke from the rear was becoming more pronounced.

Unexpectedly, there was an explosion of sound as the radar came back on, along with the KHM warning system. Then the radio crackled into life.

"…riker, do you copy?" Brognola demanded. "Dammit to hell, Striker, do you hear me? Over!"

Keeping a tight grip on the yoke, Bolan started to reach for the hand mike when a body fell from the rear of the Hercules. Had they dumped a wounded man to save on weight? No, that lump on his back was a parachute, and the man seemed to be holding a long tube in his arms. That was a Stinger!

Dropping the Saber, Bolan grabbed the emergency flare pistol from its pocket holster located under the dash. There was no time to check if the flare pistol was loaded. He had to hope for the best. Even as Bolan shoved the pistol through the left window, the falling man became enshrouded in smoke, and a rocket shot out of the tube to climb fast on a stiletto of flame.

Forcing himself to remain calm, Bolan waited long seconds as the Stinger antiaircraft missile zoomed toward the Cessna, then he gently squeezed the trigger. The pistol thumped and the signal flare streaked away for the incoming Stinger. At first, it looked as if the ploy wasn't going to work, then the heat-seeker sharply veered its course toward the sizzling flare. Instantly, Bolan slammed the joystick forward and gave the Cessna full power, angling into a dive once more and racing for distance. Come on, baby, come on...

"Striker?" the radio blared. "Do you copy?"

Aft of the Cessna, the sky lit with the exploding Stinger, the deadly shrapnel arriving just a split second ahead of the brutal concussion wave. The Cessna violently shook as one of the wing struts bent slightly and a dozen small holes appeared in the fuselage and floor. Bolan grunted as the back of his seat jerked and an object jabbed him hard in the ribs, but there was no accompanying stab of pain. Reaching down, he gingerly felt the seat to find a hot dent in the metal backing. Saved by a scant millimeter of cheap steel that slowed the shrapnel just enough.

Dropping speed to match the crippled Hercules, Bolan ignored the 9 mm rounds coming from Santarino and made a slow sweep across the damaged right wing, the 20 mm rounds blowing holes in the surface, shearing off an airfoil flap, and then a wing tank caught fire.

He banked away sharply and fed the Cessna full power. Still building speed, Bolan was facing the other direction when thunder filled the sky. The Cessna shook so hard the rear window and the dashboard radar screen both loudly cracked. For a moment he thought his luck was gone and the plane would crumple like a stepped-on tin can. But dropping the Saber, he grabbed the yoke with both hands and tried to ride out the balance of the blast as best he could. A piece of flaming wreckage shot by, nearly hitting the Cessna, and on the dashboard a warning light flashed as a fuel line cracked, a pinkish spray shooting out of the dented cowling. Gritting his teeth, Bolan strained to keep the plane on course as he reached out to flip a switch to close the ruptured gas line fast. The hydraulic pressure was dropping like a stone, but before he could do anything, it leveled out, the needle hovering just above the red zone. The Cessna lurched as a float broke free and the monoplane tilted to the left.

Fighting the wounded plane into a level flight path, Bolan risked a gentle turn in the sky and caught a glimpse of the last few pieces of the burning Hercules tumbling into the ocean. Scanning the sky, he saw no parachutes drifting downward, but there still might be survivors. With a float missing, he couldn't land the seaplane on water, but Bolan decided to do a recon.

Loosening the Beretta in his shoulder holster, he guided the Cessna lower and circled the crash area twice, looking for signs of swimmers. But there was nothing, aside from the soggy white parachute of the man who had jumped out to launch the Stinger. The material drifted listlessly in the currents and was slowly starting to sink under its own wet weight. Briefly, Bolan wondered if the lunatic who jumped had been Santarino. Then he pushed the matter from his mind and picked up the hand mike.

"Hawk One Uncle Harry—" he said and was immediately interrupted.

"Striker, thank God! Where the hell have you been?"

"Switching to seven," Bolan said, changing the setting to five.

There was a short pause. "Okay, we're secure," Brognola said. "Now what's going on? You haven't answered my hails for the past hour."

"I was busy," Bolan said, shifting in the pilot seat to try to void the dent in the chair. "Our friends had friends, but they're no longer coming to the party."

"Alphabet friends, I'll wager. Letter and a number."

"Roger that, Hal. Any news on the yachts?"

"Yes, they're all clean, which means any of them could have the Scion belowdecks, or else we screwed the pooch and they escaped some other way."

Even though he couldn't be seen, Bolan shook his head. "They used a yacht, Hal. Trust me on this. The S2 wouldn't have been out here just gunning for me. They have a major hard-on for Zalhares for political reasons."

"I hear you. I'll let you know if anything turns up."

"Roger on that, Hal. Over and out."

Returning the mike to its clip, Bolan concentrated on heading for the Cayman Islands. His fuel was low, but it should be enough.

With the S2 out of the way, there was nothing standing between him and Zalhares but a few miles of empty air. With any luck, this could all be over in a couple of hours. Once he found them, that was.

CHAPTER NINE

Fat Ed's Bar

Gritty dust blew across the old dirt road as the green Ford van rolled through the shifting desert. Evening was starting to fall, the sky turning a glorious purple on its way to the deep black of night.

As the vehicle's headlights swept along the uneven road, there appeared in the distance a large, wooden, hand-painted sign with the name of a bar, bright halogen lights illuminating it for drivers to see for miles in both directions. Bouncing along the old paved road, the van silently rolled to halt in front of the sign. The driver turned off the purring Detroit engine.

"Let's go," Zalhares said, setting the handbrake. "We haven't much time." Taking tools and weapons, the members of Scion climbed from the truck and got to their assignments.

Slinging an Uru over a shoulder, Jorgina Mizne went to the wooden sign and put a short burst of 9 mm rounds into the electrical box at the base of the main support beam. There was a shower of sparks and the halogen lights went dead. Whistling through her teeth, the woman then pulled a hatchet from a sheath on her belt and went to the first wooden support. She frowned, put the ax away and leveled the Uru. Her first strident burst chewed partially through the thick oak beam and the sign began to sag slightly. Going to the other support beam, the woman fired longer and, with the sound of splintering wood, the large sign came crashing down onto the dusty sand.

Meanwhile, Dog Mariano and Minas Pedrosa hammered a steel rod into the hard berm alongside the paved roadway. Walking across the dirt turnoff, they dragged a chain and attached it to another steel rod they had installed. Dangling from the chain, exactly at windshield level, was a sign saying in English and Spanish that the road was temporarily closed for repairs.

As the trio returned to the truck, Zalhares, having just emptied a bag of caltraps onto the ground, was using his boot to scatter them around. Invented by the ancient Romans, a caltrap was a hard piece of wood with several nails driven through at different angles so that an array of sharp steel points always jutted upward no matter how the wood rolled. Originally used two thousand years ago to stop barefoot barbarians, the ancient caltraps worked equally well against inflatable car tires.

Pulling out a pair of Starlite glasses, Zalhares surveyed the area, nodded in approval, then rejoined the others in the Ford. Mariano and Pedrosa were in their seats waiting patiently; Mizne was at the ammo case reloading her Uru. Opening the top of the stock, she dropped in a plastic-wrapped block of lead and propellant. Then closing the top, she pulled hard on a plastic tab in the butt of the stock and yanked out the covering that hermetically sealed the ammo block, keeping it bone-dry. As the indicator turned red, she switched from full-auto to single-shot, and stuck the Uru out the window to trigger a single round to make sure the electrodes were properly aligned. Ninety-nine rounds to go.

The truck was a very recent acquisition and had cost a small fortune, but was well worth the expense. The outside was worn and slightly rusted, giving it a used appearance, but the vehicle was brand-new, modified heavily with body armor, an oversize engine and extra heavy-duty springs in the rear to help handle the load—the small lead safe bolted into the rear.

Starting the engine, Zalhares froze as a car approached the turnoff. He pulled out a pistol and thumbed back the hammer. The car went by without even slowing and vanished behind a low rolling hill of the desert.

"Wretched place," Mariano muttered, lowering his rifle. "How can people live without trees?"

"Who cares?" Zalhares said, easing off the hammer and tucking away the handgun. "Soon enough we shall be back home and richer than Colombian drug lords."

Starting the powerful engine, Zalhares drove down the bumpy dirt road for a few miles before taking a curve around a low hillock. Beyond was an oasis of illumination, a sprawling parking lot full of pickup trucks and motorcycles, and in the center was a squat brick building with a garish pink neon sign proclaiming the name of the bar, Fat Ed's.

As the Ford rolled closer, the pounding music become more pronounced, seeming to throb in the darkening air. Pretending to look for a parking space, Zalhares circled the bar once doing a recon, then parked directly in front, alongside a row of motorcycles.

Lurching away from a yucca tree, a fat man smoking a hand-rolled cigarette swaggered over to the van, both thumbs tucked inside his wide garrison belt.

"Ya can't park there, jackass," he said around the joint, exhaling a long stream of smoke at the same time. "That's for hogs only."

With a soft hum, the driver's side window of the truck lowered and there was a gentle cough. The fat man jerked back his head and toppled to the hard-packed soil, the joint falling next to him as a tiny red eye in the darkness.

"Jimmy?" a voice asked from the back of a pickup. "When you coming back, honey?"

"Baby?" the voice repeated as a middle-aged woman rose from the back of the pickup, a .38 S&W nickel-plated revolver in her hand, the weapon shining like a beacon in the reflected lights of the noisy bar. Three more coughs from the van and she spun with half of her face missing, the handgun flying away into the night.

Climbing out of their Ford, the members of Scion checked their weapons as they listened to the night for a moment, ignoring the music that they could now feel pulsating against their bare skin. Gesturing with a free hand, Zalhares sent Mariano to the left and Pedrosa to the right. Drawing their silenced Imbel automatic pistols, the men disappeared around the building, then reappeared a few minutes later, easing fresh clips into their hot weapons.

Zalhares asked a question with his gloved hands and they responded then started for the shaking front door of the bar. As they reached the concrete porch, a bearded man stumbled out with a young woman on each arm, the three of them laughing. In practiced ease, the Scion stepped back until the drunk people cleared the doorway, then fired their silenced weapons directly into the backs of their heads. The people convulsed as their brains exploded and were dead long before they hit the porch and rolled limply onto the sandy ground.

The Scion waited for any reaction from the other cars. When nothing happened, they pushed inside the bar and paused as the thundering rock music hit them like a tangible force, their stomachs moving to the beat of the bass line. The biker bar was full, with crowded tables covering the floor and a line of people standing at a counter set catercorner in the rear.

Huge black speakers nearly as large as refrigerators were set into the ceiling, and posters of rock bands and famous outlaws from the Old West decorated the brick walls. Ceiling fans valiantly tried to circulate the smoky air and the floor was covered with a thick layer of crushed peanut shells. There was no other exit in sight.

Turning, Mariano knelt to lock the door with a steel shackle, while the others spread out in a firing line, looking for danger spots and marking their targets.

At a table nearby, a blowsy blonde stopped bobbing her head to the deafening music and nudged her snoring boyfriend with an elbow. The burly biker came awake with a snort and blinked a few times before looking in the direction she was indicating. Grinning widely, he stood, exposing a lean, muscular frame draped in a grimy T-shirt decorated with the rebel flag of the Southern Confederation, Nazi tattoos on both arms. The silver buckle of his belt was a screaming demon skull.

"Well, look what we got here!" He laughed, smashing a beer bottle on the table and gesturing with the jagged end. "Who let in the garbage?"

Without a word, Zalhares swung up the Uru and put a burst into the biker's face, the skull and brains blowing out through his mane of greasy hair. The blonde started to scream and everybody in the bar turned to stare in shock.

"Son of a bitch," a man said, the joint dropping from his slack lips.

As if that was their cue, the Brazilian mercenaries cut loose, the streams of silenced rounds chewing a path of destruction through the stunned people sitting at the tables or standing at the bar. Bloody clothing went flying, and people screamed as faces and bottles exploded. A group of bikers in the corner turned to pull pistols from under their vests and were cut down ruthlessly. One woman flipped over a table and ducked behind, but the caseless 4.5 mm hardball ammo punched through the Formica and wood and tore her apart.

Snarling, the bartender rose into sight, racking a shotgun, and Zalhares stitched the man across the bare chest. As the bartender crashed into the shelves of bottles along the wall, his shotgun discharged and blew apart the cash register, swirling tattered money over the gory carnage.

On and on the mercs discharged their lethal loads, until there was nobody left standing but the Scion.

Swinging his Uru to a new target, Zalhares pumped several rounds into the CD player near the dripping bar until the machine shorted out and blessed silence descended upon the building. Relaxing his tense shoulders, Zalhares slung his automatic and drew his Imbel pistol to stand guard while the others reloaded, then he did the same.

"Dog, Jorgina, recon," Zalhares snapped, gesturing across the room with a gloved hand. "Minas, check for possums."

Moving across the twitching corpse, Mariano put a burst through the plywood door and got an answering scream of pain. Kicking it open, he marched inside and the Brazilian weapon spoke twice more, closely followed by the boom of his pistol.

Meanwhile, Pedrosa strode deliberately on top

of the bodies, watching for any reactions and occasionally firing a round into anybody who didn't seem bloody enough. More than once, his suspicions were correct and the bullet got a cry of pain from somebody only pretending to be dead. A knife would have been the best for the cowards, but they were on a tight schedule, so he just shot them in the forehead and continued the hunt.

"Clear?" Zalhares asked, glancing through a dirty window at the parking lot outside. There was no motion among the still vehicles.

"Clear," Mariano acknowledged, going to the bar and pushing bodies out of the way.

"Good."

Zalhares righted a stool and took a seat before swinging a laptop from behind his back and placing it on the sticky wood counter amid the glass and teeth.

"Minas, Jorgina, stand guard," he ordered. "Watch for Army helicopters."

While the others took post at the windows, Mariano ran the power cord to an outlet; Zalhares attached the cord to the telephone. Turning on the laptop, Zalhares waited for a dial tone, then activated the scrambler and went online to access the encrypted programs already waiting for his arrival. Time to become rich.

Galveston, Texas

STEPPING ONTO THE DECK of the *Falcon Flyer,* Bolan scowled in controlled anger. The yacht was empty, the dead crew stuffed into the hold, and there was no sign of the Scion or the Zodiacs.

After refueling at the Lesser Cayman Island, Bolan had flown through the night to land on Texas A&M University's private airstrip on Turtle Island. According to the lowjack signal, the last yacht had arrived more than five hours earlier at Galveston Harbor Club, slip 37. The other yachts had already docked at various ports, the crews visually cleared by the orbiting Watchdog satellite. So this one had to be it.

But because of local cloud cover, the satellites had no idea as to the status of the crew of the *Falcon Flyer,* whether they were still onboard or long gone. Zalhares was like quicksilver, always slipping between Bolan's fingers, and the trail was already starting to get cold again.

Walking down the gangplank to the pristine jetty with its colorful canvas awning, Bolan headed for his rented Cadillac Seville parked behind a knotted rope stretched between a line of painted anchors. The whole area was decorated in the same manner, as if it were an exhibit at an amusement park instead of a working dockyard. He spotted an old man fishing off the end of the jetty and changed direction.

"Morning," Bolan said in a friendly manner. "How's the fishing?"

"So, so," the old man replied, reeling in the line to cast again. The spinning lure plunked into the gray gulf water and he started to immediately reel it back in again. "I saw you on that fancy yacht over yonder. You looking for them fellows gave a bad check for their slip charges? You a skip tracer?"

Sitting on the jetty, Bolan dangled his feet over the sluggishly gray water where the color wasn't from pollution but the local clay. If there were any fish down there, he certainly didn't see any.

"Let's just say they have something I want," he said, "and leave it at that."

"Yep, you're a collector," he said with a chuckle, casting once more. The process seemed endless. "Well, you're too late. They already left, couple to three hours ago."

"Big man with a scar on his cheek?" Bolan asked casually. "Bald guy with a mustache, another with a ponytail, a woman with them, muscular but very pretty."

"That's them. Although I wouldn't say the lady was pretty. Nice tits, though. Big, anyway, that's what counts."

"No objections there." Bolan chuckled, resting his hands on his knees. "Say, any chance you saw them leave? There'd be a reward if it helps me find them."

The conversation stopped for a minute as a pale man strolled by walking a dog, the bull terrier straining at the end of the leash, its tongue lolling from the collar around his throat holding him in check.

"No reward needed," the old man said, casting again. "It was a big green Ford truck, you know, the panel jobs with no windows in the rear. Sex vans we used to call 'em in my day. Who needed an apartment when you had a van without windows?"

"I prefer a convertible myself," Bolan said, standing to leave. "It's always nice to have the option of leaving quick."

The man smiled widely, displaying perfect teeth that had to be dentures. "Oh, a ragtop man, eh? Yeah, I should have known from that hulking big Caddy you came in."

The Executioner didn't speak for a minute.

"Sharp eyes," he said softly.

"Old, not blind," the man said, flicking the rod, the line whizzing away to splash into an unseen target.

"Did you get the license number?"

"Covered with mud, even though there ain't been rain for days. That's pretty odd, huh?" the man replied, suddenly alert as the line went taut. Then he relaxed as it came free from whatever underwater obstruction it had snagged. "Look, cousin, you might want to forget going after them, if you know what I mean. They're bad news, take my word on it."

"Can't let them go," Bolan said, the sea wind ruffling his black hair. "It's what I do."

Reeling in the wet line, the fisherman sighed and laid the rod aside to take up another. "Well, then, good luck to you, because your friends got a delivery from Jimmy G. before they drove away."

"So who does Jimmy... Wait a second, they took a package from him? Not the other way around?"

"Ayep."

"How big?"

"About the size of a shoe box."

Could be cash. But that wasn't anywhere near large enough to hold sufficient cash to buy a Zodiac. Perhaps the sale was in precious gems....

"A while ago I knew a guy in Dallas called Jimmy G." Bolan said, probing for more information. "Mean Jim Green. Big fellow, bad teeth."

Pushing back a hat covered with spare lures, the old man glanced sideways. "You got the last name right, but that ain't Jimmy. He's skinny as a crackhead and as nice as they come, unless you cross him. A blade man, likes to cut folks up. Not quite sure he's right in the head. Works as a gopher for Dillard. Mr. Ernest E. Dillard." He paused.

"Gorilla Dillard," he said, "and you know what that means."

Yes, Bolan surely did. He didn't know the name, but the situation was as old as civilization. Dillard was the local gang boss, some local tough who ran the drugs, gambling and girls in the dockyard. Oh, Bolan had met Ernest E. Dillard many times before, in many cities across the nation. He had filled graveyards with Ernest Dillards, but there were always more standing in line to take his place and to feed at the trough of human misery.

More importantly, Zalhares received the delivery of a shoe box, or something the size of a shoe box, only two hours after arriving in Galveston. What in hell could that possibly be?

"Any idea where I can locate Jimmy?" Bolan asked, smoothing down his hair with a palm. The gesture spread his windbreaker for a second, exposing the Beretta under his arm, but the old fisherman didn't seem to notice.

"Don't know where to find Jimmy. Gotta ask Dillard about that, and, son, I'd rather put my pecker in a meat grinder," the fisherman stated forcibly, then sighed. "Ernie Dillard. Now that man is mean clean through, shoot, yeah. If a rattler bite Dillard, the snake would die, not him."

"Thanks for the warning," Bolan said, turning to leave. "Good luck with the fishing."

"They have nothing to fear from me, mack." The old man chuckled, casting into the waves.

Caught in the middle of a step, Bolan almost reacted to the name, until he realized it was merely the old man's way of being friendly.

Heading to the car, the Executioner stepped over the rope divider and got inside the Cadillac. Finding the crime boss wouldn't be a problem. Men like that did everything but advertise their homes to show how well they were doing. Getting the man to roll over on Jimmy G. was another matter entirely.

CHAPTER TEN

Stony Man Farm, Virginia

The Computer Room was locked in a hushed still-
ness, the machines humming, the air conditioners
purring and the silent keyboards patting softly to
the moving fingers of the hackers. Disks were slid
into slots, software programs unleashed by the
dozens, the monitors flickering with the cascade
of data pouring through the massive Cray supercomputers below. The coffee urn was drained and
cold, plates of crumbs marking where stacks of
sandwiches had once been at each console.

Suddenly, Carmen Delahunt jerked up her head
and yanked off the VR helmet. "Got it!" she cried.
"Bear, call Barbara and Hal, the Scion are auc-
tioning the Zodiacs over the Internet."

"What?" The big man leaned forward in his

wheelchair, then waved a hand to dismiss the question and grabbed a phone on his console.

"Where is the auction?" Hunt Wethers demanded, swiveling in his chair, pipe stem tight in his clenched teeth. "I have several fake and unbreakable criminal identities to use and can join the auction to buy the bombs from the Scion. Afterward, we can settle the matter of just retribution."

"Dammit, I don't know where it is," she shot back. "In virtual space, or in the real world. The message I decoded was a reply from the Scion granting admittance to Liberty Peru to join the auction. I've got sixteen more messages found on the Internet, but each is encrypted differently. Without the key it will take hours to bust each one. They could be nothing, pornography sent between diplomats, love letters or the details of the auction."

"When is it going down?" Akira Tokaido asked.

Running a nervous hand along her leg, Delahunt glanced at her computer screen. "If this is correct," she said slowly, "then the bidding has already commenced."

Kurtzman barked a curse. "Okay, cancel all other projects. Everybody grab a random t-burst from the queue and get cracking. Maybe we'll hit gold. I'll contact Hal and see about shutting down the Internet."

The declaration was so easily said, it sent chills down the spines of the hackers. There were four deliberately arranged nexus junctions that everything passed through. The information was unknown to the general public for just this reason. In a true emergency, the Internet could be physically crashed and would stay down until it was safe to reactivate again. But the cost would be terrible, billions of dollars lost, companies going bankrupt, stock market dipping into a possible crash. Only the President had the authority to pull the plug on the world, but it was now time to alert the Man to have his finger on the button. Almost any amount of financial turmoil would be worth saving an entire city, possibly millions of lives.

Their faces grim, the hackers swiveled to the consoles and hunched over in silent fury. The monitors filled with lines of code, the submonitors flashing with codebreakers and counter-encryption algorithms.

"We're too late," Tokaido announced, angrily removing his headphones and turning off the stereo. The man ran stiff fingers through his wild crop of hair, they massaged his temples. "The auction is over."

"When?" Delahunt demanded from behind her VR helmet.

"Just now," he replied. "The buyer for Liberty Peru used the same codes for all of his e-mail and only minutes ago informed the group that they lost the bid on both of the Zodiacs."

The sentence sent a bolt of stunned silence across the room.

"'Both'?" Wethers repeated, as if never hearing the word before. "But the Scion stole four, and one was used on the *Tullamarine*. That leaves three."

"Yes." Tokaido sighed, lowering his head. "I know."

Crossing herself, Delahunt muttered a brief prayer, while in a display of self-restraint, Kurtzman lowered the receiver and hung up the phone without crushing it in his hand. His cyber team was supposed to be the best in existence and they had been outfoxed by the S2 agents like green recruits.

"Did you get a physical location?" he said, closing a hand into a fist, making the knuckles crack.

Tokaido shrugged. "Sure. The t-burst was sent all over the world and off six satellites, but I believe that the point of origin was somewhere in east Texas. Can't nail it down any tighter than that."

"Must have been a hit-and-git operation," Delahunt added thoughtfully. "The bidders previously informed of a precise time to go online and the whole thing lasted less than five minutes."

"A cyber-space commando raid," Wethers said

with a pronounced scowl. "An ingenious tactic, and damn hard to stop."

"Exactly."

"However, Striker is in Texas," Kurtzman muttered, a flicker of hope on his face. "I was tracing some lowjacks for him. He's out of touch right now, gone undercover. But it sounds like he may be right on top of things."

But the earlier statement still resonated inside the mind of the chief hacker. Both. The word had a bitter metallic taste. The Scion had placed two of the nuclear bombs in auction. So where was that third Zodiac?

Beachwood Hill Estates, Texas

COVERING SEVERAL ACRES, Ernest Dillard's estate stretched leisurely along the shoreline, a stone wall running down the manicured lawn across the white sandy beach and into the water. The eight-foot-tall barrier effectively sealed off the property from every approach except the sky and served to keep out the local riffraff. Neighbors would have complained, only both of the properties on either side of the estate had mysteriously burned down one night and no construction firm would now accept the job of building there, the workmen preferring to keep their legs intact.

At the private dock a hovercraft and several hydrofoil speedboats were moored next to a two-hundred-foot yacht that dominated the shore of Beachwood Hill.

A fence of iron lace separated the shore from the lawn, huge mosaic patios meandering through grooves of swaying trees to eventually lead to the sprawling mansion richly decorated with terraces, cool marble alcoves and red-tile roofs. But armed men stood guard on the roof, while others walked the lush grounds constantly in contact with their command center in the bomb-proof cellar.

Ernest Dillard savored his lifestyle, but steadfastly refused to be anybody's fool. Several times in the intervening years his home had been attacked. What remained of the survivors had screamed out their lives in the basement of the Spanish-style manor, their prolonged agony artistically recorded on videotape and sold on the underground snuff-film market. Dillard was famous for never missing a chance at making another buck. And the films served the double purpose of also making his enemies reconsider the wisdom of trying to whack the king of Galveston, or else they might become the "star" of his next movie extravaganza. There were no recurring roles.

Music and laughter came from the row of cabanas surrounding the free-form swimming pool, natural boulders placed in strategic positions to give protection from snipers out at sea, and to form a beautiful waterfall, behind which were hidden coves where guests could relax in private debauchery.

Several large men were swimming in the pool or relaxing in the chaise longues, and a dozen beautiful girls of various nationalities strolled around, or lay on towels sunning themselves to a golden tan.

The liquid tempo of Latin music flowed from speakers hidden in the boulders. There was a long buffet table attended by liveried staff dutifully serving the revelers from the assortment of gourmet food and endless array of liquor. A major holiday was coming soon and the Galveston crew was celebrating a few days early.

Lying facedown on a chaise longue, a red bull of a man was receiving a massage from a tall blonde in a black lace bikini. Dressed in loose satin trunks, Ernest Dillard was covered with a mat of coarse hair, the affectation giving him the secret nickname of Gorilla. But the police officer who had called him that was never seen in town again, his videotape given away free on the world sex market as a grisly object lesson. Many people tried to tell him that the time of "Mustache Pete" was long gone, you had to be smart nowadays, not merely ruthless. Gorilla Dillard didn't agree and was a living example of just how wrong that platitude was these days. He ruled Galveston with an iron fist, killing everybody he could not intimidate, blackmail or bribe.

Starting to work on the man's wide shoulders, the blonde pressed her large breasts against his furry arm.

"Lose the top, Sheila," Dillard commanded.

Reaching behind her back, the girl undid the laces and the tiny scrap of cloth fluttered to the ground. Leaning over the Mob boss again, Sheila traced her long nails gently along his spine and started moving her palms in tight circles on his lower back when one of the bodyguards walked over and discreetly coughed for attention.

"Yeah, Billy, what is it?" Dillard demanded, not even looking up.

"Tom at the front gate says we have a visitor," the man replied, touching his earpiece. "Big guy, black hair, rented car."

"That could be a hundred people I know," Dillard grunted. "He got a name?"

"Driver's license and gun permit have the name Matthew Cooper. Says he has some information you want."

"Like what?" That made the Mob boss abruptly raise his head, and Sheila backed away. The blonde made no effort to cover her nakedness and Bill clearly enjoyed the free show.

"Says it's for you only," the guard replied. "Should I send him packing?"

"No, I'm curious. Let him in," Dillard ordered, swinging his legs around to sit upright in the lounge. "But check for wires."

"Tom, the boss says it's okay," Bill said, touching a throat mike. "Harry, Tony, make sure he's clean, or it's your ass."

"It's their heads," Dillard corrected with a dark scowl. "Sheila, baby, get me a beer."

"Sure thing, honey," the blonde said demurely, then walked away with a seductive sway to her hips.

Dillard grinned at the sight. Damn, that girl was hot. Then his attention swiveled as the side gate swung open and a big man entered as if he owned the place. Dillard had seen the type before. This was a hitter, all muscle and oiled steel.

As the thick gate closed, Harry held up a palm to stop the newcomer while Tony swung a 9 mm Uzi machine gun to cover them both. Meanwhile, the bodyguards on the roof had slipped the Remington sniper rifles off their shoulders and worked the bolts, ready for trouble. But the stranger coolly used two fingers to pull back his sports jacket to reveal a belt holster with a nickel-plated Glock 21 pistol. The gun was taken, but the expert search continued until the guard was satisfied.

"Hiya, Ernie," the man said in a friendly manner, walking closer.

"That's Mr. Dillard, asshole," he said gruffly, sitting up in the chaise longue. "Smart mouth me again and you die."

Going to a nearby glass-topped table, Bolan tucked a cigarette into his mouth, picked up a book of matches to light the cigarette, then sucked in the dark smoke.

"Everybody dies," Bolan said with a smile, sliding a small booklet from inside the pack of cigarettes and tossing it onto the table.

About to drink his beer, Dillard placed the bottle aside to pick up the leather booklet. He scowled when he saw it was a bank book. Flipping through, he caught the amount in the account and tossed it back on the table.

"What is this, a bribe?" Dillard asked in disbelief, taking a swig of the imported brew directly from the bottle. "A hundred grand is chump change. I use fifties to wipe my ass."

Inhaling slowly, Bolan let the pungent smoke trickle out through his nose. "Can you still use those as legal tender?" he asked with a grin.

Choking on his beer, Dillard burst into laughter. "Shit no," he guffawed, then realized what he had said, and broke into more laughter. The rest of the men around the pool joined in, the girls following a few seconds later. Only the guards stayed grim, watching the stranger with hands tight on the grips of their weapons.

"Okay, it's not a bribe," Dillard said with a tight grin. "So what does this have to do with me?

"Check the name," Bolan said, blowing a smoke ring.

Taking the booklet, Dillard thumb through the stiff papers. His face registered shock. "Bullshit," he growled. "It's a fake."

"Suit yourself," Bolan said, grinding out the cigarette. "I just thought you'd like to know and maybe cut a deal."

"Deal? What kind of a deal?"

"That hundred grand," Bolan said, tapping the bank book, "is deposited in the name of James Harold Green. Jimmy G. is narking you out or skimming the take. Either way, you're being taken for a ride."

"Could be true, Jimmy's a snake," Dillard admitted. "But exactly how did you find out about this?"

Bolan shrugged. "I have my sources."

"My boys can beat it out of you."

"They can try."

Unaccustomed to such a response, Dillard frowned and sipped some more beer. "You got any other proof?"

"What more do you need?" Bolan said, flicking ash onto the manicured lawn. "Or do you pay

Jimmy enough for to him to save that kind of green?" The bank deposit had completely cleaned out Bolan's war chest, but would be worth it if the trick paid off. However, the old crime boss was suspicious of anything that seemed easy. Bolan could use that.

Finishing the beer, Dillard handed it away without even looking at Sheila as she took the bottle. "Okay, let's say Jimmy is skimming the till. Where do you come in?"

"Seems to me you're soon going to have an opening in your public-relations department," Bolan said, pausing to take one last drag and then flicking the live butt away. "Somebody not greedy or stupid enough to cross you."

"You want Jimmy's job?" Dillard said it as a question.

"Why not? I wouldn't steal anywhere near as much as he does," Bolan said, throwing a look at the basement door. "Besides, I'm not very photogenic."

Leaning forward in the longue, Dillard frowned at that, not sure if it was a joke. Since this had nothing to do with her, Sheila walked over to another chaise longue and laid down, crossing her long legs at the ankles. They were talking business. When the monster wanted her back, he'd let her know.

"I don't scare you," the crime boss finally said, as if the notion were brand-new.

"No," Bolan answered.

"I should."

"Same here."

Softly, the bouncy Latin dance tunes continued to play over the hidden speakers, but all other conversations had stopped. There was only the music and the splashing of the waterfall mixing with the waves cresting on the sandy beach.

"Well, you talk a good game, but I don't know you from shit," Dillard said finally. "And I don't like the idea of losing a good man."

"Mr. Dillard, you don't have a good man," Bolan stated, lighting a fresh cigarette. "You got a punk with balls for brains."

Catching the subtle change in the man's tone, Dillard glanced at the bank book. The Feds wouldn't toss that kind of change just to sneak a man into his organization. They didn't have the funds. He paid a fortune to the goddamn state politicians to make sure the cops didn't have access to those kinds of funds.

"Maybe so, but how do I know you're kosher?"

"Want me to clip somebody?" Bolan said, taking out the cigarette to inspect the tip before placing it back in his mouth. "Sure, how about Jimmy?"

"My own people can handle that," Dillard

growled. "So how about a simpler test. Right here, right now."

Standing, the crime boss walked closer to Bolan, his head barely reaching the other man's shoulder. The guy was hairy, short and wide, and Bolan could see why he had gotten the nickname Gorilla so early in his brutal career.

"See the blonde over there, without the top?" Dillard said, pointing at Sheila. Unconcerned with her partial nudity, the woman was rubbing suntan lotion into her stomach with long, smooth, motions, her painted fingernails glistening in the bright sunlight.

Bolan nodded in frank approval. He would have to be blind to miss the buxom beauty. "Sure. Nice stuff. That my reward?"

"Not even close. She's the target. Kill her and you're hired," Dillard said. "Billy, give him a piece."

Sheila went motionless as Billy reached under his coat and pulled out a Colt .45 pistol. He tossed it over and Bolan made the catch. Dropping the clip, he checked the load, hollowpoints, then slapped it back into the butt and racked the slide to chamber a round.

"Ernie?" the blonde said in a hoarse whisper. "Baby? Is this some sort of joke?"

"Head or the heart?" Bolan asked, checking the sights.

Although he was trying hard not to show it, Bolan was caught completely off guard by this, his brain racing for a way out. But if he balked, or refused, the snipers on the roof would burn him on the spot.

"In the head," Dillard said, lifting his beer and taking a sip. "Make it quick."

"No problem."

Stumbling to her bare feet, Sheila started to back away. "Please, Ernie..." she whispered, tears in her eyes. "Honey, I've been good to you!"

Striding forward, Bolan advanced upon the weeping woman and grabbed her by the hair to hold her still as he stuffed the gun barrel just behind an ear.

"Nothing personal," Bolan said blandly, thumbing back the hammer. "Just business."

"Stop!" Dillard barked, then smiled as the man eased down the hammer. "God, you are a cold bastard. Okay, you're legit. Let her go."

"Whatever you want, sir," Bolan said, releasing the girl.

Dillard heard the addition of the honorific and nodded in approval. Smart man. A stone killer.

Trembling all over, Sheila tumbled to the grass in tears; several of the other girls rushed over to wrap a towel around their friend and walk her to a cabana. Dillard snapped his fingers at one of them and a redhead left the group to rush to the buffet table and bring over a fresh beer, standing near the crime boss with a forced smile on her pale face.

Keeping his own face neutral, Bolan felt the tension drain away. That had been close. He had been stalling for precious seconds, and if pressed, he would have fired the gun near the woman and thrown her into the pool as a diversion, then grabbed Dillard as a shield and tried to shoot his way to the hovercraft at the dock.

"Anybody else here you unhappy with?" Bolan asked, looking directly at Billy. The guard blanched, then Bolan tossed the Colt on the ground near his shoes.

"Cooper, you're made of ice, a fucking ice-man," Dillard stated, slapping Bolan on the back in congratulations. "That's what I'm going to call you, Matthew Ice."

"Cooper will do fine," Bolan countered. "It holds down any unauthorized fraternizing with the staff."

The crime boss threw back his head to roar with laughter. "Goddamn it, Cooper, you are a pisser. Fraternizing with the staff, like this was a war movie, huh?" He chuckled, then reached out to loudly smack the redhead on her bikini-clad rear. "Did you hear that, Julie? This guy kills me."

"Oh, he's a killer, all right," the redhead replied, moistening her full lips, a hand resting on the string of her skimpy swimsuit. "I better be careful or he's going to just eat me up alive."

"Already had lunch," Bolan said, then politely added, "but I'll be hungry again later."

"Any time," she purred.

"Sit down, Cooper," Dillard said, gesturing at the buffet and pool. "Join the party and meet the rest of the boys. Julie, find the man a friend."

The slim redhead looked at Bolan with hungry eyes, and he got the feeling that it would be her showing the soldier a good time as soon as possible.

"Sounds good, sir, but Jimmy should be taken care of first," Bolan said, turning away from the woman. "Be happy to do it for you. I'm hot for a job now. Don't like to be called off in the middle. Makes me tense."

Smiling grandly, Ernest Dillard finally relaxed. So that was the catch. Cooper was a blood addict. He loved to kill, like other guys liked sex. Excellent. He could use a man like that.

"Sure, have fun," Dillard said, leaning back in the chaise lounge. "The little traitor is yours."

"Got an address?"

"He lives at the Golden Health Spa, it's a whorehouse over on Dulvet Street."

"Thanks."

"Have one of the girls over there if you want. On the house."

"Sounds good."

"Bet your ass it's good. Someday we'll be too old for the ladies, Cooper, and all a man will remember is every piece of tail he ever turned down."

"I'll be wearing pine by then." Bolan chuckled.

"Wearing pine, ha! Dammit, Cooper, you're a funny guy. I think we're going to get along just fine," Dillard said, scratching at his hairy chest. "And be sure to come on back when you're done. This party is just starting! Going to last for days."

For a brief slice of eternity, Bolan looked at the cabana that Sheila had taken refuge in then turned to smile coldly at Dillard.

"You will return," Julie asked hopefully. "Right?"

"Count on it," the Executioner promised, turning to leave.

CHAPTER ELEVEN

Atchafalaya Swamp, Louisiana

Throwing up a rainbow spray in its wake, the old Cajun airboat skimmed along the surface of the bayou, the thick rushes parting in front of it like wheat in the wind. Cypress and tupelo trees rose from the muddy banks of small isles, their branches heavy with Spanish moss and countless small birds.

Sitting high in the rear, Minas Pedrosa was at the helm, guiding the airboat by angling the gigantic fan that drove the craft. Cirello Zalhares and Jorgina Mizne occupied the two front seats, caseless rifles lying across their laps. Dog Mariano was back on dry land, guarding the truck and the rest of their equipment. He was also serving as a rear guard in case the customers today decided to play fast and loose. The buyers weren't famous for keeping their word; treachery was more than expected, it was nearly mandatory. But their price had been the highest and so the Scion had agreed to sup with the known devil of the German terrorist group, Volksfever.

Bolted to the deck of the airboat between Zalhares and Mizne was an old wooden box normally used to store fishing tackle or dead chickens to toss to the swamp denizens for the amusement of tourists. But now the simple crate held two battered briefcases and the harnessed power of an exploding sun.

Creepers hung heavy from the banyon trees, their raised roots exposed like a nest of snakes magically cast into wooden statues. Loons and owls called in the misty air, and thick snakes glided through the murky-green water, the insect life as dense as fog in some places. But to the Brazilians it felt like home, and they had come well equipped with various forms of bug repellants to handle the minor inconvenience of the mosquitoes.

Reaching some open water, majestic desolation spread in front of the airboat for a great distance. Cutting the engine, Pedrosa let the craft slow of its own inertia. In the crushing silence, they could hear the musical tinkling of a wind chime. Starting the engine again, Pedrosa headed in that direction, comparing the compass on his wrist with the sound of the chimes to slowly find a small island nearly lost in a maze of trees, creepers and wild vegetation. There was no dock, but a section of the shoreline was a mudflat and the airboat slowed again, heading in the new direction.

"Careful of the alligators," Zalhares said, smearing cream on his face with a bare hand, the other holding the freed glove.

Mizne gave a skeptical look. "I used to live on the Amazon River," she said, splashing her fingers in the water, "and I am supposed to be frightened of some slow American alligators?"

Suddenly there was a flash of motion under the water and Mizne jerked her hand away just in time to avoid the clashing teeth of an alligator. Splashing furiously over the missed food, the gator slammed the airboat with its tail, rocking the craft dangerously.

"Enough," Zalhares said, pulling on the glove and sliding the Uru off his shoulder. As if in understanding, the alligator quickly submerged from view.

Tracking the subtle surface waves, the man waited until bubbles appeared and then cut loose with a long, sustained burst from the weapon. The swamp water boiled from the fusillade of rounds, birds rising from the reeds to flap into the sky in fear. Then dark red blood spread outward from that spot as the riddled body of a sixteen-foot alligator slowly rose to the surface and rolled to expose its pale belly.

The gunfire seemed to echo for miles through the moist atmosphere, and Mizne returned her hand to the water, splashing in what she hoped was a pantomime of a wounded fish. But no more gators approached the smell of death in the water, and the airboat glided toward the little island without further incident.

"Woman, you endanger us with this foolishness," Zalhares said angrily. "You enjoy killing too much. Sometimes, it is wise to be quiet. Mice thrive where tigers die."

"In this noisy machine?" Mizne laughed, patting the airboat. "The Germans knew we were coming for miles away."

"And what of the Delta Police?"

She traced fingertips along the sleek frame of the Uru submachine gun as if it were a lover. "I look forward to meeting them." She chuckled softly. "Oh, yes."

"There it is," Pedrosa said, reducing their speed slightly. "Brace yourselves."

With hardly a jounce, the airboat moved directly up the slippery bank and onto the weedy lawn of a ramshackle Choctaw cabin of indefinite age. Cutting the fan, Pedrosa brought the craft to a halt and they pulled weapons while looking over the area. The cabin was in ruins, the ripped screen windows hung ajar, the roof was full of holes and the porch steps sagged as if the old wood were melting in the moist swamp air.

Then Mizne whistled sharply, and the men turned to see a group of hunters in a small patch of dry land located under the spreading branches of a tupelo tree, the Spanish moss cut away to form a sort of doorway in the natural covering.

A pile of broken bricks with a crackling fire inside served as a crude stove, a rusty iron grille supporting a galvanized coffeepot steaming gently. Sitting on cinder blocks were four men in worn hunter's clothing. Bolt-action rifles rested on their shoulders, the sewn pockets of their flannel shirts lined with shiny brass cartridges.

But the blond men weren't Cajun by any stretch of the imagination. Their Nordic skin was far too pale, their designer boots brand-new and their mirrored sunglasses and elaborate watches obviously expensive. The Atchafalaya Swamp was a wildlife preserve and river basin, and while a few poor souls tried to eke out a living here, none of them could afford the fine apparel on display among the four large men.

"You're right on time," a tall blonde said, standing. "We like punctuality. It is a sign of high intelligence."

"We like cash," Zalhares replied, lifting a briefcase and walking from the airboat. Then Mizne did the same with the other briefcase, but also slipped on a pair of handcuffs, locking the handle of the briefcase onto her wrist. Pedrosa remained in the airboat with one hand on the controls, the other resting on his lap near his open hunting vest.

"The planet Saturn was originally called George," the first German said, rubbing his smooth chin.

Zalhares nodded at the code phrase. "The official name of the moon is Luna, the sun is called Sol."

"International Astronomy Conference, London England."

"It was in 1965, and ratified again in 1985."

"That is correct."

Both sides relaxed slightly, assured that they were talking to the proper people. The exchange had almost been a formality in the situation. If either had been American agents, they would have started shooting on sight.

"Care for some coffee?" the second German asked, gesturing at the steaming pot. "It's still hot."

"There is no need for perfunctory pleasantries," Zalhares stated. "We have the Zodiac. Do you have the money?"

"We have your payment," the first German said, snapping his fingers. "Forty-two million in cut gems."

Now the fourth man stood to flip over the cinder block and lift out a small jeweler's bag of fine leather. A foot wide and some six inches thick, the pouch lay heavy in his open hand.

Stopping where he was, Zalhares frowned at that. "Our payment was to be five million in cash," he said sternly. "Plus thirty-five million in gems. Not all gems."

"Which is why we're paying forty-two million in gems," the second German retorted. "There simply was not enough time to convert enough of them into hard currency."

"The additional two million should be more than sufficient compensation for the inconvenience," the first Volksfever terrorist said, then softly added almost as an afterthought, "don't you agree?"

In the airboat, Pedrosa released the controls and placed both hands on his knees, bending forward slightly so that his vest gaped a little to expose the set of pistols holstered in his belt. Behind Zalhares, Mizne closed the briefcase and locked it tight with a loud snap.

"The gems will be fine," Zalhares decided. "Show me."

Approaching the Brazilians, the German knelt and unzipped the pouch to unroll it on the soggy ground. Folding back a section, the pouch spread wide, exposing dozens of small compartments made of a clear plastic, each completely filled with colored gems of different sizes and clarities.

"As requested, only blue-white diamonds, four to six carats," the German said, touching the gemstones in order. "Plus uncut emeralds and sapphires, but no rubies. Why not rubies?"

"The synthetic are too difficult to tell from the real gems," Mizne said empirically, as if amused by their lack of knowledge. "Actually, it is impossible to tell them apart, which is why artificial rubies have an identification code carved into them to prevent fraud."

"Really, I did not know that," the terrorist said without a trace of irony. "How interesting." He smiled at the explanation and started to fold the gems away again.

"Stop," Zalhares said, raising a gloved hand. "Minas, check the gems."

"You do not trust us?" asked the first German.

"No."

He grinned. "That is good. Trust is for fools."

Leaving the airboat, the S2 agent joined the man on the wet ground and pulled out a jeweler's loop, setting the magnifying device around his head and turning on the small light alongside the lens. Wiping his hands clean on his pants, Pedrosa started to lift out random gems to inspect them one at a time.

"And you are their expert in gems?" the German asked, watching the other man's appraisal progress.

"Yes."

"And your professional opinion is?"

Taking it slow, Pedrosa ran through several emeralds before replying. "Acceptable," he said. "Forty-two million is an accurate assessment of their value."

"Of course," the first German said. "Now show us the Zodiac."

Wordlessly, Mizne stepped forward and snapped open the briefcase to expose its complex maze of wiring and circuitry. The small German rose and moved closer to inspect the machinery before taking out a small device of some kind and running it back and forth over the bomb.

"It's real," he said at last, tucking away the scanner. "And not armed to detonate."

"Excellent," the first German said, then raised his elaborate watch and shouted, "Now!"

Four men rose from the scummy water around the island wearing alligator-colored scuba suits, their hands gripping 9 mm Steyr submachine guns, safely sealed inside plastic bags.

"Fools," Zalhares hissed, closing his fist tightly on the handle of the briefcase he was carrying. A distinct click sounded, followed by a rapidly building hum.

"Nobody move!" the first German shouted, raising a hand. "Detier, check that!"

Pulling out the earlier scanner, the small German hurried forward and worked the controls for a few seconds. "It's a Zodiac," he said, turning pale, "and it is primed to detonate."

"You brought two of them," the kneeling German snarled in controlled rage. "An unexpected move. Very clever."

"No," Zalhares replied haughtily, gazing down upon the man. "Elementary tactics."

"All right, Brazilian, turn that off!" the first German ordered in a loud voice. "Or else—"

"Or else what?" Zalhares demanded hotly, walking closer. "You'll kill me and vaporize yourselves? I think not."

His face contorting into a snarl, the leader of the terrorist group started to reply when Zalhares moved in with a boxer's grace and violently backhanded the man across the face. The other Germans swung their weapons around to the ready position as their commander fell sprawling into the mud with a crimson smear across his face.

Radiating fury, the German touched his split lip, looking at the large ornate ring on Zalhares's free hand, the jagged metal facets dripping with fresh blood.

"You'll pay for that, swine," he snarled, rising slowly.

"Wrong again," Zalhares commanded. "Now

choose your next move carefully, Nazi, because I am prepared to die. Are you?"

Nobody spoke for several minutes. The noise of the swamp mingled with the tinkling of the glass wind chimes hanging in the ruin of the old hunting cabin, as the German chewed over the situation from every possible angle.

"Am I prepared to die? Yes, I am," he said forcibly, then relented with, "But not at this precise moment. Hans, give them the jewels."

As Hans gave the jeweler's bag to Pedrosa, he returned to the airboat and tucked it safely into the wooden box between the seats, then resumed his post at the controls.

"Okay, *schiesskopf,* turn off that Zodiac and give it here," the Volksfever operative growled, extending a hand. "And we shall go our separate ways."

Waving away a swarm of annoying gnats, Zalhares simply couldn't believe the staggering arrogance of the man. And these were the Darwinian supermen who had thought to rule the world? Pitiful.

"Mine stays armed until we are long gone from here," he stated flatly. "Jorgina, give him your Zodiac."

Reaching into a pocket, she unlocked the handcuffs, then tossed the atomic bomb at the others. Two of the Germans franticly scrambled to catch the briefcase and stood panting for breath from the split second of activity.

"Satisfied?" the first German asked, looking at the Zodiac in Zalhares's hand, not directly at the man.

"Almost," Zalhares replied. "There is just one small detail to settle."

"What now?" he growled unhappily, rubbing a fist across his still-bleeding lip.

Glancing over a shoulder, Zalhares nodded at Pedrosa and the man instantly started the airboat. As the huge engine roared to life, everybody glanced its way and Mizne unslung her Uru to start firing into the German jeweler. He jerked wildly from the barrage of 9 mm rounds, walking backward and waving wildly as if being attacked by a swarm of bees. As the submachine gun stopped, he toppled over an exposed root and fell into the swamp to slowly begin to sink. The scuba drivers started toward the man, then stopped when it was clear there was nothing that could be done to assist the riddled corpse.

"There is always a price to pay for failure," Zalhares said, starting to walk away. "We left your scientist alive to operate the Zodiac, but the jeweler had served his purpose."

"He was a cousin," the first German said through clenched teeth. "A blood relative."

Contemptuously, Zalhares shrugged. "Now he is nothing."

"Move along, Adolph," Mizne prompted, gesturing with the Uru. "You have five minutes to leave before we come hunting for you."

As the Germans moved into the hanging curtain of thick green moss, the Brazilians walked backward toward the airboat, watching for more trickery. Revving the engine, Pedrosa kept a gun in hand as the others strapped themselves into the chairs. The moment they were secure, the airboat slid backward off the island in a rush of wind and moved out into the swamp once more. When they were a good distance from the moss-shrouded islands, Minas reversed the engine and began to skim along their original route at full speed toward the distance culvert near Interstate 10 where Mariano would be waiting patiently for them in the truck.

"Fools," Zalhares said, dipping his ring into the scummy water then wiping it off on a handkerchief. "Dangerous fools."

Her eyes still shining with pleasure, Mizne said nothing as she reached over and helped the man deactivate the Zodiac and safely return it to the wooden box.

"How much do we have left?" Pedrosa shouted above the throbbing engine.

"A couple of thousand American dollars, and a million Mexican pesos," Zalhares replied, massaging the hand that had been clenching the bomb's handle-trigger. "And we don't dare convert those without fear of exposing ourselves to the FBI. We shall have to find some other source of ready cash to reach our next delivery."

"Bah, we are millionaires and paupers at the same time," Pedrosa said bitterly. "Only in America, eh?"

"The lack of money is a minor problem," Mizne said, dipping her fingers into the swamp once more. "Once we reach the next state, I will scan the police bands and find us a likely target."

"I did not wish to take such actions," Zalhares stated. "It will put us at some risk of exposure."

"And what is life without risk?" The woman laughed. "Come, my friend, the risk is minimal. We have done such things before."

"But only when necessary. Personally, I shall be glad to leave this place," Zalhares said, surveying the endless misty banyon groves as they flashed by. "The stink of those German fools has made even the richness of the swamp untenable."

The airboat roared along the stagnant waterway, soon disappearing into the gray waves, reeds and the cold evening light.

red bulb on the front porch was a young woman swinging in a cane rocker and sucking on a lollipop. Dressed in a skintight Spandex top and high-cut denim shorts, her appearance left no doubt as to the nature of the intimate services offered here.

"Hi, handsome," she drawled in a strong Southern accent much too thick to possibly be real. Then she offered the lollipop. "Want a lick?"

"Perhaps later," Bolan replied, and went on through the door.

Inside, Bolan found himself in a short hallway that emptied into a front room cheaply done in wood paneling and decorated with framed centerfolds from men's magazines. The air was a terrible mixture of overly sweet perfume and industrial pine disinfectant. Near a hallway closed off with a beaded curtain was a small metal desk with a mature woman sitting behind it filing her long blue nails. Her platinum hair was piled high and stiff with spray, her white cotton dress cut low to show a lot of cleavage, but loose enough to hide her plus-size belly. Yet in spite of her ample weight, the woman still had rather shapely legs stretched out under the desk, plump toes wiggling in ankle-strap wedgies from another era. From the hard expression on her face, like a front-line general determined to make sure the troops did their job with a minimum of goofing off, Bolan deduced that she was the madam who ran the sex factory.

The carpet was bloodred and the ceiling was painted black, with a long velour couch across the room, four anxious men of various ages sitting there and trying very hard not to look at one another, even though they were all here for the same reason.

Additional centerfolds adorned the walls above the couch, and even more sex mags were stacked loosely on the end tables and coffee table for easing viewing. Not merely there to set the mood, the magazines were displayed to get the customers so excited that the whores could get them off as quickly as possible and thus service more men per night and maximum the generated revenue.

"Hi, gorgeous," the madam said with a hard smile. "Are you a member of the Golden Spa? Boy, you sure should be, I mean, a real looker like you, yes, sir."

"I'm here to see Green," Bolan said, cutting off the sales pitch. "Now."

The madam's smile froze in place. "Who was that again?"

"James Green," he said, towering over the woman. "And stop wasting my time. I work for Gorilla."

All pretense of sexuality vanished, and she reached under the desk for a moment. A few seconds later a hidden door set in the wood paneling that perfectly matched the grooving, swung open and out stepped a large man in a black T-shirt and loose Chino pants tucked into Army boots. Bolan didn't need to ask if this was the bouncer, he looked the part. His hair was cut short so an opponent couldn't grab it in a fight, and there was the leather strap of a blackjack sticking out of his hip pocket to quietly subdue the more violent customers who refused to leave or were unhappy with the services rendered.

However, there was also a slight roll of fat around his stomach from too many quiet nights on the job and sipping beer to pass the time.

"Yes, Miss Miranda?" he asked in a voice hoarse from whiskey.

She jerked a thumb. "Wants to see Mr. Green."

The bouncer looked Bolan up and down, then shrugged and turned around, going back into the disguised door. Nervously, the customers on the couch watched as Bolan followed him through the opening and closed the door.

A long stairwell stretched sharply ahead, the only other door in sight being on the third floor. Reaching the top, the bouncer swung open the thin plywood door and moved into a short hallway lushly carpeted and lined with closed doors. There was no noise coming from behind any of them, so

Bolan guessed these were private rooms for the special parties of executive guests.

"Office at the end," the bouncer said, stepping aside so that Bolan could squeeze past.

"Go wait downstairs," Bolan ordered, already walking down the hallway.

The bouncer grunted in reply and started down the stairs, the bare wood creaking at his heavy tread.

Checking the cigarette pack in his pocket, Bolan walked directly to the other door, turned the latch and walked inside. This room was radically different from the ground floor of the brothel. Clean plaster walls were painted a light pastel color that made the place seem much larger than it really was. A heavy brass bed was tucked into one corner of the room, the linens neatly made, and an air conditioner set into the wall hummed softly.

A big mahogany desk stood near French-style windows and sitting in a velvet wing-backed chair was a skinny man with wavy blond hair. He was watching cartoons on a widescreen television. His woven leather sandals were lying on the carpet, his bare feet resting on an ottoman. Everything in the room was expensive, and clashed. It was a den of wealth and absolutely no taste.

"Jimmy G," Bolan said, closing the door.

"Yeah?" the man asked without looking from

the antics on the screen, lowering the volume with a remote. "Is the pizza here already?"

"Been canceled," Bolan said, pulling his Beretta and firing.

The screen of the television exploded into a million pieces, throwing glass everywhere. Jumping out of his chair, Jimmy shouted curses as he moved from the sparking box.

"Son of a bitch!" he cried, shaking glass from his glistening clothing. "Who the fuck are you?"

When there was no reply, he turned and went pale as his gaze locked with Bolan's. All of the rebellion flowed out of the man as if a valve had been opened.

"Hey, there, I…" He started again, "That is—"

"Stuff it, Jimmy. My employers aren't happy with you," Bolan said softly, making the man strain to hear the words. It was an old trick that forced the person being interrogated to concentrate on hearing what was being said, which made it much harder for them to come up with lies.

"Your employers?" Jimmy asked, licking dry lips and glancing at the desk.

Bolan made a guess there was a gun hidden there. He walked over and started to pull open drawers until he found it, a .38 Browning Hi-Power.

"The package you delivered on the dock," he said, removing the clip and thumbing out the rounds onto the floor. "My employer is very unhappy with the quality."

"Hey, bullshit, man," Jimmy shot back, trying to rally some courage. "Those were all top quality. And legit, too. The real McCoy."

In icy silence Bolan racked the slide to eject the bullet in the chamber then tossed the useless Browning onto the bed. Jimmy darted his eyes for a second, then looked back to find Bolan pointing a Beretta in his direction, the muzzle threaded with a sound suppressor. Immediately, the Mob gopher reevaluated his estimation of the visitor and became much more submissive.

"Okay, okay, okay." Jimmy exhaled, waving both hands in defeat. "Only some of them were fakes. But there hadn't been enough time to get all fifty. I mean really, some of those weird states like South Dakota, and Iowa, who the fuck wants to go there anyway for Christ's sake?"

Bolan instantly understood what he was talking about. License plates. The shoebox-size package had actually been a bundle of license plates for a vehicle. That way, the Scion could travel across the country and not be stopped by highway patrol for having out-of-state plates. Smart.

"A few of them, Jimmy?" Bolan insisted, advancing a step.

"All right, most of them!" he cried, averting his eyes. He tried again with, "But, hey, they were top quality. You got to admit that much. Absolutely top quality. "

Reaching into a pocket, Bolan pulled out a pack of cigarettes, scowled when he realized the pack was empty and angrily crumpled it into a ball and tossed it into a wastebasket.

"Which ones, Jimmy?" he said in a no-nonsense tone.

His smile coming and going, Jimmy glanced at the smoking television set. "Hey, I really don't remember," he said, then added in a rush, "but I got it in my book!"

"One minute," the Executioner said.

Nodding his thanks, Jimmy raced to the table near the window and pulled out an expensive notebook. Licking a finger, he flipped through the pages until finding what he wanted.

"Here ya go. South Dakota, Iowa, Vermont, New Hampshire, Rhode Island, Delaware and Maine." He closed the notebook, keeping a finger inside to hold the place. "See? Nobody states. Total crap. Who needs 'em, eh? It's not like I missed New York, or California, or something important."

Scowling impatiently, Bolan had him read off the names of the states again as he filed them away in memory. Then it hit him, fifty plates. Why would the Scion need fifty if the truck came with Texas plates already?

"What about the foreign plate?" Bolan demanded.

"Hey, that Mexican plate was legit!" Jimmy snapped in righteous indignation. "I mean, shit, it's right over the border. No biggie to get a plate there."

And there it was, their escape route. Mexico. That was how the Scion planned to leave the country and drive back to South America. Or maybe stop at Panama and hop another freighter. Zalhares was going to circle, land in Texas, drive around delivering the Zodiacs and then back through Mexico and freedom.

"We want replacements, Jimmy," Bolan said, seizing the opportunity. "Real plates this time, or it's your ass."

"Sure, sure, sure," the man said with a stiff smile, gesturing with the notebook. "No problem! I can have them for you by…" Furrowing his brow, Jimmy inhaled sharply through his teeth. "Tomorrow, noon. At the very latest, one o'clock."

Bolan said nothing.

"All right, by noon, guaranteed!"

"Not enough," Bolan whispered, leveling the Beretta.

"And half the money back for fucking it up. Okay?" Jimmy pleaded desperately. "That's only fair, right? Hey, we gotta be fair. So where do you want them delivered, mister…uh…"

"Cooper."

"Right. Okay, Mr. Cooper, where do you want the plates delivered?"

Bolan gave the man a hard stare.

"Gotcha," Jimmy recanted, running a hand through his hair. "Call the boss and ask. No problem. I'm on the case. But you know, Mr. Cooper, sir, that refund is going to come right out of my cut, leaving me with shit. Old man Dillard takes all the rest. A man has got to make a living, hey, I got kids to feed."

Bolan gave a snort as he eased down the hammer and holstered the piece. "Tell me another one, Jimmy," he said. "If Gorilla knew anything about this deal, you'd be a movie star."

The man lost his smile at the very hint of the basement snuff films. "Yeah, well, you know how it goes," Jimmy admitted, generating a weak smile. "A dollar here and there, steal a little not a lot, private enterprise, the lord helps those who help themselves, and all that shit."

"Hallelujah," Bolan said, turning to leave. "By noon, Jimmy. Or Gorilla will be the least of your worries."

Closing the door behind him, Bolan paused in the hallway and slipped on an earpiece, then turned up the volume on the radio in his pocket. For a moment Bolan could only hear the crackle of the plastic expanding back into shape, then the special filter created by "Gadgets" Schwarz for the microtransmitter inside the cigarette pack kicked in and the loud thunder dimmed to the level of a crackling fireplace in the background.

There was a rhythmic tapping sound and Bolan recognized that the phone was being tapped. He only caught the last few numbers before there was a pause.

"Hi, it's me. Some guy was just in my fucking office," Jimmy said angrily. "Called himself Cooper. Isn't that the name of the new buttonman for Dillard?"

That caught Bolan by surprise. How had he learned about that so quickly? Gorilla had to have a leak in the organization, probably Sheila or one of the other girls working there. Bolan couldn't really blame them. Loyalty had to be earned, not forced with a closed fist.

There was another pause. "Yeah, makes no sense to me, either. If Dillard wanted me iced, then why was this guy pretending to be from Zalhares…oh shit, he's a cop! Christ on a crutch, that must be it, Sheila. He's a fucking cop! Gotta go."

There was a plastic clatter and then the phone was dialed again, a much longer number this time.

"Hello, Mr. Dillard? This is me. Now, don't hang up! I want to cut a deal for my life," Jimmy said, rushing out the words. "There's cop here that…hello? Hello? You son of a bitch!"

The receiver was slammed down and Jimmy punched in new numbers. "Hang up on me will ya, you hairy-assed bastard," Jimmy growled, then changed to a polite conversational tone. "Hello, I would like to leave a message for Mr. Zodiac, please."

Moving fast, Bolan slammed open the door to the office, firing from the hip. That was one phone call he couldn't let the man complete. A single mention that somebody was asking about them could send the Scion into hiding for months, and the Zodiacs would be sold and long gone before the Brazilians were found again, if ever.

Pumping blood from his chest and throat, Jimmy slammed backward into the wall, cracking the plaster for a yard in every direction. Gushing crimson, he went limp and slid lifelessly to the floor, leaving a grisly trail of vital fluids smeared along the crumbling plaster.

Picking up the phone from the carpet, Bolan wiped off the excess blood and placed it to his ear without the radio receiver.

"Hello? Hello?" a gruff voice said. "Is anybody there?"

Bolan started to hang up, then realized the old-fashioned telephone didn't have a redial button. There was no way for him to learn where the call was coming from without some cooperation from the other caller.

"Have Mr. Zodiac call me at this number immediately," Bolan said, trying to imitate Jimmy's reedy voice. Then he read off the number on the phone and hung up.

Taking a chair, Bolan waited. Now it was only a matter of time. An answering service was a smart move, they were hard to beat without raiding the office for the referring phone numbers written in a log. But there was always a way around that. Sometimes it worked, sometimes not, but it was Bolan's best chance at a fast fix on the bombs.

The phone rang.

Bolan forced himself to wait for the third ring before picking it up. Not too eager, play it casual.

"Zodiac here," a gruff voice replied.

The voice of the enemy. "Why hello, Mr. Zodiac!" Bolan answered in a chirpy tone. "This is National Cellular Phone Tele-Corporation and we want to make you an exciting offer on additional long distance and roaming charges!"

The voice on the other end cursed in reply and the call was terminated. Cradling the receiver, Bolan waited with baited breath until the telephone rang again. He couldn't do anything until Zodiac called back. If the S2 agent was calling on a cell phone, this wouldn't work, but there was always the chance that he would be using a landline to avoid speaking over the air and getting caught by a NSA Echelon satellite monitoring all cell phone calls.

When the phone rang a third time, he lifted it immediately. "National Phone," he said in a bored tone, stifling a yawn to help disguise his voice. "Our business is the world. How may I help you?"

Without any comment, the other person disconnected.

Good. Bolan exhaled in relief. Now that Zalhares had checked and was hopefully convinced the first call has been just a random sales call, he was free to tap in the *69 code, hoping that Jimmy had the service. Luckily he did and the robotic operator dutifully read Bolan back the incoming number. Tapping the phone with a finger, Bolan got a dial tone and contacted the operator to get the location for the area code. Mr. Zodiac had just called from Louisiana.

Taking out his own cellular phone, Bolan tapped in the code for the Farm and got connected to Kurtzman in the Computer Room.

"I need the street location on a phone number," Bolan said briskly. "And fast."

"Faster than you think," Kurtzman replied, then told him about the online auction.

"And it come from east Texas," Bolan said slowly, digesting the information. He was tired and hungry. It had been too long since his last food, and sleep was a distant memory. Soon enough he'd have to catch some shut-eye, whether he wanted to or not.

"That's the best we could zero it in. Oh, thanks to Akira. Okay, here it is, Striker. That phone number was for room 19, Delta View Hotel, 1498 Main Street, Baton Rouge, Louisiana."

"Baton Rouge, eh? Thanks, Bear."

"Anything else?"

Wearily, Bolan glanced at the shattered television, the sight oddly disturbing. "Yeah, better have Barbara get Able Team and Phoenix Force ready, I may need some backup on this if the nukes go in different directions."

"No problem. Call us if you need anything else, anything at all. Good luck."

Hanging up the receiver, Bolan chewed over the matter for a moment. A hotel in Baton Rouge. Why there? It was the state capital, but otherwise of no great importance. Louisiana wasn't the home to any terrorist organizations that he knew of, aside from the KKK, and they were so riddled with FBI undercover agents they couldn't buy a hot dog without Washington knowing about it five minutes later, much less a working nuke. But if there was nobody in Baton Rouge, then it had to be a meeting place. So the question became one of were there any good targets in Louisiana?

With that thought Bolan went cold inside as he

comprehended that the holiday celebration Dillard had been talking about was Fat Tuesday, the day before the start of the Catholic holiday of Lent. And in the great Southern state of Louisiana that meant only one thing—Mardi Gras. The biggest party in North America and the absolute perfect place to detonate a small-yield nuke to get the greatest number of civilian casualties covered by the world press. If the Zodiac was going to Mardi Gras, then Bolan would just have to be there first.

Ripping the telephone from the wall, Bolan placed it on the wing-backed chair and covered it with a pillow before pumping in two rounds to destroy it completely. There would be no tracing the return call now.

Leaving the office, he closed the broken door as best he could, forcing the key between the door and the jamb to help hold it in place. It wouldn't pass muster at close inspection, but it might work on a casual inspection from somebody merely glancing down the hallway.

Proceeding down the stairs, Bolan walked along the edges where the old wood would be at its strongest and creak the least amount. Reaching the ground floor, he pushed open the door and almost hit the bouncer who had been trying to listen by pressing his head to the wood. The big man smiled in embarrassment at being caught. Bolan shut him down with a steely glance and the bouncer backed away with both hands raised.

The madam behind the little desk seemed tense, her legs tucked out of sight. She avoided looking at Bolan as he left the room. All of the customers on the couch were gone, and the atmosphere of the brothel had changed. Something was wrong and Bolan could feel it. In the short hall, he checked his guns, then proceeded through the front door with extreme care.

The moment he stepped outside, the Executioner knew he was in a trap. The prostitute stationed by the front door was gone and the crickets were silent. When he arrived, the wild grass around the parking lot had been full of noise. The rows of cars were now deadly quiet.

Lashing out with a closed fist, Bolan smashed the red lightbulb alongside the door, then dived to the ground, rolling for the bushes. A heartbeat later the front porch rattled as a hail of bullets slammed into wood, the darkness around the parked cars dotted with the fiery flashes of silenced weapons.

Rolling into a crouch, Bolan pulled both of his guns and waited for the fireflies to come again. Out in the darkness, somebody was using two guns, his body faintly illuminated by the discharges. As the pistols spoke, the soldier aimed between the two flames and fired the Beretta.

The gunman gave a startled cry and slumped to the ground, losing more than merely his weapons.

"He's in the bushes!" another voice shouted before a barrage of incoming lead tore the laurel bushes apart, leaves flying into the nighttime sky.

But Bolan was already on the move, darting behind a convertible to find a large man cradling a sawed-off shotgun. He grunted at his enemy's appearance and tried to swing the alleysweeper in that direction. But the Beretta 93-R coughed just once, the 9 mm Parabellum hollowpoint round catching the man under the chin. His head snapped backward, and Bolan caught the shotgun as it fell from the man's limp fingers.

The shotgun boomed, the spray of lead pellets spraying across a dozen expensive cars, the alarm systems wailing and whooping in the night. Now the gunmen could no longer talk to one another, and that was fine by Bolan. While they were trying not to shoot one another, anybody the soldier found carrying heat was a viable target.

A big-bore handgun thundered. The soldier tracked on the revolver and answered with a Magnum round from the Desert Eagle. The lance of flame lit up the night for a second and a barrel-chested man crumpled, hitting the hood of a car and crashing into its windshield. Somebody stupidly stood while pulling out a grenade and the

Beretta sang her song of death, the gunman rolling onto the hood of a car and out of sight.

Firing the Beretta to blow out windows in distant cars, Bolan moved to the fallen man and recovered the grenade, along with two more and something else wrapped in cloth. Chancing a quick look, Bolan frowned at the sight of a lock of long blond hair, the roots still sticky with fresh blood. The light was weak, but still good enough for the soldier to see that the hair was the same color of that Sheila woman from the poolside party. It was even the same style hair clip. She had to have been caught on the telephone with Jimmy, and Dillard beat the truth out of her. No time now to think of noncombatants paying for their sins.

Screams were coming from the brothel, customers crawling out of windows and running half-dressed into the streets. One of them went flying as a machine gun chattered for a long burst, then another handgun blasted into the night, followed by the crackle of small revolvers. Wisely, Bolan stayed low, letting the fools attack each other.

When the shooting paused for them to check the damage, the Executioner stood and emptied the Desert Eagle's clip, 180-grain bone shredders sending six more men to their just reward.

"Son of a bitch must have night goggles!" a man roared over the telltale clacks of an assault rifle being reloaded.

Creeping through the blackness, Bolan realized that he knew that voice. It was Santarino! Waiting for more gunfire, he ripped off a sideview mirror from a rust-eaten old Toyota and angled it about until finding the big man. Holding a pistol, Miguel Santarino had his right arm in a sling and the left side of his face was swaddled in bandages, probably from the fiery exhaust of the Stinger. He was also standing alongside Ernest Dillard. The Brazilian killer had come looking for Zalhares and found Gorilla instead. Not good.

"Then turn on some headlights!" Dillard ordered loudly, glancing around quickly. "Blind the bastard!"

The crime boss was holding an M-16 assault rifle, but Bolan hadn't yet heard the familiar sound of the U.S. Army weapon in operation. Saving it to protect your own ass, Gorilla? the soldier wondered.

As men started reaching into parked cars and fumbling at the dashboards, Bolan pulled the pin on a fat grenade and waited for a chance for a clean throw. But civilians were everywhere, some of them actually trying to start their cars and drive away through the middle of a firefight.

"Don't move!" a gunman shouted.

Clutching his clothing, a terrified man whirled, holding his jingling car keys. "Please, don't!" he begged.

But the gunman fired anyway, then went to kick the body. "Shit, it isn't him," he complained.

Zeroing in on the voice, Bolan peeled off the spoon and flipped the grenade high above the parked cars. The nighttime shattered when it detonated in the sky, the flash and crash of the stun grenade slamming anybody standing to the ground.

Cursing furiously, the gunmen struggled to their feet again as police sirens started to howl in the distance.

"Shit, boss, we have to leave," a man said urgently, slapping off the dust.

"Finish the job!" Santarino commanded, leaning against a crumpled station wagon for support. "This man you call Cooper dies right here, or we do!"

"Fuck that noise," Dillard growled, still on his feet and apparently unaffected by the explosive blast. "This ain't the Alamo, asshole. We'll catch him some other day. You haven't paid enough for a fight with Texas Rangers. It's over."

As the men lowered their weapons and started shuffling away from the whorehouse, Santarino fired a single round into the air to get their attention.

"Nobody leaves!" Santarino cried, swinging his weapon to point directly at the crime boss. "Now do as you are ordered!"

Already running low behind the lines of parked cars, Bolan was almost in the tall grass when he finally heard the M-203 mounted beneath Dillard's M-16 go into action. But instead of a hard thump of a propelled shell, it was the ear-splitting roar of an antipersonnel charge. Basically, just a regular shotgun cartridge as big as a soup can. If there was a cry of agony from the person hit, it was lost in the sound of crumpling metal and smashing glass.

Reaching the street, Bolan took careful aim and emptied the Beretta into the tires of the line of expensive cars parked at the curb. The 9 mm rounds made short work of the puncture-proof civilian tires, and soon every vehicle was flat on the pavement. Slamming open a door, an armed driver hurriedly exited a Bentley roadster to see what was going on and Bolan coolly added him to the kill list.

Satisfied that Dillard and his men wouldn't be going anywhere for a while, except for a long chat with the police, Bolan headed away from the killing ground.

CHAPTER THIRTEEN

Little Rick, Arkansas

Turning off Markham Street, the bank truck drove through the sparse nighttime traffic to rumble onto the Broadway Bridge that arched over the Arkansas River and connected the slowly dying metropolis of Little Rock with the much older yet oddly thriving city of North Little Rock. As the heavy vehicle trundled along the smooth pavement of the bridge, a pedestrian brought a fat plastic tube up to his shoulder, aimed and pressed a button on top. Smoke gushed from the aft end of the LAW rocket launcher and a fiery dart streaked from the front to slam directly into the right side of the armored engine compartment like the hammer of God.

In a crashing roar, the front of the truck violently exploded as the front wheels blew off and the bulletproof window shattered, cutting the guards to pieces even as the concussion crushed their bodies into mangled bags of bones and flesh.

The ten-ton truck reared up onto its back tires from the force of the detonation, paused like a rampant stallion, then came slamming back down onto the bridge, flames rising up from the burning chassis as the noise of the attack rolled along the calm riverfront and quiet streets.

Across the waterway in a well-lit park, thousands of people listening to an outdoor concert looked up in shock at the horrifying sight; many reached for cellular phones. The River Police tugs came alive and started cycling open the wire-mesh gate that closed off their paddocks.

Incredibly, again from the Broadway Bridge, the pedestrian leveled another plastic tube. This time there were four fast flashes of flame that reached out to strike the police enclosure. The sizzling HAFLA rockets pounded the dock and tugs, spraying napalm everywhere, and the running police screamed as their entire world became engulfed in roiling flames.

A nondescript sedan raced along the bridge from out of North Little Rock, savagely braking alongside the burning bank truck. The Scion poured out to join Dog Mariano, who was already on the sidewalk. Heavily armed, each of the S2 agents was dressed in black clothing and wearing ski masks. Mariano tossed the spent launcher over the bridge railing, then he and Jorgina Minze hurried to the rear doors of the smashed vehicle while Cirello Zalhares and Minas Pedrosa attacked the burning engine with fire extinguishers. In only a few seconds the blaze was sufficiently under control, then a loud bang sounded from the back of the armored truck as the thick doors were opened by a shaped charged of C-4 plastique.

Pulling on gloves, Mariano climbed through the tattered opening and shoved aside the dead guards to start ripping open bags of money and toss them over the railing. Most of the packs of cash fell to the water, and started to sink out of sight. But a few of the bundles came apart in the descent and the bills went flying to spread outward on the cool breeze and flutter to the nearby park and into the watching crowd of stunned music patrons.

Using heavy-duty shears, Mizne cut open the larger bags and began tossing the individual packs to Pedrosa, who was still carrying a fire extinguisher. Standing guard, Zalhares checked the round on the grenade launcher attached to the Uru and watched for police cars or helicopters. The green snowstorm of cash had started a fight in the park, so Zalhares put a few bursts into the crowds, killing a few to increase the chaos and make the Southerners run for their lives.

One of the packs of money tossed by Mizne exploded in midair in a purple spray and Pedrosa instantly fogged it with a long burst of icy-cold CO_2 from the extinguisher. The gas froze the dye so that it condensed into a liquid and fell impotently to the pavement, unable to permanently stain the people, cars or precious cash.

Knowing that there would only be one dye pack per bag, Mizne threw Pedrosa the rest of that particular sack and started on another. Heaving the bundles over one by one, Pedrosa waited for the expected burst as the dye pack got the regulation ten feet away from the truck. When nothing happened, he made the catch and threw the money into the open truck of the waiting sedan.

As Mariano emptied another bag of cash over the bridge, there was a purple puff and the misty dye rained into the water and the bobbing collection of floating money. Following the breeze, some of the mist actually reached the rocky shoreline and bathed the more foolhardy of the fighting mob scrambling to stuff their pockets full of the stolen cash.

"Greedy fools. Let the police try to trace the serial numbers now," Mariano said with a sneer, opening another bag. "They'll have to track down half the state."

"Ninety seconds," Zalhares said, checking his watch. "How much do we have?"

"One hundred thousand," Pedrosa said, fogging another purple mist to the roadway. The collection of soggy cash and indelible dye had started to form a wet purple mound on the pavement.

"Then keep going," the S2 agent commanded. "Eighty-five seconds…eighty-four."

Softly, the wail of a police car started to grow from downtown Little Rock, and Zalhares turned to fire the grenade launcher. It soared along the bridge to precisely strike a gasoline tanker truck stolen only an hour earlier and legally parked at the street corners near the base of the overpass. The 40 mm round punched straight through the insolated side of the tanker and the gasoline ignited in an earth-shattering blast that smashed every window facing that direction and flipped several nearby cars. A torrent of broken glass fell from the high-rise office buildings blanketing the street, and several people caught in the deluge were vivisected alive.

Moving to the opposite railing of the bridge, Zalhares reloaded the launcher and pumped out another round, this time at North Little Rock. But the shell went high and impacted on a riverboat restaurant, blowing a hole in the side of the moored vessel and filling the interior with shrapnel and flame. Frowning in annoyance at the miss, Zalhares fired higher this time and successfully blew up a fireplug. The tough steel casing shattered under the grenade blast and a plume of water shot forth to block any possible view from that direction.

As Mizne tossed another pack of money, it exploded into purple and Pedrosa froze that one even faster than the first. By now the trunk of the sedan was stacked full of packs of money, mostly in large denominations. Mariano was tossing the smaller bills, twenties and fifties, into the Arkansas River, the surface thick with a spreading oval of bills moving in the gentle current.

"Time!" Zalhares snapped, shoving a fresh 40 mm shell into the launcher of the Uru submachine gun and closing the chamber with a solid snap. "Let's go."

Dropping a partially opened bag of cash, Mariano climbed out of the armored truck and headed for the sedan. Already behind the wheel, Pedrosa was revving the engine as Zalhares and Mizne yanked the pins on thermite grenades and tossed them into the smoking truck, along with the rest of the money bags and the twitching bodies of the bank guards.

Hurrying into the sedan, the Scion slammed the doors and raced away, barely reaching the end of the bridge when the grenades cut loose. The strident double blast flipped the truck sideways and sent it rolling over the railing to plummet straight into the river, catching several swimmers still trying for the morass of dyed money. Perfect.

"Now it'll take them days to find out how

much, if any, money was taken," Zalhares said, tightening his leather gloves.

"Just good luck," Mariano said with a smile.

Removing her canvas gloves, Mizne snorted. "Luck belongs to the quickest gun."

Driving through the spray of the ruined fire hydrant, Pedrosa hit the brakes and allowed the gushing stream of water to splash over the sedan, washing off the fresh coat of black water-based paint and exposing the light blue paint job underneath. The members of Scion took off their ski masks. The vehicle slowed to the legal speed limit and drove along Broadway to make a hard right onto a side street, then several more quick turns until reaching an all-night car wash.

As the sedan exited, the teenaged attendant seemed to look at the Scion quizzically, so Mizne flashed him a smile and shot the boy in the face with her silenced pistol, then twice more in the belly to make sure he died.

Rolling onto the busy streets of North Little Rock, Pedrosa pulled to the curb to get out of the way as fire trucks and ambulances went hurtling past them, the parade of city vehicles dividing between the bridge and the wild ruckus at the ruined music concert. In a wailing congo line, police cars appeared from everywhere and one squad car slowed to look directly at the blue sedan. Faking surprise, Pedrosa blinked at the officer and had started to roll down the window when the cop changed his mind and pulled away.

"I guess we don't look like killers and thieves," Pedrosa said, easing down the hammer on the pistol.

"How much did we get?" Mariano asked, pulling his ponytail from within his collar. Ah, better.

"At a guess, half a million," Mizne replied, peeling off a fake mustache and stuffing it into an ashtray. "Mostly in hundreds and five-hundred-dollar bills."

"Nothing smaller?" Zalhares demanded angrily.

"Of course," Pedrosa said, removing his brown wig. "A couple of thousands in twenties and fifties."

"We are not fools to only take big bills," Mizne added, removing her shirt to start unwinding the layers of bandages around her ample chest. The trick worked well to make her seem more mannish, but the pain was tremendous.

"Good enough," Zalhares said, pulling off his black shirt to reveal a sports coat and tie underneath. "Now while the police are busy at the bridge and park, we will visit the gun store across town."

"Are you sure they deal in illegal weapons?" Mariano asked, checking the trick stiletto tucked up his sleeve.

"According to the CIA records, yes, even though most of what we need is conventional caliber ammunition, .22s, .45s, and such. How many rounds remaining for the Urus?"

"Four blocks each," Mizne replied. "After that, they're dead. There is no way we can get more of the ammo blocks in America."

"Then we should get some additional machine guns and save the submachine guns for emergencies," Pedrosa suggested, taking a corner and then coming to a full stop at a stop sign. An impatient driver in the car behind beeped his horn, but the S2 agent completely ignored the man in the flashy coupe and waited the legal five seconds before continuing onward.

Pulling ahead of the shiny wet sedan, the driver in the Italian sports car rudely flipped Pedrosa the finger and raced off in a surge of the powerful engine.

"Bang," the S2 agent whispered in reply.

"If there is a choice, I recommend AK-47 assault rifles," Mizne said. "The ammunition will be easy to obtain and the range is good."

"Uzi machine pistols are better," Mariano countered. "Much lighter."

"But they have no range," Pedrosa added, slowing near a construction site to splash through a puddle and muddy the clean car as much as possible.

"We'll take whatever they have," Zalhares ordered brusquely, straightening his shirt collar and lapels. "Dog, you get grenades. Minas, rocket launchers, RPG, whatever is in stock. Jorgina, concentrate on the weapons and spare ammo. I will stand guard again. Remember to touch nothing in the store itself! That has many alarms. Only the illegal weapons and ammo in the rear store-room can be taken. The owners have no wish for the police to find those, and we can take whatever we want and it will not be reported."

"To steal from a thief is not a crime," Pedrosa said in a singsong tone as if reciting a famous quote, "it is merely irony."

"So you have read Cervantes, old friend?"

"Of course. Before you set me free, I had many years in jail to expand my education."

"My apologies for the delay."

"Should we kill the shopkeeper?" Mariano asked impatiently.

"Of course," Zalhares said, nodding curtly. "Afterward."

"Good."

"And then we can proceed to our last delivery," Mizne said, bending low to slip into a snug sports bra. The blonde wasn't embarrassed to be naked around the men, but she would be easily visible to the passengers in the cars passing by and that would have attracted too much attention. This was the southern United States where everybody was a hypocrite and sex was only done behind locked doors. Nudity was a part of life, just like violence. What was the point of pretending it didn't exist?

Sitting upright, the woman slipped on a frilly blouse and adjusted the shoulder straps. "God, that's better," Mizne sighed in contentment. "I hope we never have to bind me flat again."

"After this last delivery," Zalhares said with a tolerant smile, "we'll never have to do anything again."

"Except to avoid America." She smirked, and then added, "For as long as it lasts, that is."

Stony Many Farm, Virginia

IN A WHIRLWIND of cushioning air, the Black Hawk helicopter gently landed on the grassy field, the four rotating titanium and fiberglass blades slowing to a few hundred rpms. The craft was still setting its landing gear into the lawn when the door to the log cabin swung open and five men walked out carrying bulky duffel bags.

"Sure you got everything?" Buck Greene asked, matching the stride of the taller men. As the head of security for the Farm, Greene really should have been in his office watching this on a video monitor. But he liked to get his hand into the fieldwork of the teams as much as possible.

"Sure as hell hope so," Carl Lyons replied, ducking slightly as the wash of the helicopter blades started buffeting them. Powerfully built, the former L.A. police detective wore his blond hair in a short military cut.

His icy-blue eyes professionally studied the sleek helicopter. It was a sweet ship and ready to haul his combat team anywhere. Recalled from a long-overdue dinner with an old friend, Lyons was wearing tan slacks and a sports coat that seemed loud enough to be picked up on radar.

"Anything else needed can be air-dropped in the field," Rosario "The Politician" Blancanales added, pushing back the sliding door on the side of the military machine.

"Or taken from the dead hands of the enemy," Hermann "Gadgets" Schwarz added, waiting to toss in his duffel to the growing pile inside the shaking Black Hawk. "That's my preferred method."

"Just give us a shout," Chief Greene stated, pushing in another duffel full of heavy ordnance. "Anywhere, anytime."

"Especially if you need an extra hand," John "Cowboy" Kissinger added. "Always be glad to help. I know Texas better than any of you damn Yankees."

"The Scion are most likely long gone from there by now," Lyons said, tossing his duffel bag through the side hatch. It landed with a solid clank of cushioned metal. "But thanks for the offer. Be glad to have either of you at my back any day."

Greene extended a calused hand, and the five shook hands, speaking in the silent language of battlefield warriors. They all knew that every mission could be the last, so there was never any time for halfway measures in friendship. They were brothers in blood, having waded through rivers of the stuff more than once in the service of their beloved country.

Nodding farewell, the group parted, Greene and Kissinger going back inside the farmhouse and Able Team climbing into the waiting Black Hawk.

As the men took their seats, it was obvious that the adjustable interior of the craft had been configured for a combat mission. Four of the wall-mounted jumpseats had been removed and two medical litters installed in their place, along with a twelve-drawer medical cabinet that oddly resembled a tool tower system used in most garages. There was also a defibrillator and an assortment of wall hooks for hanging bags of plasma and saline to treat the wounded. But that still left seven seats for the three-man team and plenty of space for their bags of equipment.

"Got everything in here but a jukebox," Schwarz said, pulling on the shoulder straps of the jumpseat and buckling them tight across his chest and waist. "I thought we were supposed to be low profile."

"We're listed as a National Guard MedEvac unit," Jack Grimaldi shouted from the pilot's seat. "So that should cover any questions nicely. We're guardsman on maneuvers! JADD, ya know!"

"Just another damn drill." Schwarz grinned at the translation. "I hear that, brother."

"It never hurts to have a few bandages handy when lead is flying," Lyons agreed, sliding the hatch closed and commencing lock-down procedures.

With one hand glued to the joystick, Grimaldi was already throwing switches and setting the multithrottles of the military helicopter. A wide and complex control board covered the entire front of the craft, and another curved along the ceiling, with an additional panel banked with rows of buttons and dials spread between the two front seats in the high-tech cockpit.

Reaching up, Blancanales tapped a sealed container on the wall. "I see we're equipped with enough plasma for twenty men."

"Just a safety precaution," Grimaldi replied, getting grim for a moment. "In case we need to do a Lavash procedure, or full transfusion, because of radiation poisoning. This Hawk is proof to a lot of rads, EM pulses, too. But you boys will be buck-naked in the field."

"Good thing I brought my lead underwear,"

Schwarz quipped, hitching his pants. "Well, what are you waiting for, fly boy? Let's rock and roll!"

"If you don't mind," Brognola said from the front passenger seat, one hand firmly holding on to his safety harness strap.

As the powerful motors revved in sync, the Black Hawk lifted almost perfectly straight up into the sky, then angled away from the farmhouse, moving fast.

"What's the itinerary?" Lyons asked, glancing out the window.

"First, we land at a private airfield in Maryland," Grimaldi said, one hand held casually on the dogleg joystick, looking backward from his seat. As usual, the pilot had his radio headphone on tilted, his left ear covered to receive radio reports and the right clear for conversation. It was how most helicopter pilots flew, doing two things at once. Three, when it came to armed combat.

"And then?" Blancanales prompted.

"And then we wait, old buddy," Grimaldi added, returning to the windshield. "We know where Mack is at the present, and we know where he thinks Scion is, but until we get the word, we sit and wait for the go code."

Suddenly a lush hill dropped away in front of the helicopter and they were flying above a highway jammed with traffic, the cars end-to-end and horns honking. Route 65, the heart line of Washington, D.C.. A thousand or so miles to the west, Route 66 was sung about as a freedom trail of adventure and sexuality. Here in the east, Route 65 was cursed by drivers.

"Any reports of suspicious activity overseas?" Lyons asked, settling back into the jumpseat and crossing his arms.

"Overseas? No," Brognola replied, craning his neck to see the men in the rear of the machine. But the position was too awkward, so he gave it up and simply addressed the windshield. "However, Homeland Security has already stopped two groups of Arab terrorists from trying to sneak into the country."

"Were they from Unity?" Blancanales asked, naming a recent enemy they hadn't encountered for a while.

"Unknown," Brognola said grimly. "But from their equipment it was clear that the men were here to obtain the Zodiacs and to smuggle them out undetected."

"Faraday nets?" Schwarz asked.

"Exactly."

"So they want to duplicate the Zodiacs," Lyons said slowly, fighting to control a rush of his famous temper. "Crack the cascade design and start flooding the black market with these damn things."

"That's my conclusion, too," Brognola agreed.

"Which makes it a cast-iron necessity that the Zodiacs are recovered—or are destroyed in the field."

Nobody spoke for a few minutes. This was more than the ancient battle cry of come back holding your shield or lay dead on it. Able Team had just been authorized to lose one American city to save a hundred more. The soldiers had dealt with these sorts of odds on a personal level before, but never on such a scale with civilian lives.

"This comes from the top?" Lyons asked for clarification.

"Authorized by the President," Brognola replied. "Nobody likes it, but what other course do we have?"

"Get them all back," Lyons stated, "and kill the Scion where they stand."

"Good plan," Blancanales said resolutely. "Gets my vote."

CHAPTER FOURTEEN

New Orleans, Louisiana

Crowds and noise filled every street as Bolan rode the purring BMW motorcycle through the growing celebration. Walking was completely out of the question, and driving a car even more so as the city was packed solid. If he could have skimmed over New Orleans in the Cessna, Bolan would have done so gladly, but the EM scanner he was using only had a range of four blocks. Which put it far outside the operational deck of any airplane and well within the fireball of an exploding Zodiac.

Arriving at a private airport just outside of New Orleans where questions were never asked about unexpected visitors, Bolan exited the plane and hurried to the brand new BMW K-1200 LT motorcycle Hal Brognola had arranged to have waiting for him. Bolan had decided to handle the Big Easy himself and had Barbara Price send Able Team to Baton Rouge.

The Beamer was a windswept, black beauty, wide and comfortable, with all of the amenities. But more importantly, while a Yamaha was faster, and a Harley had more brute power, the BMW possessed the special feature being driven by a piston instead of a linked chain. The machine whispered through the crowd, attracting a minimum of notice, while a conventional bike would have become the unwanted center of attention. Especially since motorized vehicles were frowned upon on many streets and outright banned on a lot of others. During Mardi Gras, the city belonged to foot traffic and the few mad souls willing to ride a bicycle through the jostling, pushing, shoving morass of inebriated people.

"Hey, gloomy!" a young girl called.

As Bolan turned at the hail, the busty redhead lifted her shirt high and wiggled, then lowered the garment and broke into a gale of laughter as numerous onlookers tossed her beaded necklaces as if she were the winner of a contest.

Allowing himself a brief smile, Bolan rolled on past the jubilation, cymbals clanging and bottles passed freely among strangers, with more college girls flashing their breasts. It was one hell of a party, that was for sure. However, it was his job to make sure it didn't become Hell on Earth.

Pausing at an intersection, Bolan watched as an amateur parade of homemade floats trundled by, the outrageous costumes and hot music of the dancers more than making up for any lack in the aesthetic quality of the construction. There was only so much that even the most talented artist could do with papier mâché and fresh flowers. But then a deliberate motion in the crowd caught his attention and Bolan turned to see a frowning New Orleans cop stride over with an expression of pure trouble. Before the uniformed officer even spoke, Bolan flipped open his FBI commission booklet and gave the man a good long look before tucking it away again.

"Trouble brewing?" the cop asked, putting away his ticket book. Then he hastily added, "Sir?"

"Purely a ballerina visit," Bolan lied, working the throttle of the bike.

The cop frowned, then broke into a grin. "Keeping us on our toes." He chuckled. "Gotcha. Nothing important happening for sure now, right?"

"Nothing that needs police assistance," Bolan stated truthfully as a group of topless women walked by arm-in-arm singing loudly. Video cameras followed their every move and the air was full of confetti and streamers thrown from the second-story balconies of hotels and homes.

"But it sure would be nice if I wasn't on duty," the soldier admitted. "A man could gain a lot of wisdom here."

"Carnal knowledge, at least. I hear that," the cop agreed, starting to leave. "Well, you drive careful now, sir. And best stay away from Bourbon Street."

"Why's that?" Bolan demanded curtly, rolling a few feet closer to stay with the walking man.

The cop stopped and pushed back his cap. In the throbbing ocean of costumes and flash photography, only Bolan and the police officer stood in conversation, a small island of self-control in the joyous throng.

"Well, sir," he drawled, "the DPW is doing some emergency road work there. Seems a drainage pipe broke, so now Bourbon Street has got more water in it than free beer. Swamp water, too, and that'll foul the electronic carb on that supercharged Schwinn you're riding faster than blackstrap molasses."

"Thanks for the tip," Bolan said with a nod. "I'll keep it in mind."

"Sure 'nough," the cop said, touching two fingers to his cap as a salute. "No drinking and driving now, y'hear?"

Still waiting for the parade to pass by, Bolan

watched the cop move effortlessly through the mob, then suddenly dart forward to grab a man by the arm making him drop the wallet he had just lifted from a drunken fat man. Pinning the pickpocket with an arm lock, the cop hustled him out of sight and the endless party continued, completely unaware of the many little dramas happening within its very midst.

With a flare of trumpets and clowns, the parade finally ended and Bolan rolled through the intersection to continue his methodical sweep of the boisterous city. Under ideal conditions, he would have liked to check New Orleans in two-block sections, but there wasn't any time for that. If the new owners of the Zodiac were already here, then the hammer could fall at any moment. He had to trust the team at the Farm, and check the city in four-block patterns. There wasn't time for anything tighter. If he missed by a block somewhere, or went right by the briefcase before it was taken out of its Faraday net, then the Big Easy would suffer a disaster that would make the deadly floods of the last century look like a balmy summer day.

The blocks rolled by in endless procession, the crowds all starting to resemble one another as the hours slowly crept past. Twilight was approaching, the city starting to unleash its glory of colored lights before Bolan was even halfway through his first reconnaissance. Stopping at a quiet garage,

Bolan topped off the tank of the bike as a group of college-age boys walked toward him carrying a boom box large enough to serve as a footlocker, the thudding bass of the rap song so loud that their necklaces rattled. Even Bolan felt it in his chest from across the street. As they turned a corner and the volume dropped, a subdued vibration came from the EM scanner in his shirt pocket. Bolan yanked it out to see the meters fluctuating into the green. A Zodiac had been activated within a three-block radius! The bomb wasn't just uncovered, but live and ready to blow!

Moving the scanner, Bolan got a definite reading and hopped on the bike to start driving that way as fast as possible. More than one person made angry complaints about the rude guy on the bike forcing his way through the crowd, but he ignored them, concentrating on the little beeping device held in the palm of his hand.

Starting down Bourbon Street, Bolan saw the meter indicate the other way, so he parked on a corner and started to walk. The Zodiac wasn't moving; he had almost gone past it. The bomb was here within less than a block. Leaning against a wall, some drunk Hells Angels staggered over and started to laugh at the fancy BMW, so Bolan tossed them the keys and headed directly into the corner hotel. This was it, ground zero.

The lobby was wildly decorated in every imaginable color, with a group of singers in the corner clustered around a grand piano, where a middle-aged man was belting out some classic jazz rifts. A big sign advertised a buffet in the main dining room, and every member of the staff seemed to be carrying their body weight in beaded necklaces.

However, the scanner was registering upward, so Bolan ignored the crowded elevators and took the stairs, stopping at each floor to confirm a negative reading until reaching the ninth level. The scanner indicated slightly to the left. The Zodiac was in a room facing Bourbon Street, overlooking the main path of the big parade tonight. Of course. That would be where all of the television cameras would be pointed.

Going down the hallway, Bolan got a strong reading from room 912, which weakened as he went past. This was the place. Mentally reviewing the procedures for shutting down a Zodiac, Bolan tucked away the scanner and quickly checked his weapons. The soldier knew full well that this was going to be a fight unlike any other he had been in.

If he shot the wrong man, the real triggerman would drop the briefcase and New Orleans would vanish. And the same thing might happen if he got the correct man and he died too quickly, or too slowly, for that matter. Timing was everything here. Bolan needed to shock the enemy senseless for a few vital seconds, to hold them still until he could locate the Zodiac and move for a capture. A stun grenade would only make them trigger it instantly, as would using sleep gas, a flash canister, BZ gas, or damn near anything else that came to mind. Bolan had only one chance at getting this right, and it was about as big a long shot as the Executioner had ever taken in his life.

"The Scion is here!" he shouted, going flat against the wall alongside the room. "Zalhares is here!"

Bolan waited, watching the door of 912. It burst open, revealing a blond man holding an ordinary briefcase, the knuckles on that hand clenched white.

"Dumpkopf bastards!" the blonde snarled, pulling out a 9 mm HK pistol. "Trying to steal it back, eh?"

Stepping into view, Bolan fired his Beretta through the wrist holding the gun, then dropped the Beretta and grabbed for the man's other hand, which was holding the Zodiac. The blonde with the German accent screamed in pain as his pistol fell away from limp fingers, dark blood pumping from the collection of severed arteries in his wrist. Bolan grabbed the handle of the Zodiac with both hands and the blonde realized what was happening. Snarling in fury he simply released the handle.

But Bolan was already there with both hands holding on for a million lives. Yanking the briefcase away from the stunned man, Bolan lashed a side kick directly in the German's throat and sent him tumbling backward into the room to smash into another man rising from a chair; they crashed to the floor in a tangle of limbs.

Pulling out the Desert Eagle, Bolan stepped into the room to look for any other briefcase, and the door was slammed shut behind him by a little man wearing glasses standing there holding a 38-caliber Walther PPK.

"Achtung!" the runt gritted. "So I see that the CIA has…"

Angling the silver barrel, Bolan triggered the Desert Eagle and blew off the man's face, eyeballs and teeth shotgunning into the wallpaper like an explosion at the morgue. Then Bolan was tackled from behind and slammed into a mirror, the glass shattering from the impact. He dropped the Desert Eagle as pain sliced his cheek from the crackling shards. But he still held on to the Zodiac. Nothing was going to make him let go of that.

Ramming out an elbow, Bolan crushed the big German's nose. As he staggered back, Bolan then kicked him in the groin, making the fellow double over in pain. Raising his knee fast to meet the man halfway, the Executioner was jarred to the bone by the force of the impact, but it flipped the

German backward and he hit the floor with all the animation of a rag doll.

Outside the room the crowds cheered and laughed, horns blared and bells rang in wild celebration.

"Die, swine!" the first German screamed, bringing up a duplicate of the briefcase.

A second Zodiac? If so, there was no logical reason for the man to gesture it like a weapon, so Bolan played the odds and dived sideways, going over the bed.

Squeezing the handle of the briefcase, the German cut loose with a stream of 9 mm rounds from the MP-5 submachine gun hidden inside. Wildly raking the room, the copper-jacketed slugs knocked the paintings off the wall and splintered the headboard, the pillows bursting into a whirlwind of feathers before he got the jerking recoil under control.

But by then Bolan was on his feet and already moving. Coming out with a decorative end table, Bolan lunged for the German, but the trick briefcase pounded the flimsy furniture out of his grasp and sent it crashing through the outside window. The sounds of the celebration filled the room as Bolan desperately swung the Zodiac and smacked it into the bleeding wrist of his attacker. The blonde went stiff with pain and the soldier charged, ramming a shoulder into the terrorist, driven by all 220 pounds of muscle. Losing the trick briefcase, the German crashed into a tall armoire and rebounded, reeling weakly. A river of blood poured down his face, and a wet clump of hair jutted from the sharp corner of the antique hardwood dresser.

As Bolan went for the Desert Eagle, the bathroom door slammed open and out strode a giant man wearing a sleeveless T-shirt, the tattoo of a Nazi swastika on his hairless chest.

"Filthy bastard!" he roared, and charged with both hands raised for a choke hold.

Sidestepping the rush, Bolan let the giant go by, then kicked him in the small of the back, adding new force to the original momentum. The Nazi hit the wall hard, grunting from the brutal impact. But he smoothly pivoted, fists now raised in a boxer's crouch, and threw an expert jab that was only a blur of motion. The soldier dodged out of the way, the scarred knuckles grazing Bolan's cut cheek as he moved with the strike to spin and raise an arm just in time to catch haymaker on his forearm. It was like being hit with an ax, but he took the pain and swung the Zodiac behind his back and out of reach. Ever shifting position, Bolan blocked two more jabs, then found an opening and buried two stiff fingers into the man's left eye, the orb bursting into colorless ooze.

Immobilized with the shock and pain, the Nazi

went stock-still, his convulsing mouth forming a wordless howl of agony as his entire body shook.

Ramming the side of his hand into the man's throat to crush the windpipe, Bolan next kneed him in the groin, then the nose, as he had the other German. Incredibly, the giant Nazi lunged forward and wrapped his massive arms around Bolan in a crushing hug. Pinned and unable to breathe, Bolan drove his forehead into his adversary's face, hitting the broken nose once more, but with diminished results. The big man had to be past his threshold of pain, raw adrenaline blocking the nerve impulses. The terrorist was horribly wounded, but for a brief slice of time, he was totally invulnerable to any additional pain.

Switching tactics, Bolan kicked out with both of his legs and went down, dragging the giant along with him to the littered carpet. Then he threw himself sideways, forcing his captive to roll over the broken slivers of mirror, one of them piercing the man's leg as he tightened his death grip.

The world was starting to take on a red fog for Bolan and his lungs were bursting for air from the combined exertions. His hand clutching the Zodiac was also weakening, his fingertips beginning to tingle from lack of circulation; he only knew for certain that the handle was still depressed by the irrefutable fact that he was still alive. But the nanosecond he let go, all of downtown New Orleans died.

Clawing on the floor with his free hand, Bolan found a sliver of jagged glass and sliced down the spine of his opponent, cutting the shoulder muscles. Incredibly, the German still refused to relinquish his crushing hold. But the hug lessened, and Bolan managed to gain a sip of air before summoning his last ounce of strength to savagely bury the makeshift dagger into the man's kidney. Merely grunting at the lethal wound, the German tightened his hold as Bolan made a fist and shoved the shard of mirror as deep as it could go.

Breath exploded from the Nazi as he started to shake, his arms weakening as dark blood began to run from his mouth. In a surge of motion Bolan was loose. Panting for breath, the soldier staggered across the hotel room, searching amid the debris of the frenzied combat. Out of the corner of his vision, Bolan saw the giant Nazi raise a leg to fumble at his ankle, exposing a small pistol in a hideaway holster.

Bolan found what he had been looking for. Dropping to a knee, he grabbed the Heckler & Koch gun case and pressed the handle, a stuttering stream of 9 mm bullets racking along the ceiling as he fought to control the unwieldy weapon. The recoil was uncontrollable, but by sheer muscle strength, Bolan got it to track on the giant and stitch him across the chest just as he racked the slide on the tiny .32 pistol.

Going over backward from the multiple hits, the Nazi fired the backup piece just once, the tiny bang lost amid the jubilation of the noisy throng outside. The slug hit the light fixture and an explosion of glass tinkled down upon the lifeless corpse.

Then from out of nowhere, gore-streaked fingers grabbed the Zodiac and tugged hard, trying to get it away from Bolan.

Slamming the trick machine gun against the head wound of the first German, Bolan forced the man away; he fell sputtering and weeping. Then his hand closed upon the dropped Walther PPK and he started to fire blindly. Moving the Zodiac behind him for protection, Bolan kicked a chair in the way of the incoming rounds and the wood shattered. As the gun ran out of ammo, Bolan walked to the dropped Desert Eagle and leveled the weapon, knowing full well there was only a single round remaining in the clip.

Casting away the useless Walther, the battered German sneered contemptuously at the American standing amid the corpses and broken furniture of the ruined hotel room.

"I s-surrender," he panted, blood dribbling from the hideous head wound. "N-now arrest me...I need m-medical attention."

"Too bad for you I'm not a cop," Bolan said without any emotion.

That took a moment to sink in, but as the bleary German finally came to understand, his face contorted into an expression of horror and Bolan stroked the trigger, ending the discussion forever.

Almost as if on cue, the happy crowd in the streets below roared into life and music from a dozen bands swelled into a deafening cacophony as the Grand Parade of Bourbon Street officially began.

After wearily checking the rest of the room for any more people, Bolan moved the bodies out of the way and locked the hallway door. Reclaiming the dropped Beretta, he then holstered the Desert Eagle and sat on the bed with the CIA briefcase. There was a small dent in the side where it had caught a ricochet, but the damage was only superficial. Anything worse and the Zodiac would have automatically detonated.

In spite of the pain of his clenched hand, Bolan took a moment to gather his thoughts before commencing the disarming procedure. Moving with surgical precision, he repeated each step twice in his mind before actually doing it, knowing that there would be no second chances if he made a slip. The soldier refused to release his grip on the handle until the internal indicators went dim and his pocket EM scanner registered zero activity. However, it was still a tense moment as he let go and waited for a full second for total annihilation, but nothing happened.

Massaging his hand for a few minutes, Bolan

went inside the bathroom to wash his cuts and administer some battlefield first aid, before drinking a glass of tepid tap water and sitting in the only unbroken chair to place a call on his cell phone. The casing of the device was badly cracked, but it was still functioning.

"Brognola," the man answered on the first ring.

"I have one," Bolan said simply, flexing some circulation back into his left hand.

"Great news, Striker. But, Jesus, you sound terrible!"

"Been better," he admitted. "That's enough for now."

"Yeah, I guess so. Any breakage?"

"Nothing that can be traced back to you."

"Fair enough. Was it our alphabet friends from down south?"

"More the iron eagle type," Bolan said with a scowl.

"Adolph's boys, eh? Should have known the Volksfever would be after it. Just their sort of weapon. Need anything?"

"Just getting this damn thing off my hands will be fine, Hal," the Executioner said in grim humor.

"Hold it a minute," Brognola said, and there was silence on the line for a brief while. "Okay, Bear has your location. I can have the local FBI bomb squad at the hotel in twenty minutes."

"Not here," Bolan said, glancing at the confetti

drifting in through the busted window. "Security is impossible today. We'd better do this someplace outside of town."

"Wherever you want."

"There's a car park near the northern cemetery. I'll call back with detailed instructions later. You'll be the relay between us, and give constant report until the FBI arrives and I know for sure it is them. If there's anything suspicious, I'm taking them down."

"Now hold on, Striker…no, wait. Okay, I agree, this is much too important for any half-assed security measures."

"Damn straight," Bolan growled, standing and starting for the door. "And should have been from the very beginning."

"Ain't that the truth, old buddy. Ain't that the goddamn truth."

CLOSING THE DOOR to the hotel room, Erich Strumfield and his team went to say their goodbyes to the rest of the Volksfever down the hallway when they noticed the spent brass shells on the carpeting in front of the closed door.

Pulling silenced weapons from under their civilian clothing, the kill team burst through the door and swept into the room using a standard two-on-two formation for coverage. They stopped in their tracks at the sight of the carnage and destruction. Every member of the Volksfever was dead, and the Zodiac was plainly gone. Only the Heckler & Koch briefcase with that trick machine gun inside still remained, the carpeting coated with empty brass.

"Good God," Cort Rutland muttered, lowering his piece. "How could this be? We were gone only a few minutes!"

"Fifteen," Strumfield corrected, holstering his weapon. "We should go. There is nothing to do here."

"But, sir—" Paul Krieger frowned.

"We know who did this," Strumfield growled, cutting off the reply. "It was those S2 cowards. Who else could it be?" The barrel-chested German terrorist gestured grandly at the corpses. "The FBI, perhaps? The CIA? They always take prisoners."

Leaving the room, the grim men closed the door and moved down the hallway toward the elevator banks.

"What shall be our response, Commander?" Kreiger asked, pressing the call button.

"Find the Scion and kill them all, as painfully as possible," Strumfield answered coldly. "Then we come back with a Zodiac and finish the job."

"But, sir, that was not our assignment," Rutland said slowly as a set of elevator doors opened wide. "We are merely the guards for this project."

"Well, now it is our assignment!" he said as the

doors closed behind them. The men were alone here, and it was safe to talk plainly until reaching the busy public lobby. "We are the Volksfever! The hammer of the people, and we shall not let our comrades fall alone."

"Honor and blood," Krieger intoned, giving a stiff-arm salute in the privacy of the elevator.

Repeating the oath and gesture, the rest of the terrorist killers began their slow descent into the bowels of the jubilant metropolis.

CHAPTER SIXTEEN

Oklahoma City, Oklahoma

Parking the van in a secluded section of the Will Rogers Airport, the Scion took a city bus to the downtown area and walked along the peaceful streets, doubling-back every now and then to make sure that they weren't being tailed.

As the mercs cut through an alleyway, the homeless man who seemed too inquisitive about their passing was ruthlessly eliminated purely as a precaution. Not finding any hidden weapons or microphones on the corpse, the Scion hid it inside a refuse container for the evening collection. Americans were quite fanatic about such things as garbage, and were always complaining about the filth in their major cities. Meanwhile the rest of the world marveled at the nearly antiseptic conditions of the North American suburbia.

Dressed casually to blend in with the local citizenry, the S2 team was wearing deliberately scuffed sneakers, with white T-shirts tucked into faded blue denims and loose shirts hanging unbuttoned on the outside to cover their holstered weapons.

Prepared for trouble, all four S2 agents carried briefcases; Mariano and Pedrosa armed with a Heckler & Koch gun case, Zalhares and Mizne each carrying a Zodiac. This time one of the bombs was armed for detonation. The Scion had been almost caught in a trap once and they had no intention of ever allowing such an unthinkable catastrophe to occur again.

The sun was high and hot overhead, the sky a clear blue without cloud coverage of any kind. Pausing on North Meridian Street, Mariano glanced at a thermostat in the window of a drugstore and struggled to convert the weird Fahrenheit into the more logical Celsius. Meanwhile, Zalhares looked over the civilians streaming around and nodded in approval. Aside from the expected male glances of appreciation at Mizne, the mercs didn't seem to be garnishing any undo notice.

However, their contact was another matter entirely. From a logistic standpoint, Tulsa was a better city to conduct their clandestine business. But there were very few people of Chinese descent in Tulsa, in spite of the horde of coolies forced to build the great network of railroads across the state. There were some, but nowhere near enough to make the Chinese Red Star operative indistinguishable amid a crowd.

On the other hand, Oklahoma City was bordering on becoming a metropolis, with a justifiably famous Chinese restaurant on North Merdian Street that boasted a wild mix of Tex/Mex and Cantonese food. The eatery had received a four-stars rating for the past ten years from the city newspaper, and was conveniently located near the downtown Civic Center, an equally short walk from the mammoth Cox Business Conference Center.

Reaching for blocks, the staggering Cox pavilion of white stone and mirrored walls housed a combination exhibit hall and arena capable of holding crowds in excess of sixty thousand people. And directly across the street was the world-famous Myriad Botanical Gardens and two luxury hotels. Strangers went unnoticed in this part of Oklahoma City, even tall, scarred strangers carrying identical briefcases.

Personally, Zalhares was never happy when dealing with the Red Chinese. Their standards of honor were flexible to say the least. However, the Communists had offered the highest price online, and since he was unable to think of a plausible reason to deny the bid, he had been forced to accept. Pity. Uganda always kept their part of a deal and desperately wanted a nuclear weapon, but the destitute nation didn't have the money. Then some Japanese terrorist group Zalhares had never heard of before offered a staggering hundred million dollars, payment to be handled as an electronic bank transfer. Since those were becoming notoriously easy to track these days, the bid had been refused.

Unexpectedly, and at the very last minute of the Internet auction, there had come a serious bid from the Sicilian Mafia, the highest cash actually, an offer for fifty million, but in gold bullion. The amount was right, but the tender was totally unacceptable. Aside from the size and bulk, the sheer weight of the gold would need an armored truck for conveyance, which in turn would have been completely impossible to sneak past the Mexican border guards. Regretfully, Zalhares had passed on the offer, and in retrospect, it seemed like a wise choice.

Always suspicious, Minas believed the gold could have been a ruse, a trick to slow them down and become exposed to the American secret police. That was an unlikely but not untenable possibility. Still, fifty million in shining gold bullion would have been quite an impressive sight, like something from the lost Inca treasure fortress and, unlike diamonds, or cash, bullion was accepted everywhere. Gold and lead were the only true universal languages.

Suddenly alert, Mizne spun and stepped closer to the others. "The man in the black silk shirt and cowboy hat," she said quickly, scratching her taunt stomach to keep a hand near her silenced Imbel pistol. "He's carrying a weapon on his belt."

"FBI?" Pedrosa asked, turning the gun case to point at the man standing on the street corner.

"He is nobody," Zalhares said calmly, watching as the light changed and the cowboy strolled away through the thin traffic. "Give it no concern. Most of the people around us are armed today."

"Why is that?" Mariano asked, glancing about in concern.

"They are holding a gun show at the Cox Center," the S2 agent explained, gesturing a gloved hand at the marquee of the white building. "It is an annual event, and excellent coverage for us. In a crowd of armed people, we are invisible. Nobody can notice a fish in the ocean, eh?"

"A gun show," Mariano repeated slowly. "This is a joke?"

"No, my friend, it is not," Zalhares said, giving a cold laugh. "These Americans love weapons, especially firearms, and often gather in crowds of hundreds of thousands to buy and sell them. It is a very big business, and quite legal."

"But I thought most Americans were not allowed to carry guns," Mariano insisted, studying the people passing by.

Until now he had been scrutinizing the traffic for police cars or military transports, but many of the men and woman walking by were wearing shirts and hats bearing the logo of a weapon manufacturer—Smith & Wesson, Heckler & Koch, Glock, Colt and so on. Some even carried a political slogan about weapons and freedom. And they were doing so in broad daylight without being immediately arrested by the police. It was unbelievable.

"Few are allowed to carry concealed guns without permission," Mizne explained. "But most of them own guns."

"Are they members of a militia? Criminals, perhaps?"

Impatiently, Minas snorted. "Of course not."

"Then for what purpose?"

"To look at them, hold them, revel in the fact that they can own such things," Mizne said with a shrug. "How should I know the workings of such minds?"

"Incredible," Mariano muttered. "We would have a revolution if such a thing was allowed to occur in Brazil."

"Which is why it does not," Pedrosa growled, then he pointed. "Look there, it is the restaurant we seek."

Studying the building for a few minutes, Zalhares ordered Mariano to stay in place while the others walked past it and took positions near the front door. Then Pedrosa went around the block once, looking for hidden observers. Upon returning, the man gave an all-clear signal and Mariano joined the others before the Scion proceeded into the restaurant.

Golden dragons were painted on the glass doors fronting the hot sidewalk, yet the vestibule inside was icy-cold thanks to a strong draft blowing out of a ceiling vent. The next set of doors was more functional, clear glass without decoration, which allowed an unobstructed view of the interior of the restaurant.

Past some velvet ropes adorned with golden tassels was a waiting area with black-and-silver embroidered couches. Next was a ridiculous wooden bridge that arched over a babbling creek to reach the artificial island full of tables that composed the majority of the establishment. The ceiling was an ornate array of sculptured plaster in classic Mandarin lettering and raised Imperial dragons. The walls, sweeping murals of the Yang River Valley. Sadly, that was now a historic scene from the past since the Communist government had built a massive dam to flood the ancient valley to create a hydroelectric generating station that would supply vitally needed power to a dozen cities, a hundred factories and several hidden missile bases.

Chatting and eating in very un-Chinese loudness, the customers were a mix of Orientals, whites, blacks and quite a few Latinos. However, the staff were all Orientals, although Zalhares noted that only a handful were actually Chinese. Most of the waiters and busboys appeared to be Mongolians, with a few Laotians and Cambodians. He also knew that few non-Asians could tell the subtle differences.

"Good afternoon, sir," said a pretty waitress beaming a smile as she approached the waiting Brazilians. "Do you have a reservation?"

Studying her coldly, Zalhares observed that while the woman was in a tight red dress that showed off her slim figure to its full advantage, she was also wearing the flat shoes of a professional who stood all day long, not decorative high heels. The female was a waitress, nothing more. Good.

"Goldsmith," Zalhares replied without preamble.

Now stretched taut, the smile froze on the woman's face and she gave a short, respectful bow. "Of course, sir. This way, please."

Leading the way, the waitress crossed the delicate bridge and moved through the maze of tables to a second bridge to finally pass through a set of red-lacquered doors marked Private. The room inside was empty, bare to the walls, without a scrap of furniture in sight. Nor was there another door, or even a window for ventilation.

"What is this?" Zalhares demanded, stopping at the entrance.

"Your private dining room, sir." She smiled quizzically. "As requested. Is something wrong?"

"No," Zalhares said slowly, glancing at the other members of the Scion. "It will do fine."

"Enjoy your meal, sir," the waitress said with a bow, exiting and leaving the door open.

Motioning the others inside, Zalhares used his foot to block the door as the mercs, weapons drawn, spread out for a fast recon of the premises.

"Clean," Pedrosa announced after several minutes. "There are no trapdoors, microphones, gas bombs or anything else hidden that I can find."

"Then there are none," Mizne stated confidently. "What do we do now?"

"We close the door," Zalhares said, removing his foot.

With a sigh, the door swung shut and for a moment nothing happened. Then there came a hiss as a pneumatic bolt thudded home, locking the exit tight, and the entire room began to gently shake. Instantly the Scion pulled handguns in response, but there came a definite dropping sensation as the walls started to rise.

"This is an elevator," Dog whispered, impressed, then he tried to show bravado by joking, "Perhaps it leads all the way down to China, eh?"

"That is probably closer to the truth than you know, my friend," Zalhares said, flexing the gloved hand holding the Zodiac. "These are not those silly German fools from before. We are now dealing with the only superpower in the world aside from America. Stay sharp."

Slow and stately, the disguised elevator continued downward, the wallpaper ending at the molding to be replaced with bare cinder blocks. Then another door came into view. As the room was still descending, Zalhares pushed the door open to see a vast, empty, private dining area.

As that rose above them, a third door appeared, behind which the Scion could hear the steady thumping of loud dance music. Zalhares tried the door, but it seemed to be locked.

Acting on impulse, Mariano raised his gun case to shoot the lock, but Pedrosa kicked out sideways and the portal crashed aside, exposing a boisterous club filled with flashing lights and rows of startled Chinese men wearing expensive business suits, all sitting along a circular stage with a dozen different girls dancing stark-naked. Rising from the darkness, a large man that could only have been a bouncer surged forward to throw the door shut again as the elevator kept going.

The following level had a glass window in the stained door, and the Scion could see a steamy kitchen of sweaty Chinese cooks shouting orders over fiery stoves as they stirred the contents of boiling pots and sizzling woks.

The next doorway was open, showing a dimly lit room filled with row upon row of bunkbeds stacked three high, each closed off with chicken wire. Shoeless men lay asleep on a thin mattress or reading technical books under small lights. A few were playing cards, a single woman dressed as a waitress was slowly brushing her long hair as if she had eternity to do the job.

"It's an entire secret world under Oklahoma," Mizne breathed.

"Under most cities," Zalhares corrected. "There are a great many more Chinese in America than the government will ever know about. Most of them slaves."

"Slaves?"

"Indentured servants." Zalhares snorted in disdain. "Which is the same thing. They get loans to pay for their journey to America, then spend the next twenty years paying it off."

"An odd practice for social Communists," Pedrosa said bluntly.

"They are Communists in name only," Zalhares responded, lowering his voice to a whisper. "Bejing worships power and nothing else."

A black line formed around the base of the moving room and the Brazilians could only see blackness past the edge of the carpeted floor. Moving so that they stood in a tight group facing outward, the S2 agents waited for the elevator to finally stop. Hinged panels lowered from the sides of the overhead shaft, closing off the hole and sealing them in total darkness.

Nobody moved or spoke. Then bright lights crashed on, showing a large room full of young men holding AK-47 assault rifles and an older man with slicked-back hair who stood unarmed amid the small army. The others were wearing T-shirts and khaki trousers, but he was dressed in a linen suit, the shirt unbuttoned at the collar showing just the tip of a tattoo on his hairless chest.

As his vision adjusted to the differing light levels, Zalhares calmly looked around. The walls were old brick, dark with age, and the ceiling was veined with pipes and electric cables. In the far corner sat an enormous furnace, a dull red glow emanating from its wide grating. Nearby stood a line of oversize, electric water heaters, the white containers resembling a bank of missile tubes. If there was more to be seen in the subbasement, it was hidden by the crowd of men and the thick shadows.

"You're late," the man said, tilting his head slightly.

"No, I am early," Zalhares recited. "The world is late."

"But since we are born into misery," the Chinese man continued, "being late is a blessing."

One of the young men in the group snickered at the exchange as if it were comical. Mizne shot him a puzzled glance, then realized he was looking directly at her, amused by the presence of a lowly woman. She felt a rush of cold fury and shifted her stance to press her breasts forward. Instantly the man's attention moved there and Mizne chuckled softly with the sure knowledge she could eliminate the fool whenever she wished.

"Satisfied?" the unarmed man asked, tilting his head to the other side.

"For now," Zalhares said, yielding nothing.

"Good," the man said, smiling at that. It was the grin of a predator about to feed. "I am Colonel Yang Shunrao."

"Zodiac," Zalhares replied, taking a step closer. "Do you have our payment?"

"I'm afraid that I have bad news," Shunrao said, slipping a hand partially into a pocket, but keeping his thumb on the outside. It was as if he were posing in a clothing catalog, the artifice of a model turned affectation. "The sale is off."

"Then prepare to die," Zalhares stated, hunching his shoulders.

In a wordless snarl of outrage, a young man moved from the surrounding group and raised the stock of his Kalashnikov as if about to strike. Lashing out with amazing speed, Mariano smashed the fellow in the temple with the silenced barrel of the Imbel and the gunman dropped with a muffled cry, blood on his face. The sound of well-oiled arming bolts being worked filled the basement in metallic chorus.

"Your people move well," the colonel said, completely unperturbed by the exchange. "And I see they are not afraid."

"Of this rabble?" Zalhares sneered in open defiance. "You have too many people jammed down here, Colonel. If a firefight should start, they would be shooting each other more often than us. No, we are not frightened of your cooks and waiters, but are tired of your games. We are not fools, you are not fools. Now tell us why you are reneging on the deal, old man."

"And why we shouldn't remove this shithole from the face of the earth," Mizne said, slightly raising her briefcase.

His black eyes shining brightly with avarice,

Colonel Shunrao stared hard at the piece of luggage, then glanced briefly at the others held by Pedrosa and Mariano, until settling on the one carried in a gloved fist by Zalhares.

"So that is it," the colonel breathed. "The size is amazing. Simply amazing. You brought two, of course, but that was only logical."

The number was whispered among the crowd of armed men and their stern faces lost some of the arrogance.

"Lee Wa!" the colonel snapped. "Bring chairs for our guests!"

"We'll stand," Zalhares countered. "Now talk. My patience grows thin."

The crowd parted as a thin man approached with an old wooden chair. As Lee Wa set it down, the colonel sat sideways and draped an arm across the back. Scowling at the posturing, Zalhares said nothing. It was too contrived to be natural, merely an illusion to mask his body language and to hide his true feelings. With that realization, the Brazilian suddenly understood that he was facing a truly dangerous man.

"As for canceling the contract, I really have no choice in the matter," Shunrao said, gesturing with his free hand. "The use of the Internet was expedient, but foolhardy. Too many now know about the Zodiacs and have sent people to steal them from you."

"Let them try," Pedrosa rumbled ominously.

"Ah, but they have tried already," Shunrao corrected. "Several groups have been caught by the new Homeland Security, not to mention the FBI and the hated CIA. And for them this is a personal matter, although not of reclaiming their honor, but more a matter of covering their ass. The Americans know you are here and will do anything to find you and recover the bombs."

Then the colonel added, "There have even been some references heard to your own S2 operating in the country. A big man with many scars, and even more identities."

"Santarino? Yes, I know the fool, and he could not find wet in the rain," Zalhares said confidently. "He is of no concern to us in this matter."

"So you say, but that does not mean it is true," Shunrao averred. "However, my friend, this is not our only operation in this country, and with so much pressure on this particular project, I do not have the people to see it through to completion. It is a simple matter of manpower."

"And what of this lot?" Mariano asked, indicating the crowd of armed men.

"Waiters and cooks, as you said earlier," the colonel admitted. "Street soldiers I have, trained operatives I do not. The deal is off. If by some miracle you manage to smuggle the item out of the country, then please contact me again."

Zalhares couldn't believe this was actually happening. He had naturally assumed this was merely some sort of renegotiation tactic, perhaps for a lowering of the price. But the Red Chinese agent had only wanted to pump them for information to ascertain the true level of danger involved, and now was dismissing them like field-workers who hadn't brought in enough crops.

"Goodbye," Shunrao said, standing. "Lee Wa, allow our guests to leave unharmed." With that command, the men eased off their weapons and assumed a more relaxed stance

"Yes, Comrade Colonel," Lee Wa said with a bow, and started walking into the shadows beyond the bright lights.

By sheer willpower, Zalhares kept his expression neutral. This was a disaster! They were low on funds and needed the cash from this sale to get back home. Another bank robbery was possible, but with every public exposure, the noose of the American secret police drew tighter around their neck. They needed this deal. It could not fail.

"And what," Zalhares said in a tightly controlled tone, "if we were to assist you in your mission?"

Slowly walking away, Shunrao stopped, then turned and reclaimed his vacated chair.

"I'm listening," he said.

"We're mercs, and the best in the world," Zalhares stated bluntly. "We will hit the target, and then you pay us."

"For an additional fee," Mizne added hastily.

Shunrao waved that trifling matter aside. "Of course. But how could I know that you would not simply take the money and leave with the Zodiac?"

"Come along with us," Pedrosa said in explanation.

"Interesting," the colonel muttered. "Of course, I would also need to bring along some of my own people. For our mutual benefit and protection."

To maintain the balance of power, was more like it, Zalhares mentally translated. The Brazilians were short of cash and the Chinese were low on trained people; it was an equitable solution for both sides. In theory.

"As long as the number is equal," Zalhares stated firmly.

"Naturally." Shunrao smiled. "Then we are partners now."

"Agreed," Zalhares said, tightening his hold on the Zodiac. Partners. There was an ugly word. But the Brazilians really had no choice in the matter.

"So where are we going first?" Minas asked, flicking on the safety of the briefcase and setting it down to release the handle. Informed of what a Zodiac could do, the simple action visibly unnerved the Chinese men, which had been his intention.

However, the colonel frowned more at the interruption than the distraction. He disliked having to address several people on the same matter. It seemed that the Scion was a team of equals. They would have to be watched closely. The true danger of the mythical hydra was not its deadly fangs, but the fact that one blow could not kill all seven heads at the exact same moment.

"We shall leave for New Mexico in the morning," the colonel said tolerantly. "Where you will receive your payment as agreed upon in the auction. Then we proceed directly to the target."

"The sooner the better," Zalhares said, flexing the muscles in his arm so that his hand holding the Zodiac didn't become tired and weaken. Part of the price in the auction had been the disclosure of what the Zodiac would be used for. That way the Scion could plan a safe escape route and be far, far away from the strike zone when the nukes shook America to her knees.

"Agreed." The colonel smiled, then called, "Lee Wa!"

Dutifully, the thin man returned from the dim recesses of the huge subbasement.

"It appears that the people of China will need your total assistance in this matter after all," Shunrao said formally.

Lee Wa nodded and turned once more to shuffle away.

"And where is he going?" Mariano demanded, watching the man disappear into the darkness.

"Nowhere," Shunrao said without any noticeable emotion. "He is going nowhere at all."

CHAPTER SIXTEEN

Metarie Road, New Orleans

Wearing a camouflage-colored ghillie jumpsuit, Mack Bolan was hidden inside the branches of a leafy tree across the street from the Metarie Cemetery. Holding an Army monocular, he watched the roadway, and kept a very careful check on the old red Buick parked near the entrance to the world-famous graveyard.

Located on the west bank of the new basin canal, the entrance to the Metarie Cemetary was a somber brick house flanked on either side by tall brick arches that blended into the wall that surrounded the estate. Far outside of town, the grave-yard would seem to be an unlikely favorite among the visiting tourists, but hundreds flocked there every day, many coming because it was supposedly haunted by dozens of ghosts, among them, the restless spirit of the mother of New Orleans voodoo, Marie Laveau. However, a lot of folks came just to view the astonishing collection of mausoleums. Past the plain brick entrance the cemetery was an outdoor art museum of marble and granite, with statues everywhere and in every conceivable shape and size and design.

Directly behind the gatehouse was a soaring white marble spire with larger-than-life female statues on each side: Faith, Hope, Love and, supposedly, Mrs. Merrilman, the dead wife of the local banker who had erected the monument. Past that was an Egyptian-style pyramid of gleaming stone suitable for a pharaoh from biblical days. Over in Millionaire's Row there was a plain column for the Army of Northern Virginia, and underneath was a mass grave that held the remains of more than two thousand Confederate soldiers. Yes, the Metarie Cemetery had a lot of ghosts, but even more memories.

At night, the graveyard was a favorite hunting ground for muggers and rapists waiting in ambush for foolish wannabe voodoo witch doctors who had read one too many books and lacked any common sense. But during the day Metarie held an almost carnival atmosphere thanks to the countless visitors photographing the beautiful memorials. But then, Bolan knew that in N'Orleans, as the locals called their beloved town, a funeral was usually a happy occasion, a wild party celebrating the departure of a friend on a long journey, not a somber affair of speeches and tearful regrets. As a soldier he considered both appropriate, a meaningful funeral service, followed by a farewell party that lasted for weeks.

A city bus rumbled to a stop at the cemetery, a group of people still decked out in Mardi Gras regalia stumbling off to head into the graveyard. Bolan wished the drunks good luck on finding their way back out of the marble maze. He went tense as four black cars appeared down the roadway.

Focusing the monocular, Bolan saw that the windows were tinted to a mirror shine, making it impossible to see who was inside. But he also noted that the tires were military-grade and the vehicle rode low, as if heavy with armor. That could be them. Checking the arming circuit of the radio detonator strapped to his forearm, Bolan donned an earpeice and pulled out a cell phone to place a call when the device shook in his hand.

"Go," Bolan subvocalized into the throat mike wired to the phone as the black sedans parked around the red Buick, blocking it from sight on the ground but not from above.

"The FBI has arrived, Striker," Hal said. "Four cars, black sedans, twelve agents in business suits. Want the license plate numbers?"

"Describe them," Bolan growled, lifting monocular scope to his eye and listening carefully as Brognola detailed the eight men and four women, each done in turn.

"By the way, Striker," Brognola said over the sound of rustling paper. "The Scion hit a bank in Little Rock, so they must be desperately low on funds."

"That's good news," Bolan replied, starting to frown as he spotted another person with the group of FBI agents, a middle-aged man in a rumpled suit. A thirteenth man.

"Unfortunately we can't trace the bills, and I have also some bad news from…"

"Hal, we have a security breach," Bolan said calmly, taking a Remington bolt-action rifle from an overhead branch. "There's a thirteenth man."

"What? Could you have miscounted?"

"Negative, Hal," he said, laying the weapon on a branch and looking through the Zeist telescopic sight to center the crosshairs on the face of the thirteenth man. Tipped with a sound suppressor as big as a coffee can, the Remington was covered with bits of bark and leaves to mask its presence and already had a depleted uranium round loaded in the chamber, the super-dense slug more than capable of punching straight through the side of an M-1 Abrams tank.

"I go the moment they touch that car," Bolan

said, shifting the angle to adjust for the wind. "Talk to me, Hal."

"Just a minute, Striker. I'm checking with Quanico, just in case the bomb squad has been compromised."

By now the FBI agents were around the Buick and starting to looking through the windows.

"You don't have a minute," Bolan stated, placing a finger on the trigger. "I want an ident fast or—"

"He's CIA!" Brognola blurted in relief, through a crackle of static. "The guy is David Osbourne, the head of the Zodiac reclamation project."

With the leaves rustling all around him, Bolan studied the stranger through the crosshairs of the scope on the Remington sniper rifle. "That's the guy from England who lost them in the first place," he said as a question.

"Yeah, that was Osbourne," Brognola admitted. "Now he wants a crack at saving what is left of his career." Then the top cop of the Justice Department described the CIA operative in full detail, right down to his shoes.

"Okay, I'm standing down," Bolan acknowledged, easing off the pressure on the trigger. "Tell them to open the trunk. But to go slow. No sudden moves. I'm not going to allow an Osbourne mistake to occur on my watch."

"Sure, sure, no problem." There was a short pause. "They want to know where the key is."

Motionless in the tree, Bolan gave a snort. "Hal, if they're actually the FBI, then they can open a damn car faster than I could an MRE pack."

"Fair enough. Hold on."

Bolan watched as the team leader nodded to the cell phone, then called over one of the women and pointed at the car. The woman pulled out a very advanced model of a keywire gun from her pocket and opened the trunk without any trouble. But then she dropped the keywire gun and backed away, clawing for the pistol under her jacket and turning around fast.

"What the… Striker, they say there's a Claymore mine in the trunk along with the Zodiac," Brognola said quickly.

"Just some insurance in case of trouble," Bolan said, checking the radio detonator on the forearm of his ghillie suit. "The Zodiac is safe under a couple of bulletproof vests. If the Claymore detonated, it wouldn't be harmed any more than dropping it on the sidewalk."

"Don't miss a trick, do you, Striker?"

"An ounce of C-4 is worth a pound of cure," he stated, working the controls on the detonator until the green light turned red, then went dark. "Okay, it's safe. They can take it away now."

The head FBI agent closed the cell phone and Osbourne went to the trunk himself. Shifting the vests, the CIA agent extracted the Zodiac as a FBI agent removed the Claymore mine and expertly defused the detonator. The rest of the government agents stood in a semicircle around the Buick, forming a living shield to save the Zodiac from any possible attack. The irony of men dying to protect a bomb wasn't lost on Bolan the soldier.

"Okay, Hal, what was that bad news you mentioned earlier?" he asked as Osbourne got back into the armored sedan, the leader of the FBI team removing his sunglasses and looking around at the rooftop of the cemetery, the towering granite spires, trees and other cars parked along the roadway. The federal agent then gave a thumbs-ups sign to his unseen associate and climbed into the sedan with the rest of the agents.

"I checked the police and morgue reports. There was no body found at Dulvet Street that matched Santarino's description."

Watching the convoy roll out of sight, Bolan started to gather his arsenal of equipment and weapons. "There wouldn't have been much left after being hit with a 40 mm AP round," Bolan stated.

"Yeah, I know. But there wasn't any corpse in that bad a shape, although one officer did report finding a Honda hatchback damn near cut in two with an AP charge."

"Dillard missed," Bolan growled, climbing out of the tree.

"Seems likely, Striker. Which means Santarino is still hunting for you, along with the Scion and those last two bombs."

Reaching the ground, Bolan pulled on a stained overcoat to hide the ghillie suit and started toward the nearby canal. So the big Brazilian was alive. Twice the S2 agent had faced Bolan and lived. There wouldn't be a third time.

Sliding the backpack off his shoulders, Bolan dropped it into the storm sewer and waited for the splash before starting down the rusty ladder.

"I'm going out of range, Hal," Bolan said abruptly. "I'll contact you after I fly north and connect with Able Team in Little Rock."

"Stay sharp, Striker. Santarino is a stone-cold killer."

"Aren't we all?" Bolan growled, cutting the connection.

Reaching the bottom of the ladder, Bolan stepped into the sluggish flow of watery mud, grabbed the backpack and began wading through the ankle-deep muck, heading for the pumping station and a waiting car. Now that the Zodiac was safe, he could fly the Cessna to Little Rock and continue the hunt. The noose was tightening around the Scion, while Kurtzman and his team were still trying to find out who the other buyers were at the auction, Phoenix Force was waiting for the Scion along their escape route in Mexico, and

Able Team was at Baton Rouge checking the rendezvous site in the swamp. One slip on the part of Zalhares, and it would be all over.

However, time was short. As soon as the Scion realized that Mardi Gras wasn't going to be destroyed, they would scatter and run, possibly using that third nuke to fake their own deaths again. Yeah, that made sense, Zalhares would use the last Zodiac to blast his way out of the country. Which meant Bolan was only tracking the one sold Zodiac and the Scion. Three options had become two. He was another step closer. So far, Bolan had managed to stay hot on the trail of the elusive Brazilians, always one step behind, nipping at their heels. But that wasn't enough anymore. He needed to rip out their hearts, and that meant finding an exact location. This whole thing was going to fall apart unless he found some way to pinpoint the terrorists. Bolan desperately needed a clue, a rumor, some scrap of hard data that would give him an edge. Anything would do, anything at all.

Approaching the pump station, the steady thumping grew to a deafening level and Bolan stopped dead in his muddy tracks. Osbourne. How the hell had a CIA operative based in Washington, D.C. gotten to New Orleans so quickly? That was flatly impossible, unless he had already been in the area. Starting to move through the processing machinery, the truth hit Bolan like a fist in the dark. He knew! That son of a bitch had known Mardi Gras was a possible target. The CIA had a hit list of targets perfect for a Zodiac. Still playing politics, Osbourne was holding back intel again, trying to salvage his career at the expense of lives.

Now racing past the clamorous pumps, Bolan burst out the access door and into the bright sunlight, the cell phone already in his hand.

"Something wrong, Striker?" Brognola asked after the first ring.

"Have the FBI hold Osbourne," Bolan ordered, heading for his rented car. "He has a hit list for the Zodiacs!"

There was a stunned pause.

"Then he's going to jail for treason," Brognola growled in unaccustomed savagery. "But more importantly, we finally have the Scion by the balls!"

"So let's start squeezing," Bolan said, starting his car and driving for the airport. "I want that list, Hal."

"You'll have it in ten minutes!"

"Make it five."

TURNING ON THE ITS directional blinker, the Louisiana Department of Public Works' truck began to slow and move over to the side of the highway to roll to a stop on the berm. As the humming traffic flashed by, the members of Able Team climbed from the state vehicle and walked to the right side of the truck and out of the sight of the other cars. Working undercover, the infiltration team was dressed as state workers in yellow hard hats and rough workclothes, their orange safety vests untied to allow access to the handguns tucked into their belts. With a little cybernetic assistance from Carmen Delahunt at the Farm, the team actually had a government work order on their clipboard, and the vehicle was registered as on patrol. Which it was, but not for potholes.

"Okay, according to the maps Mack found on the Volksfever," Gadgets Schwarz said, checking the PDA minicomputer in his hand, "this seems to be the best place for the Scion to launch an airboat for the rendezvous at the Choctaw cabin."

"Culvert down below," Rosario Blancanales said, holding on to his hard hat and looking over the side of the steel railing. "Good place for an airboat."

"So were the last three culverts," Carl Lyons commented, casting a glance downward.

Situated below the overpass was a shiny expanse of black mud, dotted here and there with tufts of swamp grass and the occasional beer bottle or other bits of rubbish. Over by a rotting tree, there was a buzzing swarm of wasps. The murky water lapped along the irregular edges of the mud island, spreading outward in every direction to become the primordial wildlife preserve. Somewhere in the far distance, an alligator gave a loud baw for its mate and was immediately answered.

"Swell place for a picnic," Blancanales said, waving away a cloud of stinging gnats. "No wonder the state has so much tourism."

"I'm just glad we're wearing hats," Schwarz replied, watching a flock of birds fly directly overhead.

"That's a fifty-foot drop," Lyons continued. "Hell of a climb for you boys. I'll get some rope from the truck."

While the ex-cop got the tackle, Blancanales and Schwarz did a fast recon along the berm, but there were no overt signs of anything having occurred here. No Brazilian cigarette butts, no empty shell casings, but considering who it was they were after, it would have been very surprising if the Scion had made such a beginner's mistake. Still, it never hurt to look.

Exiting the truck, Lyons attached the rope to the tow bar and tossed it over the railing. Easing over the railing, Schwarz went down first, gliding expertly along the smooth length of nylon rope, using his gloved hands to control his descent. He landed with his legs spread and stepped aside just as Blancanales arrived right behind.

Staying on the overpass, Lyons stood guard while the others separated to search the muddy flatland, Blancanales moving along the edge of the water, while Schwarz pulled out a compact bundle of rods that quickly became a portable metal detector. Sweeping the slimy black soil, the soldier frowned as the device gave a beep on every single pass.

"Aw, this is useless," Schwarz complained, turning off the detector and folding it back into a pocket. "There's too much trash down here. It must be a favorite spot for folks to toss their old junk. I'm finding mufflers, bed springs, all kinds of useless shit."

"Maybe a little too much junk," Blancanales said cryptically. Wary of the nearby wasps, the man moved slowly as he lifted a discarded license plate and studied it for a moment. Then he rose and walked to the edge of the mud to rinse off the plate in the greenish water. As the crud washed away, it was revealed as a brand-new license plate for the state of Florida registered for this year.

"He dumped them here," Blancanales said in astonishment. "Zalhares had the Scion dump their extra plates in the swamp to get rid of them!"

Careful of his step in the slippery mud, Schwarz rushed over eagerly. "If that's all of the plates, then maybe we can—"

Suddenly, Schwarz broke off, and raised a clenched fist, then pointed. As Blancanales stood, he saw that the wasps were gone, vanished in a single moment. Glancing at the overpass, he jerked his head at the swamp. Lyons nodded and disappeared.

"Freeze!" a stern voice commanded from behind.

Turning about halfway, Schwarz and Blancanales spun at the sound of the voice, reaching for their guns, but they stopped at the sight of several men in scuba suits rising from the murky water in a curved line around the mud island.

Raising their hands, the two members of Able Team backed up until they were against the concrete abutment supporting the highway overhead. Damn, they had figured there was somebody in the water, just not this many! Trapped in an expert cross fire pattern, there was nothing they could do at the moment.

Two of the men spit out their breathing mouthpieces and walked onto the black island. Instead of cumbersome swimfins, they were wearing rubber sneakers, useless for swimming underwater, but perfect for walking on the slippery mud.

"These men are not the Scion," Erich Strumfield growled angrily, his features distorted by the diving mask. "They were not at the meeting."

"Perhaps one of them is called Dog," Heinrich Gutterman snarled impatiently.

"Hoo boy, another damn robbery. Just take the

money, okay?" Schwarz said, starting to reach inside his work vest as if going for a wallet.

Two of the armed men fired in unison, the slugs ricocheting off the concrete, kicking out a stinging spray of dust.

"Keep both hands on top of your head," Paul Krieger ordered, gesturing with a Heckler & Koch submachine gun safely wrapped inside a plastic bag, slimy swamp water dripping off the outside. "We can see that you are armed, fool."

"This is Louisiana! Hell, boy, everybody packs heat down here," Schwarz replied in an artful display of scorn. "There's gators and snakes in the bayou kill a man faster than my ex-wife."

"Y'all calm down," Blancanales drawled in a perfect New Orleans accent. "We just be a road crew. If y'all are poaching you some gators, that be fine by us, lawd yes. I likes dem gators me self."

"Very convincing. Officer." Strumfield sneered. "And if I had not heard you speaking earlier without the accent I would have believed you."

One of the gunmen still in the water removed his mouthpiece. "Officer? Do you think they are FBI?" Cort Rutland asked.

With the regulator of his scuba tank clicking slightly, Krieger shrugged. "Or CIA. What difference does it make?"

"Kneel," Strumfield commanded, shaking his weapon for emphasis. "Now very slowly place one hand on top of your head, and with the other, open your vest. Keep it easy and you may live through this."

"Then you will tell us about the Scion," Krieger added. "Are they actually Brazilian? Who are their known contacts? We want to know everything!"

As Blancanales and Schwarz kneeled on the soggy ground, there was a flash of movement from the other side of the culvert and Lyons appeared, sliding down the second rope, holding on with his left hand while the other leveled a massive Atchisson autoshotgun.

Startled by the sight, the Volksfever members paused for a single second and Lyons used that to aim over the heads of his kneeling friends. Then he cut loose, the Atchisson ripping a roaring burst that sounded like the end of the world, firing all seven 12-gauge shells in less than a second. In an explosion of blood, the hellstorm of steel pellets virtually disintegrating Rutland and Gutterman, tatters of flesh and scuba suit blowing into the swamp.

Recovering from their shock, Strumfield and Krieger fired across the culvert, but before they could track on him, Lyons touched ground and dived for cover behind the concrete abutment. Instantly, Blancanales and Schwarz drew their handguns and fired, hitting the men several times and eliciting only the telltale grunts of lead hitting body armor; they tracked the pistols high and shot both men in the face. Already dead, the German terrorists fell backward, their automatic weapons wildly throwing lead until the corpses splashed into the swamp and the nerveless fingers eased on the hair triggers.

The noise of the brief gun battle echoed across the weedy water and into the moss-draped tress, mixing with the steady rumble of traffic on the highway.

"Now who the hell are these assholes?" Lyons demanded, coming around the abutment, sliding fresh shells into the hot breech of the Atchisson.

"German nationals from their speech patterns," Blancanales replied, watching the bloody bodies start to sink into the quagmire of the Cajun swamp. "And they knew Zalhares by sight."

"Must have been part of the Volksfever," Schwarz suggested, lifting a plastic-wrapped SMG. "They learned about the deaths at the hotel and came here to lay in ambush." The subgun was an MP-5, the exact same model used by Phoenix Force. Just another deadly example that the soldier behind the gun was more important than the weapon used. Expensive guns didn't make a person braver or a better shot.

Resting the shotgun on a broad shoulder, Lyons looked around the little muddy island. "So why did they choose here?" he said thoughtfully.

"Because this is where the Scion landed their airboat," Blancanales said, going back to reclaim the license plates. "And here's the proof. Mack mentioned that Zalhares bought a stack of fifty in Galveston. These must be them, all brand-new and never been used. See? There are no scratches around the bolt holes."

"So after the Internet auction, the Scion waited until they were in a secluded area before dumping the rest of the plates," Lyons concluded, joining his friend and pulling out more plates from the sticky mud. "The plates for the states they weren't going to travel through."

"No sense hauling around deadweight," Schwarz agreed, yanking one free from underneath the moss-covered tree. However, the disturbance started an angry buzzing from the wasp nest.

"Oh, gentlemen," Schwarz said, retreating slightly from the area. "I do believe that the Republicans aren't happy with our being here."

"The bugs are Republicans?" Blancanales asked in confusion.

"Well, they are wasps."

"Aw, for the love of… Can I shoot him?" Blancanales asked, facing Lyons. "Please? Just once?"

"Maybe later," Lyons said with a small smile. "But get the plates first."

The wasps, now completely agitated, were

ready to defend their home to the death. With no choice in the matter, Able Team went back to the DPW truck and hauled down enough fogger to do the job. Soon the nest was still and the men were able to safely recover the rest of the license plates. Laying them out in a crude map of the country, they found far too many missing states, so Schwarz used his metal detector to search the shallow water around the island. He located several more plates that had slipped underwater. In short order, the Stony Man team had an almost complete map of America covering the muddy island.

"Okay, we're missing Texas, but that would have been abandoned when they rolled over the state line into Louisiana," Lyons said, standing. "Same thing with Louisiana when they crossed into Arkansas."

"Now they wouldn't do a bank job in Arkansas if that was a delivery site," Blancanales said, committing the map to memory. "Which leaves Oklahoma, Colorado, Arizona, New Mexico as their delivery path out of the country."

"Four states is still a lot of ground to cover," Schwarz commented, logging the data into his PDA. "But this makes no sense. Why should they have kept the Arizona plate? Oklahoma borders on New Mexico, which borders on Mexico, so that's the shortest, fastest, easiest route out of the country."

"Which means Arizona must be a delivery site," Lyons said grimly, wiping the mud off his hands with a handkerchief. "And that's where the next Zodiac is going to be detonated."

"This is pretty damn thin, Carl," Blancanales said.

"Obviously transparent," Lyons agreed. "But if you've got a better idea, I'm ready to listen."

"No, I agree. It has got to be Arizona. But that's a mighty big state. Hell of a lot of places where a small nuke could cause real damage."

"Too damn many," Schwarz agreed unhappily. "I've read the Army Corps of Engineers manual on nukes in the field. You wouldn't believe what these things are capable of in the right hands."

"We have a choice to make here," Lyons stated in a tightly controlled voice. "If this is getting out of control, we should contact the President and ask him to shut down the state and declare martial law."

"Which would stop the Scion but also cause rioting in the streets when the truth got out. There could be hundreds of civilian casualties in the mob violence, and the Scion would escape to use the Zodiac somewhere else."

"Yeah, I know. But it would buy us more time to find the bastards," Lyons stated. "The question is, are we there yet? Are we ready to kill dozens to save a million?"

"Hell of a choice."

"Part of the job, *amigo*."

"The worst part, yeah."

Just then Schwarz glanced at his pocket and pulled out a vibrating cell phone. "Able Security," he answered, then listened for a moment, his face growing more grim by the second.

"Hold it a sec, Barbara," he said, then covered the mouthpiece. "Listen up, guys. Mack got a nuclear hit list from the CIA on Zodiac sites. Hal thinks it was used in the Internet auction to help make the sale. We'll sell you the weapon, plus tell you where to use it for maximum effect, too, that sort of shit."

"Clever bastards," Blancanales growled. "Any targets in Arizona?"

Schwarz took his thumb off the mouthpiece and told Barbara Price at the Farm about the license plates. "Yes, one," he said, and gave the name.

Impressed by the sheer audacity of the idea, Blancanales let out a long low whistle at the target. "The Scion doesn't play small, does it? We have got to take out these animals as fast as possible."

"First we get that bomb," Lyons told him, picking up the Atchisson and cradling the weapon in his calloused hands. "Okay, where does Mack want us to meet him?"

"We go to St. George in Utah," Schwarz said, turning off the phone and closing the watertight cover to tuck it away again. "He's landing in Las Vegas. That way we can converge on Lake Mead and head straight for Hoover Dam."

As Blancanales started up the rope, Lyons glanced at the swarm of dead insects covering the dark ground, their bodies twitching from the aftereffects of the deadly poison that invaded their homes. The symbolism was chilling, but he shook off the unproductive thoughts and concentrated on the task at hand—finding the Scion long before they reached the dam and pulling an unarmed Zodiac from the very dead hands of Cirello Zalhares, along with whoever purchased the infernal thing.

There would be no second chances on this, no fallback position and no backup. This mission had to be balls to the walls, a full-out blitzkrieg. Win or die. That was all. Because if they failed, resulting death toll would be beyond imagination.

CHAPTER SEVENTEEN

Missouri-Iowa Border

Approaching the toll plaza, Lee Wa shifted the newspaper from the passenger seat of the stolen Corvette sports coupe to partially expose the pile of automatic weapons and sticks of dynamite. As he eased to a stop alongside the booth, the Chinese agent deliberately didn't smile as he handed the attendant a dollar and waited for the change.

"Receipt, please," Lee said gruffly.

The attendant merely nodded in reply, but then his eyes went wide as he gave back the change and printed slip.

Satisfied that the weapons had been seen, Lee pocketed the coins and receipt, then drove away, knowing that the government wheels were already in motion.

Keeping to the middle lane, Lee maintained the speed limit as he crossed into Iowa and reached out a hand to tug on the steel hook installed in the dashboard just that morning. It was well anchored, and no matter how hard he pulled, the blunt hook wouldn't budge from its position. Good. It would be needed to serve the People of China soon enough.

Aside from a few semi trucks hauling produce and livestock, the traffic was light; there had been an early-morning rain that had left the air smelling clean and crisp. Use of the radio or CD player was strictly forbidden, but the big motor of the powerful Corvette purred through the floorboards and up his legs like a sexual beast, and Lee allowed himself to enjoy the ride. He had never been to Iowa before and was simply amazed at the size of the farmlands he was passing. There seemed enough food here to feed the world. Yet the imperialist warmongers denied their own people access to this abundance. The Russian Communists may have failed in the great task of liberating the oppressed masses of the world from the yoke of the American Paper Tiger, but the Chinese would not.

In a wail of lights and sirens, a state cop suddenly appeared behind Lee. Calmly, the man reached into the wooden box on the floor of the sports car and lifted a grenade. Catching the pin on the hook attached to the dashboard, he yanked hard. The pin came free, the spoon dropped and he tossed the grenade out the window.

Eight seconds later a fireball exploded into existence behind the speeding Corvette and the police car. But an SUV caught the blast full underneath and was flipped into the air like a broken toy tumbling over and over then landing in a tremendous crash to continue tumbling sideways along the road. Another car veered wildly around the burning wreckage, but another slammed headlong into the SUV and there was another explosion from a ruptured gas tank.

"You are under arrest!" an amplified voice bellowed from the P.A. of the state police car. "Pull the car over to the side of the road, now!"

Increasing his speed, Lee tossed out another grenade, then pulled the pin on a third, but waited four long seconds before lobbing it out the passenger-side window.

The second grenade cut loose into a fireball that just missed a Mack truck, but the second one caught the state police car like a guide missile. The vehicle burst into flames and the burning driver lost control, the car angling straight off the highway and crashing through a safety railing to sail away and disappear into the thick fields of green spring corn.

Now all of the other vehicles on the road started

braking hard, the squealing of brake pads from the cars mixing with the keen of pneumatic brakes on trucks. Then one BMW shot out of the pack along the side of the road and tried to race past the humming Corvette. Lee allowed the fool to get directly alongside, then lifted an Uzi machine pistol and sent a burst into the other driver. The sideview window shattered under the hammering 9 mm rounds, and the driver was torn apart as the Beamer swerved out of control and headed straight for the Corvette. Slamming the accelerator to the floor, Lee fed the engine gas and the sports coupe streaked away from the Beamer as it crossed the pavement and went off into a billboard advertising a local restaurant.

Never having been in a running car battle before, that was a most unexpected reaction. But a valuable lesson learned. If he was to complete his mission, Lee could never allow that to happen again. The Corvette was a most excellent machine, and with its many safety features he could survive such an impact, which would simply ruin everything.

Nervously, Lee started to reach for the plastic cup of soda sitting in the cup holder, but stayed his hand. The soda was gone, replaced by ice water, and that had a much more important task ahead than satisfying his thirst.

Trucks were pulling over onto the side of the

road ahead of him, probably communicating on their famous CB radios. Good. He needed a fast road, and took advantage of the clear stretch of pavement to see just how fast the Corvette could go.

Streaking by an overpass at 90 mph, Lee wasn't surprised when four police cars charged onto the highway from the on ramp, two of the state police and two of the sheriff's department from whatever was near. He didn't really care anymore, his heart was pounding, adrenaline pumping, and he prepared for the final moments of his life.

Impulsively, Lee turned on the radio hoping for some rock and roll, but he only found gospel and country music. In disgust, he turned the radio off. Bah, he should have purchased a CD of something appropriate. No man should die without music.

Sirens wailed as the police gave pursuit, one car loudly demanded his immediate surrender while another kept shooting with a pistol. Tossing out a few more grenades, Lee caught a sheriff's car in a thermite explosion, but the others dodged the bouncing military spheres. Lifting the Uzi, he sent a burst of lead out the rear window, the ejected brass bouncing all over the car and one landing on his cheek, burning the flesh. Startled, Lee cried out and lost the Uzi, the machine pistol tumbling out the shattered rear window and vanishing down the road.

Cursing, Lee gave the Corvette more gas and started pulling away from the police, which prompted an increase in the lead coming his way. The Vette was hit in the trunk, the lid flying open to block his view of the other cars, and then the sideview mirror was shattered on the left side. In cold realization, Lee understood that the American police were doing these things deliberately. They were blinding him to their approach!

Flashing under an overpass, additional shots rained down upon him, and even more police cars joined the chase, one of them some sort of a sleek racing car. In panic, Lee tossed out more grenades to fill the highway with flame, but held on to the very last one for five seconds before finally letting go. The resulting explosion shook the Corvette, and antipersonnel shrapnel peppered the car like machine-gun fire. But his brand-new tires held and the gas gauge didn't show a puncture in the tank. Excellent! He was still good for the final assault.

Rising in the distance, a helicopter appeared, and Lee knew he'd reached the end of his journey. Snapping off the lid of the plastic cup, the Chinese agent poured the ice water onto the maps tucked into the sleeve of the door, soaking them completely. Then he pressed the accelerator flat to the floor, and kept it there, turning the steering wheel to aim the car directly at a Mack truck parked alongside the road. Closing his eyes, Lee Wa waited to slam into the rear of the truck. The Corvette had been chosen for its height as well as its powerful engine. The rear loading ramp of most eighteen-wheel trucks would just miss the front hood and go through the windshield, beheading the driver, giving instant death with a minimum of pain, and causing little damage to the sport coupe and the precious documents inside.

Minutes seemed to pass and finally the man couldn't wait any longer. Opening his eyes, Lee got a brief impression of the loading ramp of the truck coming across the hood of the Corvette on an angle. Frozen in terror, he shrieked as the corner of the truck punched through only half of his head. The man was still horribly alive as the Corvette went flying off the road and out over the lush Iowa cornfields. The pain was beyond imagining and Lee pitifully begged for forgiveness from the universe for what seemed like centuries until the airborne car mercifully slammed into the ground, ending his existence on this plane of reality.

Seconds later, the police arrived in force to extinguish the burning wreckage. They soon found the wet maps, safe and completely undamaged in the pocket of the driver's-side door.

The FBI was called immediately and within minutes the information was on the desk of Harold Brognola of the U.S. Justice Department.

Hoover Dam

STANDING ON THE ROOF of the Visitor's Center, Jack Grimaldi and Mack Bolan quietly looked down at the panorama of Hoover Dam. Bolan was in full combat rig, with the Beretta and Desert Eagle at their accustomed spots and a crossbow slung across his back. Grimaldi was in flying togs, with a Glock 21 pistol tucked into a shoulder holster and the handle of a knife sticking out of his left boot.

Rough hills formed the landscape to the west and the east of the stately dam, Highway 93 meandering through a series of switchback curves before arching along the top of the monumental concrete monolith. More than twenty thousand men had labored for five years to build the Hoover Dam, which became Boulder Dam and, finally, Hoover again; just another victim of the whims of politics. But whatever it was called, the dam stood as strong as the Nevada mountains and as powerful as the wild Colorado River, a testament to the tenacity of Man to overcome any problem. The dam was also a work of genius, a single, seamless slab of concrete rising 726 feet high that used the pressure of the artificial lake behind it to stand firm. A combined unit of force, lake and dam formed a symbiosis of technology and nature unparalleled in the history of the world.

In the distance, the majestic Fortification Mountains rose, looming over the landscape like a granite king surveying his subjects. Even the awesome majesty of Hoover Dam was feeble in comparison to the titanic works of Nature.

Parked just behind the two men, the Black Hawk helicopter was quiet at the moment, its General Electric engines turned off to conserve fuel. Specially armed for this mission, the gunship was equipped with weapon pylons on each side and could deliver a massive punch wherever needed. But it couldn't stay aloft forever and, without a timetable on the attack, the forces of Stony Man had no choice but to stand down and stay alert.

Walking to the edge of the roof, Bolan looked out across the Black Canyon, with the Colorado River directly below and the soaring dam to his left. The twin power plants were situated on either side of the white water river, their seventeen generators faintly audible even from this great height. Earlier in the day, the engineers had done some routine maintenance and flushed out one of the jetflow gates set into the side of the gorge, the rush of water from the four titanic vents sounding louder than thunder and creating crisscrossing rainbows that filled the canyon with breathing beauty. Reborn at the bottom of the Herculean dam, the Colorado River rushed by the twin generator stations and past the jetflow gates to simply become a river once more, stretching into the far distance and vanishing from sight.

Thankfully, the Colorado River was an impossible approach and, more importantly, useless. Setting off the Zodiac at the very bottom of Hoover Dam would be like kicking an Abram tank really hard—more damage would be done to the foot than the tank. At its base, Hoover Dam was hundreds-of-yards-thick, steel-reinforced concrete under millions of pounds of static pressure and dynamic sidereal force merging at the rock walls of the canyon and deep into the bowels of the earth. Attacking the dam from the river was the only path Bolan didn't have to worry about.

"That river flows through three states and Mexico before reaching the Gulf of California," Grimaldi said grimly, joining the man at the edge of the round roof. He rested his folded arms on top of the yard high concrete fence. "The Zodiac would pollute the drinking water for about ten million people and kill enough farmland to cause a nation-wide shortage of food."

"And that's if the dam holds," Bolan added darkly, shifting the crossbow to a more comfortable position.

"Hey, no offense, Sarge," Grimaldi said, squinting toward the colossal dam. "You know weapons a hell of a lot better than me, but can a quarter-ton-yield nuke even dent that man-made mountain?"

"Yes and no," Bolan answered truthfully. "The Zodiac doesn't have enough brute force to blow the dam apart, not even if it was sitting directly on top. But if was submerged under water, the blast would blow the whole thing apart like a house of cards."

"Like a firecracker in your hand," Grimaldi said, thinking out loud. "Set off a firecracker in your open palm and you'll be hurt bad, maybe even seriously. But light one and close your hand into a tight fist and that same firecracker will blow off your fingers, possibly the whole hand."

"Basic physics," Bolan agreed. "And there's not a thing we can do about that."

"Well, we could always lower the water level in the dam," Grimaldi started, then frowned. "No, that would tell the Scion, or whoever they're working for, that we're wise and they would leave to strike someplace else."

"The Chinese," Bolan said unexpectedly, frowning. "They sold the bomb to the Red Chinese."

"Chinese terrorists?"

"No, spies, Red Star agents working in America to pave the way in case our nations go to war. That call I received a while ago was from Hal. A known Chinese agent killed a bunch of police in Iowa, then crashed his car in a cornfield. The cops found maps of Green Bay, Wisconsin, in the

wreckage, showing where a nuke could be detonated to pollute the watershed for northern America and Canada."

"Damn," the pilot muttered. "But you don't believe it."

"They were wet," Bolan answered curtly. "But
not wet enough to make the ink run much, so the
driver must have dampened them down just before
crashing. It was ruse. We also got a hot tip from
the Mob that the Scion are dealing with the Chinese."

"Which mob? The Mafia?"

Bolan nodded. "Leo Turrin."

"Leo The Pussy," Grimaldi said, breaking in a
grin. Leo "The Pussy" Turrin was an old friend of
Bolan's who had infiltrated the Mafia and reached
a position of power. Although, semi-retired, he
still had contacts within the Mob and passed on
pertinent bits of information.

"Leo heard a rumor and told Hal. It matched the
intel we received from other sources, so it seems
solid."

"On top of which, there are the license plates
that Able Team found," Grimaldi added, studying
a tiny sailboat skimming along the surface of Lake
Mead. "Dammit, Sarge, if rumors and hunches
are the best info there is, we could be pissing in
the wind here."

"Don't I know it," Bolan growled, reaching into

a pouch on his belt to pull out a monocular scope and check the sailboat. "But at least we know where the wind is blowing. It's more than we had yesterday."

After a moment he lowered the scope. "No, this is the place. It's only 'when' that we don't know."

"Okay, we wait," Grimaldi said.

Taking up the monocular scope again, Bolan did a fast recon over the highway leading to the dam. To the east and west, the switchback road snaked through the rough countryside. There was no easy approach to Hoover Dam, which gave the covert operatives a fighting chance. Anything coming their way would be seen long before the Zodiac was in range. If the Scion was identified in time, that was.

"So it has to be in the lake," Grimaldi said softly, squinting against the harsh Arizona sunlight.

"And damn close, too," Bolan added. "Too far away and the shock will dissipate, too shallow and the force wave will skip off the surface and fail again."

"That narrows the battlefield somewhat, but it's a mighty big lake."

"A hundred and ten miles long, eight wide at the middle, several hundred feet just before the intake towers. The prime location would be no more than a half mile away," Bolan continued. "Somewhere between the Fortification Mountains and the intake towers."

"Easy approach. Simply send down a diver. No, what's the point of a scuba tank on a suicide, eh? Just hand an anchor to the poor bastard and toss him overboard, count to ten and—"

"Ten million people pay the price," Bolan finished, studying the sky. "And, yeah, we've thought about scuba divers, especially after tangling with the Volksfever. But the Department of the Interior already has Navy P3 sonar down there, and Able Team dropped about a hundred underwater mines to form a firewall across the inlet passage. Anything coming from that direction gets blown to Hell long before reaching the killzone. We're well protected from that direction."

"What about crashing a plane into the water? Pol and Gadgets got enough Stingers?"

"Absolutely. Do you?"

The pilot snorted. "Sarge, I could knock an aircraft carrier out of the water with the armament my Hawk is carrying," Grimaldi said with a touch of pride, casting a look at the sleek black gunship. Barely visible between the landing rails was a long green tube, its marking cryptic military jargon. "No worries there. I got you covered."

"Which leaves the obvious route, driving up in a car and tossing it over the side."

"Occam's Razor, pal. The simplest answer is usually correct."

"But not always," Bolan said, pulling the Desert Eagle to check the clip. "And so we stand, and wait for them to come to us."

Listening to the rumble of the river and the whine of the power plant, the two men didn't speak for several minutes, each thinking about the task ahead of them.

Just then the radio on each man's belt crackled into life.

"Go," Bolan said, touching his throat mike.

"Heads up, brothers," Lyons said briskly. "The P3 sonar shows heavy surface activity, source unknown, and Gadgets reports Geiger activity on Highway 93 at the five-mile marker, and coming fast."

"Nothing from the west?" Bolan asked, swinging the monocular scope that way. As far as he could see, the winding road was clear of traffic until it went behind the jagged Nevada hills.

"Pol reports the Geigers read clean."

"How fast are they traveling from the east?" Grimaldi demanded, raising a hand to shield his face from the sun.

"Exactly the speed limit," Lyons replied. In the background came the sound of a motorcycle roaring to life. "So they don't suspect anything yet."

Or did they? Bolan wondered. Zalhares was no

fool, and the Chinese were the acknowledged masters of trickery. Was the noise on the lake a diversion, or the second nuke? He didn't have the manpower to cover every approach.

"What's the word, Striker?" Lyons asked, gunning the engine of the bike. "Your call. Do I stay or go?"

Yeah, his call. This was it, all or nothing. "Have Pol cover the top of the dam," Bolan directed. "Carl, you help Gadgets. Jack and I will check the lake."

"Roger that. See you in Hell, boys!"

Finished on the radio, Bolan pulled out the cell phone and glanced at the top of the dam. He could just barely make out the tiny figure of Carl Lyons already racing to the east on a Harley-Davidson. This was no job for a dignified BMW. The man had a need for speed.

"The weather is lovely, wish you were here," Bolan said into the phone, giving the code phrase for contact with the enemy. Then he cut the call in case the enemy was monitoring local transmissions.

Turning, Bolan saw that Grimaldi was already in the pilot seat, wearing sunglasses, headphone halfway on, and flipping switches to start the Black Hawk into operation. Good man. As he headed that way, there came a steadily growing rumble from the river valley below as all four of the jetflow gates were opened to full aperture to lower the lake water as fast as possible. Brognola had to have had the chief engineer of the dam holding on a landline, waiting for authorization to open the gates. Now that the enemy was committed to the attack, there was no danger of the Scion or the Red Chinese spotting the trap, and every foot less of height in Lake Mead meant the Zodiac needed to be another yard closer to the dam to work.

Reaching the Black Hawk, Bolan climbed in through the side hatch and grabbed a safety harness with one hand. In spite of the increasing beat of the blades, he could now hear a faint alarm clanging from inside the Visitor's Center. The guides would soon be hustling the tourists down into the cellar for a "hurricane drill" as they had been instructed by Washington.

"Let's go," Bolan shouted over the growing noise of the spinning props.

With the weapon systems coming alive on the control board, Grimaldi nodded in response and the armed gunship lifted smoothly into the clear Arizona sky, heading quickly over the dam and out across the crystal-blue lake.

CHAPTER EIGHTEEN

Highway 93, Arizona

Standing on an escarpment in the Arizona hills, Gadgets Schwarz lowered his binoculars and picked up the .50-caliber Barrett sniper rifle.

Through the scope he could see the approaching riders as if they were only feet away. To handle the bright sun, their helmets were mirrored. But one guy was big, there a woman with a hell of a figure, and two smaller men who had to be the Chinese Communist agents. The woman had to be Jorgina Mizne, the big guy could have been Pedrosa or Mariano. He wasn't wearing gloves, so it wasn't Zalhares. The leader of the Scion had to be in the second group on the lake. Bad news for Bolan. Even worse news for Zalhares.

All four were riding low-slung Yamaha speedsters, just about the fastest bike in the world. The rider had to virtually lie down on his or her belly in the saddle to handle the sheer velocity the machine was capable of reaching, which made it hard as hell to shoot them from this angle, but also made it tough for them to fire back. Another stalemate.

However, according to the Geiger counters buried along the road, and now his flickering EM scanner, the Zodiac was here and live. As expected, each of the riders carried an identical briefcase and, at this range, there was no way to tell which was the real Zodiac and which the fake.

Okay, forget the bombs, concentrate on the riders. The Brazilians were almost definitely the guards, muscle hired to deliver the nuke. So which of the two Chinese men was the suicide bomber? Zooming in on their faces with the rifle scope, Schwarz couldn't tell any difference in their expressions behind the mirrored face masks. Both were armed, and racing side by side, with nobody in the lead.

Now, Blancanales could probably tell at a glance from their clothing or something, Schwarz fumed, but the master of psychology was miles away. It was his call. Okay, take them all down or try for a capture? He had the firepower to blow the whole group off the road, but that would also ignite the nuke. Best to go for the capture first.

Schwarz had no qualms about dying for his country, but that was the absolute court of last resort.

Hunkering back down under his tarp, the Able Team commando placed the .50-caliber rifle aside and waited impatiently for the sound of the speeding bikes. They were traveling really fast, but he had chosen the attack point well. This was the sharp bend in the largest switchback, and if the riders didn't slow, the bikes would go straight off the road and into the side of the hill.

Time seemed to stand still, then he heard them coming closer, their engines getting louder, the harsh buzzing sound filling the air. Wait for it, dogface…now. In an explosion of motion, Schwarz stood, throwing off the camouflage-colored tarp. The riders were only yards away, coming straight for him on the curve. He raised the heavy crossbow.

Pedrosa and Mizne swung out their Urus and started to fire. In spite of the angle, the man was hit a dozen times in the chest, his NATO body armor absorbing the energy of the brutal impacts and throwing him backward, yet he still fired the crossbow.

However the shot went high and the trident slammed directly into Pedrosa's faceplate, the three prongs piercing the Plexiglas and stabbing deep into his face. Grabbing his helmet, Pedrosa screamed from the white-hot pain and the Yamaha went right off the road at full speed to crash into a boulder. Pedrosa went flying to hit an outcropping and splatter like a bug on a windshield.

As the crumpled speedster burst into flames, the others raced past and put on speed, reaching the straight section of the serpentine road. The three riders spotted something large lying in the middle of the pavement and realized it was a Harley-Davidson on its side, the motor still running. The rider was sprawled at a broken angle, his helmet lying nearby. Immediately, Mizne and the Chinese agents slowed, searching for an oil slick, caltraps or whatever had taken down the Harley. But there was nothing in sight. As they arched around the fallen bike, Lyons stood and checked his EM scanner before firing his crossbow at point-blank range.

Dead on target, the trident slammed into the hand of the real bomber, piercing the bones and pinning his hand permanently to the handle-trigger of the CIA weapon.

Screaming more in rage than pain, the Communist agent tried to pull the barbed trident free and nearly lost control of the bike in the process. Firing from the hip, Mizne sprayed Lyons with hardball rounds, but he was behind her and had ducked behind the Harley for protection. The hail of 4.5 mm lead hammered the machine mercilessly, puncturing the gas tank and blowing both tires. With the engine still running, fuel poured out like pale pink blood, and Lyons raced for distance as the gas ignited and the Harley burst into flames.

Drawing his .357 Magnum Colt Python, Lyons lay a barrage of hollowpoints at the gunner, but the other Chinese agent got in the way and took the hit, blood erupting from the triphammer strikes. Then he sagged and the bike toppled sideways to begin tumbling down the roadway, leaving a gory trail of arms, legs and machine parts.

"Faster, fool!" Mizne shouted, revving her bike to the red danger line.

Shaking in panic, the suicide bomber twisted the throttle all the way and streaked away on the sleek Yamaha speedster, then insanely pulled out a knife and began hacking at his own flesh as Hoover Dam came ever closer.

Lake Mead

As THE THROBBING Black Hawk skimmed the surface of the lake, Grimaldi whistled and Bolan looked his way from the open hatch of the gunship.

"You might need this," the pilot said, pulling the knife from his boot.

"Got one, thanks."

"Not like this," Grimaldi said, pressing a stud on the handle. Instantly, the blade snapped apart into three stiletto-thin blades.

"Cowboy pulled these out of his arsenal. Its

from the Middle Ages, for Christ's sake, and called a swordbreaker. Designed to catch and break the other guys sword in a fencing duel." Then he smiled. "But this model is made of a tungsten alloy and tougher than tank armor."

"Yeah?" Bolan asked. "Expecting to double-H a Sherman?"

The Stony Man pilot shrugged. "Might also be pretty good at skewering a guy's hand to the handle of a CIA atomic bomb so that he can't let go."

While the crossbow on Bolan's back was armed with a trident for the same purpose, a trick blade could come in handy. When facing the unknown, it paid to be prepared for anything.

"Thanks," he said, pulling the Gerber from its sheath on his shoulder and replacing it with the swordbreaker. "But I hate to leave you naked."

Reaching to his left side, Grimaldi pulled out another and tucked it into his boot. "Don't sweat it, Sarge. I always have a spare."

Just then the radar began to beep, the tones coming faster and stronger.

"There she is," Grimaldi said, slowing the Black Hawk and swinging around the ragged peninsula that cut across the man-made lake. "What the… Son of a bitch, it's a hovercraft!"

"Which explains why the P3 went crazy," Bolan said.

The powerful fans set underneath the craft

caused it to skim above the lake on a cushion of air. But it wasn't in the water, or even on the surface, but flying above with the lake as support. No wonder the Navy sonar couldn't figure out what was coming.

Through the binoculars, Bolan could see several figures in the craft, two looked Chinese and two had dark skin. Sounded like the right mix. Checking his EM scanner, Bolan found that the hovercraft was too far away to register on the portable device.

"Geiger is clear," Grimaldi shouted over the props, pointing at the larger, more powerful model mounted in the modular control board. "But the EM scanner is off the charts, big guy. That's a Zodiac and it isn't armed!"

Moving fast, Bolan climbed into the co-pilot's seat, pulled on the gunnery helmet and inserted the plug. Instantly there was a grid of lines on the faceplate and a floating crosshairs appeared in front of the man. As Bolan turned his head, so did the M-134 7.62 mm minigun slung under the nose of the Black Hawk in perfect synchronization. Then he switched to the missile guidance system and got a green light to go on the Sidewinders.

Suddenly a Stinger rose from the hovercraft and Grimaldi barely was able to move out of the way in time, leaving a cloud of chaff and flares behind. The deadly rocket detonated in midair, the shock wave shaking the gunship as the halo of shrapnel arrived. But the composite hull of the Hawk was proofed to 23 mm rounds and the hot metal debris only noisily peppered the craft to no effect. "Blow the underwater mines," Bolan directed, trying to get a positive lock on the targeting grid. "Keep them busy!"

Swinging around in the sky, Grimaldi flipped a few switches and suddenly the entire section of the lake jumped, boiling gouts of steam rising all across the inlet as muddy geysers shot out of the lake. Starting to weave, the hovercraft lost its plumb and one of the men went flying overboard, the rocking craft gliding back over him, the spinning air turbines leaving only bloody chum in its wake.

"Show time," Grimaldi growled, shoving the joystick forward and going into a steep attack run.

Checking to make sure the Zodiac still wasn't armed, Bolan set the controls, targeted the grid, got tone and lock, and fired.

Flashing forward on fiery contrails, the Sidewinders crossed the distance in under a heartbeat and dived into the water to violently explode. The hovercraft was thrown high on a white plume, the men tumbling free to splash back into the lake as the hovercraft landed upside down, exposing its belly fans. Switching to the minigun, Bolan put a long burst into the hovercraft, the spinning blades shattering under the AP rounds, and the engines bursting into flame as the wreckage began to sink into the churning waters.

"Okay, land me on that escarpment," Bolan directed, yanking off the gunnery helmet and going into the rear of the craft. "Time to search for the Zodiac and any survivors."

Slinging the crossbow over a shoulder, Bolan added a Saber combo-assault rifle to his web harness, racking the bolt to first chamber a 5.56 mm round, then a 20 mm shell.

Without further comment, Bolan went to the hatch and watched the muddy waters below for any sign of life.

Hoover Dam

As the two bikers reached the final curve on Interstate 93, Mizne suddenly cried out and flew from her bike like a puppet yanked on a string. She hit the roadway landing flat on her face, her helmet shattering. The woman scraped along the ground at seventy miles per hour, leaving a crimson trail behind as the rough asphalt abraded her down to the bone. Her bike continued onward for several yards, then lost its balance and went off the road to crash into the pipe railing above an empty parking lot.

A second later a rolling boom echoed across the terrain from a high-powered rifle in the ragged eastern hills.

Now alone, the Communist bomber started slowing to zigzag in expectation of another bullet hitting between his shoulders. Then he realized that was what the gunman wanted, and instead twisted the throttle of the Yamaha speedster to all the way.

Rapidly building velocity, the bomber tried to ignore the searing pain in his hand. But the blood was going everywhere, and he was starting to feel sick to his stomach, plus a little cold in spite of the hot sunlight. Time was pressing. His guards were dead, and soon he would pass out. What to do? Because of the pitchfork-like thing embedded in his flesh, the original plan of simply going over the retaining wall of the dam and releasing the Zodiac was impossible. There was a gun under his leather jacket; he could shoot the Zodiac to make it detonate. That would work. But first he would have to stop the bike to reach the pistol, and the Americans could kill him with immunity. The hand with the Zodiac was going numb and weak….

Wait, he could crash the bike into something. The top of the dam was a curve, he would drive straight into the retaining wall on top. That should certainly be enough of a blow to set off the nuke! Now he grinned fiendishly. Victory could still be seized! The enemies of China would now feel their wrath and there was nothing the Americans could do to stop him!

As the Red Chinese agent came roaring around

the final switchback curve, there was Blancanales standing in the middle of the road, holding a crossbow loaded with another trident. Sneering in contempt, the biker fed more power to the machine. The Able Team commando dropped the crossbow to swing around an M-16/M-203 slung across his back. He leveled the weapon but didn't fire. Cursing loudly, Blancanales shook the fully functional assault rifle and worked the bolt to eject a round as if struggling to clear a jam.

Laughing in triumph, the biker streaked closer, staying on a straight course right past the man. Then Blancanales leveled the M-16/M-203 and triggered the 40 mm grenade launcher. But instead of a primed shell, the launcher blasted out an antipersonnel cartridge, the hellstorm of steel pellets blowing the left arm off the rider. Set free, the Zodiac and attached limb went flying, and Blancanales dropped the assault rifle combo to dive under the tumbling bomb as if making a football catch. Streaking by, the biker shrieked at the unbelievable agony, blood spurting from the ragged stump at his shoulder.

Scraping painfully along the pavement, Blancanales got under the tumbling Zodiac and caught it in his arms just as the Yamaha speedster and its dying rider slammed into the low retainer wall. The bike violently exploded, but impelled forward, the Red Star agent went through the windshield and over the wall to fall screaming for a very long time before finally reaching the bottom.

A few minutes later the Black Hawk landed on the roadway on top of the dam, just as Schwarz and Lyons came racing into view from around the switchback curve, weapons at the ready. Kneeling on the concrete, Blancanales was just finishing the procedure to deactivate the Zodiac, and he looked up at their arrival.

"We're clear," he announced, rocking back on his boot heels. "It's turned off."

"Hell of a shot there, Rosario," Schwarz said as a compliment, nudging the tattered human arm with the barrel of his sniper rifle.

"Thanks. Better than you could have done with that popgun."

"Ha! In your dreams, old man."

Holstering the Colt Python, Lyons walked to the helicopter and leaned in through the open side hatch. "What's the status on Mack?" Lyons shouted over the noise of the rotating props.

"Dropped him off a few minutes ago to search for the Zodiac," Grimaldi replied, flipping a few switches on the control panels. "No word yet on how he's doing."

"Yeah?"

"But there is no way anybody could have survived the missile strike," the pilot continued, over

CHAPTER NINETEEN

Lookout Point

Crawling out of the muddy water along the rock bank, Colonel Yang Shunrao staggered onto dry ground holding the Zodiac. When the black helicopter appeared in the sky, the Chinese operative had known it was his chance, and had immediately shot the Brazilian mercenary in the back, stolen the atomic bomb and dived overboard. Naturally the other fools fought the American gunship, and just as naturally it literally blew the hovercraft out of the water.

The others had to be dead, and that was good. The stupid S2 agents had been convinced that this was merely a dry run to test the feasibility of attacking the dam, when in reality it had been the actual attack. The fools coming along for the ride just in case the first team failed, the second Zodiac would be right on hand to finish the job. Shunrao had planned for failure, which was the only true course to success.

Trudging through the residual boulders, the Red Star spy was delighted at the outcome of events. Now he had a Zodiac and wouldn't have to die. The other Chinese man in the hovercraft had behaved as an underling, but in truth had been Red Star director Pai Ho Yee, his hated superior, a total fanatic who relished the idea of dying for the glorious cause. Well, Shunrao had no qualms about allowing others to die, but he saw no reason for him to join the ranks of the dead. Unless it was absolutely necessary.

Rummaging in his clothing, the man unearthed a long length of greenish cord brought along for just such a contingency. Wrapping it tightly around the handle of the Zodiac, he next set the controls and activated the bomb. There was a low audible hum as the capacitors charged, and then silence.

Staggering back toward the jagged hills, Shunrao headed for the observation point overlooking the scenic lake. He would light the waterproof fuse and simply throw the accursed bomb into the lake from there. More than heavy enough, the Zodiac would sink of its accord and when the fuse burned through all the way, the handle would release and the bomb would detonate. But by then, he would safely be behind the Fortification Mountain range and far from the death shroud of radioactive steam that would rise to sterilize this section of the state like a laboratory autoclave. With any luck, the cloud would drift over to Las Vegas and slaughter even more of the fat greedy fools. As Chairman Mao said, the path to freedom was paved in the blood of others. True words, indeed.

Reaching the Nevada-side parking lot, the colonel went up the zigzagging flight of stairs to reach the observation deck carved from the living stone of the hills. There were benches, a coin-operated telescope and a simple pipe-railing along the edge facing the picturesque lake and dam to keep idiots from trying to dive in from the great height. Pausing to light the fuse, the colonel smiled as it came to sputtering life, and he headed for the railing.

In his opinion the mission was already over and Shunrao was starting to think of the next attack on America when Bolan charged from the rocks and grabbed the handle of the Zodiac. Although startled, Shunrao turned with a Norinco .45 pistol in his grip, only to find the black-haired stranger was pointing a huge silver .357 Magnum Desert Eagle right back at him.

"Fool," Shunrao said, sneering, clicking back the hammer. "I am prepared to die."

"Really?" Bolan queried. "If that was true, you never would have tied that fuse to the handle. You don't have the guts, and we both know it."

"Do we, Officer?"

"Yes," Bolan stated coldly.

Softly, the burning fuse sizzled, slowly burning its way around the handle. Shunrao tried not to flinch from the flame touching his skin, and found himself ashamed when the other man didn't react. Was he made of ice? Who was this American thug?

"Here's the deal," Bolan said gruffly. "Drop the weapon and you can leave alive. That's a promise. I've come after the Zodiac and don't want you."

"When that fuse burns through—" the colonel started.

"Then I shoot you and we both die," Bolan said, cutting the spy off. "It's better for the bomb to detonate here than in the water, and I'm ready to pay that price."

"Indeed?"

"Choose or die," Bolan said. "Your call."

Chewing a lip, the Chinese agent was obviously considering his options, then Bolan saw the man's attention flick away. Shoving his gun into the spy's throat, the Executioner turned to see a dripping wet Mariano charge from the parking lot, a rifle in his big hands.

"Kill him!" Shunrao commanded, spittle flying from his mouth.

Grinning in blood lust, Mariano leveled the weapon at Shunrao, not Bolan, and pulled the trigger. Nothing happened.

"Your ammo block is wet," Bolan said, stepping back to cover both men with the Desert Eagle.

"Die, traitor!" Mariano screamed insanely as he charged, holding the rifle like a club.

The Chinese man hissed at that and started to lift his pistol at the Brazilian. Then he paused to glance at Bolan and the Zodiac held between them, the fuse burning steadily.

"Unless we cooperate," Shunrao said quickly, "he will kill us both."

"Then let go," Bolan said, trying not to show his apprehension. Things were getting out of control fast. The S2 agent called the Red Star agent a traitor, so he had to have reneged on a deal.

Screaming in Portuguese, Mariano arrived and swung the rifle at the Chinese man. Bolan almost reacted to that, but stood his ground. The other man finally moved the Norinco pistol and shot Mariano in the throat. The Brazilian jerked back, dropping the rifle as both hands grabbed his ruined throat, blood spurting from the severed arteries.

Then Bolan fired and the colonel doubled over,

revealing that he was wearing body armor. Quickly, the Executioner aimed at the head, then Mariano collided with Bolan, knocking the Desert Eagle aside, the slug intended for the Chinese agent going into the Brazilian.

But the distraction had given Shunrao his chance. In a surge of strength, the colonel yanked the Zodiac free and sent it sailing over the railing toward the lake. Shoving the dying Brazilian away, Bolan fired once into the Chinese agent's grinning face, and the back of his head burst apart from the staggering point-blank impact of the 180-grain hollowpoint round. Holstering the heavy gun, Bolan raced along the pavement, hit the railing in a bound and soared away from the cliff, angling his dive into a steep incline. He hit the water clean, missing the boulders that lined the shallows and disappearing below the choppy surface.

Down into the murky lake Bolan swam, moving as fast as he could, eyes wide to keep track of the tiny ember of the burning fuse. There was a strong current toward the dam, and Bolan followed along, knowing that the Zodiac would go with the flow.

Suddenly something came into view, reaching for him with a giant gnarled hand, and Bolan swam around the dead tree sticking out of the side of the old Black Water canyon. The current toward the dam was more powerful now, dragging in the silt. For a moment, he lost sight of the fuse. Raw adrenaline flooded the man, but Bolan forced himself to stay calm. Excitement only used more oxygen, and he was nearing the end of his supply, heart pounding, lungs starting to ache. Then the murky darkness parted, leaving a zone of clear water and there was the briefcase! Lying on the edge of a small cliff, slowly being dragged along by the current toward the dam and a yawning expanse of deep water that became total blackness. The shadow of the dam. A low rumble could be heard coming from below, and Bolan knew it was the turbines of the power plant, and certain death.

Kicking hard, Bolan knifed through the water and caught the briefcase just as it was about to go over the edge. Locking a hand around the handletrigger, he wasted no time underwater with the fuse, which still had minutes to burn. Besides, it helped keep the handle engaged. Instead, the suffocating man started instantly for the surface. Fumbling at his belt, the buckle finally came loose and the Desert Eagle fell away. Now the man rose higher and faster without its heavy weight. Then the Beretta went, the spare ammo, radio and both grenades. He had to make it to the surface now.

Moments later the Executioner exploded from the lake gasping for breath, his aching lungs pulling in gulps of cool sweet air. For a moment he sank below the waves again, then surfaced once more and began to wearily swim with the current. He knew where it was going and could use the help. Time passed as Bolan did nothing but stroke with his free arm and kick steadily, then without warning, he slammed against the outer screening of the Nevada-side intake tower. The steel grating that covered the intake vents ripped at his clothing, but the metalwork also gave him handholds, and Bolan soon worked along the side to reach an access ladder.

It felt like climbing Mt. Everest, but Bolan finally got up the eighty feet and reached the catwalk platform that formed a ring around the structure. Sixty feet wide, the ring was enormous, but then everything was gigantic at Hoover Dam, even the danger. Levering himself onto the perforated flooring, Bolan lay down, catching his breath and resting, except for his left hand that maintained its iron grip on the Zodiac.

Now that he was safe, Bolan very carefully switched hands and gently flexed the aching left, inspecting the score of blistered red marks from the burning fuse.

Footsteps sounded on the catwalk of the intake tower and Cirello Zalhares came into view. His clothes were dripping wet, and the man was horribly burned on half of his face, the skin blistered and split open with raw oozing cracks. Most of his hair was gone and his left eye was a milky-white dead orb. The gloves were gone, showing the horribly scarred hands, but the blue-steel Imbel pistol in his hand looked in perfect working condition.

"So the currents also dragged you here, eh?" Zalhares snarled, advancing in a stagger, something obviously wrong with his left leg. "Thank you for delivering the Zodiac to me personally. Now it is time for you—"

Cutting him off in midsentence, Bolan kicked out with both boots and Zalhares went down with a curse. Kicking out again, the soldier drove a heel into the other man's crotch. The breath exploded from the Brazilian in anguished cry and he dropped the gun. Scrambling to snatch the pistol, Bolan started to aim at Zalhares when the S2 agent lurched forward to grab his adversary by the throat and wrist, crushing both in a powerful hold. Struggling to turn the weapon on the Brazilian, Bolan found that was impossible, so he flipped the gun over the side of the catwalk toward the lake below.

"No!" Zalhares cried, releasing Bolan's wrist to try for the flying gun.

But the merc was too slow. The soldier reached out with the Zodiac and pressed the burning fuse against the unmarked side of Zalhares's face. Recoiling fast, the man shrieked and released his stranglehold. Backing away, Zalhares then pulled a curved blade from a sheath behind his back, the steel glinting evilly in the sunlight.

Going into a crouch, Bolan pulled out his own blade and steel hit steel as the knives clashed, each deflecting the thrust of the enemy. Shifting his stance, Zalhares feinted to the right, then lunged from the left, but Bolan was ready for that and meet the other man's knife with an upward thrust that drove his hand against the intake tower with ringing force. Zalhares snarled as he lost the blade but then caught it with the other hand and slashed across Bolan's vulnerable stomach. The soldier moved fast, but the curved blade sliced open his shirt to leave a crimson trail across bare flesh.

Lashing out with an elbow, Bolan rammed Zalhares on the burned side of the head. But the nerves had to have already been deadened from the hovercraft fire because he merely grunted at the blow and then stabbed for Bolan's throat, but only scored another bloody scratch.

Their blades met again and again, each receiving minor grazes and barely escaping lethal cuts. Zalhares was smart enough to keep his blind side to the tower where Bolan couldn't use it to his advantage. Zalhares slashed, Bolan blocked then lunged, and the other man dodged, to slash in return. Equally matched, both men were at the limits of their strength and the outcome of the match was beyond anybody's guess.

With a sputtering hiss, the waterproof fuse burned through the last knot and a short length of the smoking green cord dropped from the handle of the Zodiac onto the perforated catwalk.

"It's live!" Bolan shouted, raising the briefcase.

In spite of himself, Zalhares glanced at the bomb for a split second, dropping his guard, and Bolan lunged, burying the blade into the man's chest. He pressed the stud. The three blades snapped apart, literally tearing the Brazilian's stomach apart. Dropping his knife, Zalhares went pale and sagged slightly, then he jerked an arm forward and a derringer snapped out of a sleeve into his palm. But Bolan kicked sideways as the man fired both barrels, the .44 slugs merely hitting the tower to noisily dent the metal.

"By the god of my fathers!" Zalhares screamed insanely. "What does it take to kill you?"

Casting the useless weapon at Bolan, the dying man clutched the flow of life from his gaping stomach and stabbed out two stiff fingers for Bolan's eyes in a martial arts move. But Bolan swayed under the attack and used his momentum to get closer and punch the gushing belly wound with every ounce of his fading strength. Spilling out his life onto the catwalk, Zalhares reeled from the incalculable agony, but then screamed insanely as he pulled the splayed swordbreaker from his own belly and raised it high to strike when he suddenly jerked to the right with a trident sticking out of his throat. Gurgling horribly, the man dropped the triple-blade knife and batted feebly at the quarrel through his neck, but then two more tridents slammed deep into his chest. Wordlessly, the Brazilian S2 agent eased to the catwalk and toppled over, the blood ceasing to flow from his ghastly wounds.

A powerful throbbing began to be heard above the roar of the dam, and Bolan gave a salute of thanks as the Black Hawk gunship lowered into view, Grimaldi at the controls and Able Team sitting in the open side hatch, dutifully reloading their crossbows.

Schwarz touched his throat mike and said something, but Bolan pulled at his collar to show the communications device was gone. Nodding understanding, Lyons passed Blancanales his crossbow, then jumped from the gunship, changing his fall into a swan dive. He hit the water clean as an Olympic swimmer. A few moments later there was the sound of footsteps on the access ladder and a dripping-wet Lyons walked into view with a pistol in each hand.

"He's dead," Bolan reported, struggling to stay upright.

Moving past Bolan, Lyons fired both guns into the S2 agent's chest, the rounds making the corpse slam against the steel wall, the skull cracking loudly as the bones shattered.

"Just making sure," Lyons said, holstering the piece, then he kneeled. "Easy now. Let me have that, Mack."

But even after Lyons had a sure grip on the handle, Bolan grimly made certain of the fact twice before he would finally allow his cramped hand to stop clenching.

As the lake swirled and drained below them into the sucking vents of the intake tower, the weary soldier slumped against the railing as Lyons started the disarming procedure. The internal indicators soon went dark and the infernal machine was turned off.

With that, Bolan sighed in relief.

EPILOGUE

Somewhere Over Texas

With a start, Bolan came awake on a litter in the rear of the throbbing Black Hawk. Able Team was strapped into the jumpseats and the two Zodiacs were lying in a box on the deck, the handles removed and partially dismantled. Looking around, Bolan saw that the plasma bottles hadn't been used, so his injuries had to be minor. But he felt as stiff as hell and there were bandages wrapped around his stomach, left hand and both legs.

"I see you've been busy," Bolan said, rising up onto an elbow. "So when do you ram the red-hot poker up my nose and finish the mummification process?"

"He's up!" Grimaldi called from the pilot's seat, glancing over a shoulder. "And it's under an hour. Told you so. That's twenty bucks you owe me, Gadgets."

"Put in on my tab." Schwarz grinned, releasing the straps. "How you feeling, Mack?"

"Been better," Bolan admitted, swinging both legs to the deck. "What's our situation?"

"We stopped them," Lyons said, reaching into a frosted case and pulling out a water bottle. He offered the chilled plastic bottle and added, "Or would you rather have a beer?"

"Beer, thanks." Bolan smiled, accepting a bottle from the same refrigeration unit. He took a long draft. "Okay, any breakage on our side?"

"Not a soul," Blancanales said. "Although I don't think we'll ever be allowed to visit Hoover Dam again. The director was delighted we saved the dam, and mad as hell about all the explosion damage."

"I think all the potholes add a nice touch to the road," Schwarz said with a grin. "Makes it look more like Route 65 back home in D.C."

Bolan took another drink from the beer bottle. He was feeling more like his old self by the minute. "Any word from Hal about the bombs?"

"Damn right there is," Lyons said, leaning forward in the jumpseat. "These remaining two Zodiacs are being delivered by us to the Red Ridge Nuclear Arsenal."

"We'll be there in a couple of hours," Grimaldi announced. "So sit back and enjoy the ride."

"Good."

"And our pal Osbourne has been cashiered out of the CIA," Blancanales added.

"Good riddance," Bolan stated, dismissing the matter. "Anything to eat in this eggbeater?"

"Only some MREs," Blancanales said in apology.

His stomach rumbling, Bolan considered that for a moment. "Pass," the soldier decided. "But thanks anyway."

"Hey, I like the beef stew," Schwarz said in defense.

"You would," Blancanales shot back. "I think your taste buds got shot off in a firefight."

"As long as I keep my mustache," he replied, stroking the growth like a small pet. "The ladies love it."

"Yeah, lady orangutans."

"Hell, we're all due some real chow after this," Lyons said, leaning back in the seat. "Also been a while since we took R&R. Hey, Mack, want to join me and do some fishing up in Canada? Gary also has a great cabin in Quebec that he lets friends use for vacations."

"Fishing any good?" Schwarz asked eagerly.

"Great, trout as big as your arm," Lyons stated, showing the dimensions using both hands.

"Thanks anyway," Bolan answered. "But after a few days at the Farm, I'm going back to Galveston. Gorilla Dillard and I have some business to settle."

"The mobster?" Lyons asked curiously. "Yeah, I heard about him. Screw it, let him wait a few weeks."

"Can't do that," Bolan said, closing his eyes. "That's one loose end I want to tie up."

James Axler
Outlanders®

MASK OF
THE SPHINX

Harnessing the secrets of selective mutation, the psionic abilities of its nobility and benevolent rule of a fair queen, the city-kingdom of Aten remains insular, but safe. Now, Aten faces a desperate fight for survival—a battle that will lure Kane and his companions into the conflict, where a deadly alliance with the Imperator to hunt out the dark forces of treason could put the Cerberus warriors one step closer to their goal of saving humanity...or damn them, and their dreams, to the desert dust.

Available August 2004 at your favorite retail outlet.

Or order your copy now by sending your name, address, zip or postal code, along with a check or money order (please do not send cash) for $6.50 for each book ordered ($7.99 in Canada), plus 75¢ postage and handling ($1.00 in Canada), payable to Gold Eagle Books, to:

In the U.S.	In Canada
Gold Eagle Books	Gold Eagle Books
3010 Walden Avenue	P.O. Box 636
P.O. Box 9077	Fort Erie, Ontario
Buffalo, NY 14269-9077	L2A 5X3

Please specify book title with your order.
Canadian residents add applicable federal and provincial taxes.

GOUT30

THE DESTROYER

UNPOPULAR SCIENCE

A rash of perfectly executed thefts from military research facilities puts CURE in the hot seat, setting the trap for Remo and Chiun to flip the off switch of the techno-genius behind an army of remote-controlled killer machines. Nastier than a scourge of deadly titanium termites, more dangerous than the resurrection of a machine oil/microchip battle-bot called Ironhand, is the juice used to power them all up: an electromagnetic pulse that can unplug Remo and Chiun long enough to short-circuit CURE beyond repair.

Available July 2004 at your favorite retail outlet.

James Axler
Outlanders®

SUN LORD

In a fabled city of the ancient world, the neo-gods of Mexico are locked in a battle for domination. Harnessing the immutable power of alien technology and Earth's pre-Dark secrets, the high priests and whitecoats have hijacked Kane into the resurrected world of the Aztecs. Invested with the power of the great sun god, Kane is a pawn in the brutal struggle and must restore the legendary Quetzalcoatl to his rightful place—or become a human sacrifice....

Available May 2004 at your favorite retail outlet.

Or order your copy now by sending your name, address, zip or postal code, along with a check or money order (please do not send cash) for $6.50 for each book ordered ($7.99 in Canada), plus 75¢ postage and handling ($1.00 in Canada), payable to Gold Eagle Books, to:

In the U.S.	In Canada
Gold Eagle Books	Gold Eagle Books
3010 Walden Avenue	P.O. Box 636
P.O. Box 9077	Fort Erie, Ontario
Buffalo, NY 14269-9077	L2A 5X3

Please specify book title with your order.
Canadian residents add applicable federal and provincial taxes.

GOUT29

DEATH LANDS®

Separation

*Available June 2004
at your favorite retail outlet.*

A struggle for survival in a savage new world...

JAMES AXLER

DEATH LANDS

Separation

The group makes its way to a remote island in hopes of finding brief sanctuary. Instead, they are captured by an isolated tribe of descendants of African slaves from pre–Civil War days. When they declare Mildred Wyeth "free" from her white masters, it is a twist of fate that ultimately leads the battle-hardened medic to question where her true loyalties lie. Will she side with Ryan, J. B. Dix and those with whom she has forged a bond of trust and friendship…or with the people of her own blood?

Or order your copy now by sending your name, address, zip or postal code, along with a check or money order (please do not send cash) for $6.50 for each book ordered ($7.99 in Canada), plus 75¢ postage and handling ($1.00 in Canada), payable to Gold Eagle Books, to:

In the U.S.	In Canada
Gold Eagle Books	Gold Eagle Books
3010 Walden Ave.	P.O. Box 636
P.O. Box 9077	Fort Erie, Ontario
Buffalo, NY 14269-9077	L2A 5X3

Please specify book title with order.
Canadian residents add applicable federal and provincial taxes.

GOLD EAGLE®

GDL66